Finding
the lost woman

Also by Anna Buckley

AWAKENING the lost woman
(book one of the lost woman trilogy)

CAPTURING the lost woman
(book two of the lost woman trilogy)

Finding

the lost woman

(book three of the lost woman trilogy)

august
XXIX

Anna Buckley

Published by august XXIX, an imprint of August Twentynine pty. ltd.
mail@august29.com.au

First published 2014.

1-3-1.00

National Library of Australia Cataloguing-in-Publication entry: (paperback)

Author: Buckley, Anna, author.

Title: Finding the lost woman / Anna Buckley.

ISBN: 978 0 9924781 2 4(paperback)

Series: Buckley, Anna. Lost woman; no. 3.

Subjects: Women—Fiction, Erotic fiction.

Dewey Number: A823.4

ACKNOWLEDGEMENTS

Thank you to my family who have been so supportive during the entire process of writing all three books. Without your love and encouragement nothing would have been possible.

ABOUT THE AUTHOR

Anna Buckley is an author based in Melbourne, Australia. Her previous career was in design.

Her aim is to write books about women taking control of their lives, financially, emotionally and sexually. Her books are set across the world and feature art, architecture, design, fashion, food and wine.

Anna Buckley has a blog where she posts stories and pictures behind her books. Find it at annabuckley.com

Contents

Part 3   154

Part 4   228

Part 1

Free

There was no sense of time or place. I woke in a sterile white room, confused. My body ached. Pain shot through my shoulder like a knife blade twisting between the bones. I began to retch, bitter tasting bile filled my mouth. My head throbbed with each involuntary spasm. The feeling was like no brain tumour hangover I'd ever had.

'Oh you poor darlin', here, let me clean you up,' said a kindly voice with a lilting Irish accent.

'There there, that's better,' she said as she wiped my face and brow with a cool cloth.

'You've been asleep for quite some time. I was wonderin' what we might have to do to wake you up. Welcome back, Christina. There'll be a lot of people pleased to see you.'

The smell of disinfectant, the beep of monitors, the bland interior, told me where I was. Hospital.

Drifting back into sleep was my preferred state, but the nurse would have none of it and she began slapping, squeezing my hand and speaking more authoritatively.

'Christina, come on girl. It's time to wake up.'

'What happened, where am I?' I croaked, my throat parched, my lips painfully swollen, cracking as I tried to speak.

'You're ok, you're gonna be fine. You're in the best hands.'

She gave me some ice to suck to relieve the thirst and called the doctor in. As I tried to move, I realised my left shoulder was tightly bandaged, painful, preventing me from sitting up. The nurse helped me, propping me with pillows, giving me a better view of my surrounds. The doctor picked up the notes at the end of my bed and checked the monitors.

'How do you feel, Ms. Maxwell? It's good to see you awake, you've had a bit of a rough trot.'

He told me I was in hospital in Hobart. I had been shot in the shoulder, the bullet narrowly missing my heart. Shot? What was he talking about? Then the memories started to flood back. Moses, the shack, the beating, the fear, the betrayal. The guilt. My mind was racing. I didn't know how to process the confusion of thoughts buzzing round my head.

'Please, I don't want to see anybody yet.'

'It's the middle of the night. Your family was sent home, we'll let them get some sleep. I'll call them in the morning when you'll be feeling a bit better.'

'No, no one, I want to be left alone.'

Thankfully she let me drift back into my comatose sleep. I would face my demons in the morning.

When I woke the same nurse was on duty. Emma was the name on the tag, pinned to her uniform.

'Mornin' darlin'. Feelin' better today?'

I rolled over to avoid her upbeat cajoling. I was no ones darlin' and still didn't want to talk to anybody. She was becoming concerned, saying there were many people wanting to see me. Wondered if I should talk to someone professional first? Thankfully she did not bring in the clergy. Some sanctimonious buffoon praying over me was the last thing I wanted. A tall, elegantly suited woman entered the room.

'Hi Christina, you've been through quite an ordeal. I'm told you don't want to see anyone yet. Do you want to talk about it?'

I resented her being there. Didn't want to play into the hands of some know all psychiatrist who thought she'd gotten her hands on a textbook case of Stockholm Syndrome. What happened between Moses and me ran so much deeper than that. Staring blankly at the wall, I was in no mood to be analysed. I hadn't decided how to process all the shit going on in my head and wasn't ready to talk until I had some answers myself. She sat waiting for me to open up. I rewarded her with silence. I didn't need to hear her patronising comments about how it would make me feel better if I started talking.

How could I tell her that I had rejected my daughter, my lover, my friends, my life? Betrayed all those around me for someone who I thought offered everything. That I'd felt real desire for a man who had forcibly held me captive. Who I had willingly fucked. A man who violently bashed me almost to death. How on earth could I tell anybody what had really gone on in that place where I'd been held prisoner?

'You cared for him didn't you?'

My eyes burnt with tears, she was right. I still didn't want to talk. 'Just let the nurse know if I can help,' she said as she stood, realising that her patient was not going to open up to her.

A new nurse came in and went about her tasks. Asking the same questions. Checking I was ok. Dressing the wound on my shoulder. Refilling the morphine drip I clicked endlessly. The thing was, that although it didn't really stop the pain, it helped me forget and I was happy to remain in my drugged haze for the rest of the day.

The staff had respected my wish to see no visitors, but they could not keep out the police. The detective spoke first.

'Ms Maxwell, the doctors have told us that you are up to giving a statement.'

I feared what Moses had already told them, tears filled my eyes. I felt panic, didn't know where to start.

'It's ok Ms Maxwell, Christina, you've got nothing to fear. He can't hurt you now. We found his body yesterday. He tried to escape into the bush, didn't get very far. He'd been shot, bled to death.'

They had misinterpreted my reaction and, thank God, I now knew that Moses would never tell them the real story. I felt a great sense of relief.

The statement I gave was vague, I could never reveal all. I filled them in on my attempt to get off the island to get help for Adam, being lost, and of my eventual kidnapping. I told them I had been incarcerated in the cellar, tied up for a long time, heard the helicopters above, was powerless to get help. Told them enough to let them know that, at the beginning, I'd been a very reluctant hostage. They saw the bruising, my swollen face. I told them Moses had done this when he discovered my attempt to make contact with the outside world. I didn't tell them that, before the savage beating, he had offered me freedom and I had chosen to stay.

'Ms Maxwell, we have one more thing we need to do before we leave. We need to take some photographs of your injuries and remove the metal band around your ankle.'

I wriggled my foot and felt the heavy metal ring Moses had attached the chains to. I'd become so used to it I'd completely forgotten it was there. The nurse pulled back the covers and they photographed the bruises on my face and stomach and the rope burns around my wrists. So much of that last horrible hour with Moses was coming back to me in vivid detail. Then the detective consulted with a guy in overalls. They slid a protective cover between my skin and the metal and with a pair of bolt cutters, snapped off the ring and placed it in a clear plastic evidence bag.

I was glad of the bruises and the metal ring, because this would be the evidence they needed to show I had not been a willing hostage.

'Thanks Ms Maxwell, that will be all for now. We'll take a more detailed statement when you're feeling a bit better.'

They got up and left the room.

I wept into the pillow for a man I'd grown to like, and for whom I'd almost been prepared to give up everything. His seduction had been so clever. He made me think I had all the control, that I would be with him by choice. And when he'd discovered that my almost forgotten plan had caught him out, he bashed me senseless, a clear message telling me exactly who was in charge. How could I have been so prepared to pretend that what Moses offered was love? Was it all the years I'd spent in a passionless marriage? Just like with Paul, the sex with Moses had been completely unfulfilling. I had tried to convince myself it would get better, that I could change this most fundamental flaw. Had I become so conditioned to this way of life, that it was my default position? The choice of a simpler life, when the one I'd created was getting too complicated? The sobs were now for the realisation of my own weakness.

Click, click went the button as I pumped in more morphine. Numbing the pain and the guilt.

A change of shift and another new nurse, observing my slowly healing body. Offering to help me eat my untouched food. Encouraging me to see the people outside.

Hours and hours passed and nothing changed.

'Oh pet, look at you.'

The gentle Irish voice, that lovely nurse, Emma, had returned. Her motherly tone giving me a sense of security and trust.

'Darlin', you've not touched your food. How are you gonna get better if you don't eat?' she said fussing, stroking my forehead with her cool hands.

'Wouldn't blame you though, the muck they serve in here isn't fit for a mongrel dog. Just wait a minute, I've got something that might help.'

The creak and whoosh of the heavy door signalled her return. She sat me up and asked me to open my mouth. I reluctantly complied. Soup, chicken soup. That comforting and oh so familiar flavour my mother had given me when I was a child. Sick, upset or just out of sorts, she always knew it would cure all that ailed me. And here was this beautiful woman doing the same. I burst into tears, overwhelmed by the emotions it brought flooding back.

'There, there, sweetie, it's ok. Have a nice big cry. Just let it all out, it'll make you feel so much better,' she gently coaxed.

She was just what I needed, holding me close as the sobs convulsed through my body, releasing wave after wave of pent up emotion. She sat rocking me gently, like a baby, until I finally calmed.

'I'm sorry, I didn't mean to cry.'

'That's alright, sometimes it's good to get it out. Are you feelin' a little better?'

'Yes, a little, thank you.'

The soup was offered again and I wolfed it down. Emma looked on, satisfied that the healing process had finally begun.

'Has anyone offered you a shower?'

'No. It hadn't occurred to me to even ask. I'm hooked up to all this stuff. I feel disgusting. Do you think it would be possible?'

'A good cry, chicken soup and now a shower. We'll have you dancin' around the room in no time.'

She checked with the doctor, then slowly started to pull out the tubes. A catheter had been inserted and I gasped at the strange and intimate sensation of having it removed. She took out the drip and mentioned something about not getting too attached to that evil little concoction. Then expertly covered my dressings with waterproof bandages. Carefully she helped me off the bed and supported me as we walked to the shower, my jelly legs barely holding up. She sat me down on a chair and let the hot water run over my body. Happy to stand by until I'd had enough. She towelled me dry and dressed me in a clean gown, making me sit up in an armchair as she stripped the bed and remade it with fresh sheets. She helped me back into the cool crisp linen, tucking the sheets firmly in a drill I'm sure some cranky old matron had taught her many years before. It made me feel secure.

She sat on the bed and looked me straight in the eye.

'Christina, I came from Northern Ireland, immigrated when 'the troubles' were at their worst. Lots of kidnappings. Worked in a hospital in Belfast and spoke to some of the people who'd been taken hostage. They told me they didn't always hate the men who'd taken them. Is this what's been troublin' you so much, darlin'?'

I nodded unable to speak, choking back the tears. Emma was safe, she felt like the mother I'd lost. The protective shield wasn't just the result of my loveless marriage, it was a defence against the hollow loneliness of an orphan's abandonment.

'Big breath angel, your story's safe with me.'

She heard everything. I let it all come out. Telling her my innermost thoughts, relieving me of the torture of guilt. After what seemed like hours, she gave me something for the pain, something to help me sleep. She left, knowing that now I could begin to move on.

Trust

When the surgeon did his rounds, he said he was pleased with my progress. The bullet had stopped at the bone and had been easily removed. It left only a small entry wound that he assured me was healing well, only a few stitches were needed. He was reluctant to let me leave until the swelling and bruising had gone down and was sure that the injury had not impacted on my heart.

'I hear you still don't want to see anybody,' he said, broaching the subject I'd been avoiding.

'I just need to sort out a few things in my head before I'm prepared to face the world. But there is someone who I would like to look after me. She is the only person I feel I can trust.'

Emma, the lovely Irish nurse, was that person. He told me he would see what he could do. By late afternoon all was in place. Emma would look after me in twelve hour shifts during the day, no other duties. A trusted night nurse would supervise during the evening when I slept. At long last, control was coming back into my life.

When Emma arrived the next morning it was as if a long lost friend had returned.

'Darlin', this business of hidin' yourself away is no good for you. I've been wondering why you won't at least see your daughter?'

'The newspaper articles, Moses showed me them all. Nobody spoke out, nobody defended me. It seemed that everybody had moved on. It made the idea of leaving them all so much easier. He'd convinced me that we were alike, so much of our pasts were similar, and I did feel a connection, us against them. I'd been trying to find where I fitted all my life. He made me think I could discard the people I loved and find sanctuary with him. The longer he held me captive, the more fond I grew of him, believed him, felt I belonged. And now I can't bear this feeling of guilt. The ease at which I could justify abandoning Kate, my friends, everyone and everything, to stay with him. I feel so ashamed.'

'You had no choice, and quite frankly you could not possibly have read all the articles. It was the biggest news, on the front pages for ages, it was covered by everyone. Lands End was a sea of reporters, people couldn't get enough of the story. Whatever that man showed you should have been enough to fill a library. Has it occurred to you he only showed what he wanted you to see?'

Slowly it dawned on me that what she was saying could be true. Why would Moses show me anything other than the stories that would support his claim on me and reinforce his hatred of Adam?

'Last night, when I was thinking about coming and working for you, I did a bit of research of my own. It seems that those closest to you spoke only through your blog. It pissed off some of the papers, they had to scrape the bottom of the barrel to get anyone to talk. Looks like that woman called Fiona had her fair share of rants. You must've done something pretty major to piss that one off! Look, here. You can see for yourself,' she said, as she handed me an ipad.

And it was all there. I scrolled down. Hundreds of pages, telling the whole story. Moses had most definitely only shown me a small piece of the picture. He'd cherry-picked the articles to manipulate me and my way of thinking. He'd managed to capture so much more than just me, he'd almost successfully captured my mind as well. I was a fool to think I had any control over him. He had been the master puppeteer all along.

What an idiot I'd been.

'Kate? How is she?' I croaked through shameful tears.

'She's been waiting outside everyday since they brought you in. I'll go and get her.'

Within seconds my gorgeous daughter ran to my bed, hugging me, crying, holding me tight, afraid to let go.

'I'm sorry darling. I'm so glad to see you. I love you very much.'

'It's alright mum, I'm here. I can't believe you're still alive, I love you, too,' she said quietly, choking on the tears.

When we had calmed down, Emma broke the intense emotional scene by making a cup of tea. She had an almost sixth sense.

'Kate, this is Emma, she has been wonderful.'

'I know, she's been keeping me informed of your progress. She is lovely, I don't know what I would have done without her. She even baked cookies for me yesterday,' said Kate, looking at Emma with an affectionate smile.

'She told me you were too fragile to see anyone, that your heart was in danger and that I would get to come in when you were no longer at risk. I knew you'd be ok, you're a fighter,' added Kate.

'They kept everyone away except me. There are reporters everywhere. It's complete madness outside, far worse than when you went missing.'

Emma was an angel beyond compare. I had no idea she'd been carefully filtering the information to Kate, protecting her and me from my irrational decisions of the last few days.

'Where are you staying? Is anyone looking after you?'

'Cindy, she's been great, she's organised everything. We have an apartment in a building connected to the hospital. She's handling the media, liaising with the doctors and police. Nothing is getting past her eagle eye. She's been holding everyone and everything together since you disappeared.'

We spent the next few hours talking about what had happened while I was gone. Kate was very careful not to pry too deeply about my capture. Again, Emma must have spoken to her. By lunchtime I was starting to doze off, a good time to say farewell. The return to normality had begun.

Cindy arrived in the afternoon.

'Bloody hell, you should've told me you needed a longer break!' she said, grinning with relief.

'None of us at the office could accept you were dead. We didn't even entertain the thought, there was no plan B, we just kept on going,' she exclaimed.

'And of course boss, you hitting the headlines has been very good for business. Things are going crazy back in Melbourne.'

'Why don't you hook me up to my computer? I could write some stuff for the readers?'

'Tina, you nearly died... twice! They can wait. I'll write something brief, give a bit of a progress report, say Hi from you. Everything is under control, trust me. You need to rest now. Take your time. We just want you to get better, so you can eventually get back to the office and help us deal with the Tsunami you've created.'

It was good to be reminded of her no nonsense approach.

Emma suggested that I needed to have my wounds dressed and Cindy understood the hint. She left me with a phone.

'Use this if you need it, only Kate, Emma and I know the number. I've put in our details. See you later, maybe tomorrow?' she said cheerily as she walked out the door.

'Two down, one to go. You haven't mentioned Adam? Why don't you want to see him?' said Emma, as the door closed shut.

She had pointed out the elephant in the room. How could I see him? What did we have left? I'd slept with my kidnapper, been unfaithful, fantasied about an escapist life that did not include Adam. Pouring my heart out to Emma was the only way I was ever going to begin to unscramble this emotional torment.

'Well, do you love him?'

13

'I don't know what I feel, he tears me apart. We've tried to be together, but things always get in the way and now I've committed a betrayal from which I see no redemption.'

'You weren't in your right mind,' she said consolingly.

'But I was, all my decisions were completely clear.'

'No, you're not looking at it logically. Take your mind back to the time before you were kidnapped. You were trying to get help. What would you have done if you'd made it back to the main road, to Moon Bay, to Joe's place? None of this other malarkey would've occurred.'

She had a point. I'd never thought of it that way.

'You should try to imagine what things would be like if you'd made it out safely and got help for Adam. What would have happened next?'

'We had talked about a life together...'

'Do I still sense your reluctance to think about what that might be?'

'Well yes, because we've never really had the chance to even begin.'

I told her about the unlikely way we'd got together. About the riots and the stranding on the island. She laughed with the absurdity of it all. But it wasn't just about the lack of time Adam and I had spent together in the real world. I told her about his fucked up family and the brother who would always come between us.

'Do you think you're the first woman to have ever encountered these issues? Family is often the biggest stumbling block, clashes of personality, simple misunderstandings. This fairy tale shite is hard wired into us. Don't you think Prince Charming had some annoying little brother in the background, getting in the way, pissing him off?'

As usual she was right, it was a relief to be given a new way of thinking about things. Of what might have been.

'The one thing I don't understand is his silence? I feel like he let that bitch Fiona do all the talking, stomping all over me.'

'Perhaps he chose not to talk on their terms. He had no control over what others said. I think he works differently. He has made a very generous donation to the hospital, because of him you've been given these conditions. Don't get me wrong, I would've looked after you for nothing, but I've never seen the rules bent so much for anyone before. This room is on the top floor near the conference centre, away from the wards and the other patients. It's a suite that's usually used for visiting specialists. He paid for it to be fitted out while you were in intensive care. He's even made sure there are security guards preventing any unnecessary intruders.'

'But he's rich, anyone with that kind of money can do what he's done.'

'That's not all, while you were missing he organised the search to continue way after the police had given up. We'd see him on the television, directing the searchers. It was only when a shoe was found washed up on the beach a month later that he stopped.'

'He may not have talked to the papers, but his actions spoke louder than any words. That land at Moon Bay, he bought it. Sent out a press release saying it would be replanted. That it would be a fitting final resting place for a woman he loved deeply. That he had always felt a strong connection with the land. He even mentioned something about the two of you replanting trees. Everyone who watched that broken man knew his grief was intense.'

The extent of Moses' clever brainwashing was now becoming evident. Even the story about mining had probably been fabricated. When I'd read through the articles on the search, the land at Moon Bay was always described as former forest, once owned by the bankrupt timber company, no mention of Adam's father. Surely the press would have had a field day with that story if all Moses told me was true? The only truth was that Adam had fought against the land being logged all those years ago. The press had mentioned this. And now I find out, Adam only purchased it after my capture. He hadn't lied about the land. Moses had probably seen the surveyors and knew it was being prepared for sale. In his sick mind he'd been able to create a plausible scenario he knew I'd accept. How close I'd come to falling into his trap. But now that I knew the truth and understood how cleverly I'd been manipulated, I could finally start to forgive myself. My heart flooded with relief, I was beginning to chart a course through this emotional minefield. Doubts about a future with Adam began to slip away. I would take Emma's advice and create a new beginning.

'Darlin' girl, I also think you've forgotten how to be loved,' said Emma. She was right.

'Tomorrow, tell him to come tomorrow.'

She let me sleep, it had been a truly exhausting day.

Into the Night

The night light was on. How long had I been asleep?

'Now that's what I call a good rest. Would you like a shower, a cup of tea?'

'A shower would be great, maybe I could do it myself?'

'I don't see why not, here let me fix your dressings.'

Emma kept the door ajar as I luxuriated under the hot water. The toiletries were from his hotel, the towel not your usual hospital issue. I had failed to even notice such details last night. I called her to help wash my hair, still reluctant to raise my injured shoulder.

'Try lifting it a little, it's healing nicely, you need to get it moving.'

I cautiously stretched out my arm and fingers, pleased the bullet had not damaged the nerves. Slowly I lifted my shoulder and realised the pain was not as bad as I thought. Emma stayed and watched me tentatively begin to use my left arm.

'Good girl, they'll be letting you out of here before you know it,' she said and walked away confident I would be quite capable of showering without her help.

She had dispensed with the hospital gown and a beautiful pair of pyjamas, like the ones from The Imperial, lay folded on the chair. His presence was everywhere. I was beginning to feel human again.

A comb was found and I looked into the small mirror above the sink. A rainbow of bruises covered my face, my split eyebrow stitched neatly to close the cut. The reflection was hideous and I needed no convincing about the brutality of my abductor or the beating he'd given me. Moses was an animal and I hated him for what he'd made me become. I was no longer under any illusions about what had occurred and what it might have been like if I stayed.

It was getting close to the end of her shift, Emma must be getting exhausted. I had been a very demanding patient.

'Is there anything I can get you before I go?'

'Actually I'm starving. Could I get a bite to eat?'

'Already done. I've called up one of those fancy little restaurants off Salamanca Place, they're bringing over some food. Probably be another forty minutes. The night nurse will let them in.'

I thanked her and she winked as she left the room smiling,

'Just doin' my job darlin'.'

A quiet knock, I must have dozed off, the food was here. The waiter pushed the trolley towards my bed, I could barely see his face in the muted evening light. The aromas whetted my appetite. I was curious to see what Emma had ordered. He had his back to me as he lifted the cloches, assembling the food.

'It's ok, you can leave, it must be quite late, the nurse will help me.'

He silently shook his head.

Sitting up in bed, I closed my eyes, wincing at the discomfort of trying to move the shoulder. As the pain abated, I opened my eyes and gasped. He stared at me tenderly, it was Adam. I began to weep. He swept me up in his strong arms and held me close. I felt the trembling of his sobs. For what seemed like ages we didn't move, not wanting to let go. He gently kissed my bruised face, his lips brushing away the ugliness. I saw the anguish in his eyes, in his dark brooding, beautiful face and knew nothing could compare to this most visceral moment of love. Nearly lost, but breathtakingly found. He kicked off his shoes and climbed into bed with me, holding me, rekindling our connection. That is how we stayed all night.

No food was eaten. No night nurse knocked. I was now truly safe.

A New Day

As the dawn light began filtering into my room, I woke to feel him against my back, cradling my body. I reached for his arm, running my fingers along his hand, intertwined, he squeezed back, awake. He held me, kissing the back of my neck, then sat up and brushed the hair from my face, staring intently, his eyes filled with the wonder of our reunion.

'Good morning,' I whispered, our first words, and smiled faintly.

'Good morning,' he replied.

'I can't believe I've got you back. I can't bear to think of what might have been. I never want to be away from you again,' he whispered.

'I need you with me, too.'

He touched my face, traced my lips with his fingers, reassuring himself that I was here. Real. We lay together silently until my stomach growled, reminding us both that we had not eaten, the trolley remained untouched.

'I'll see what I can salvage from last night's dinner,' he said getting up, a faint grin lifting the mood.

'Hmm, what have we got here? Some bread and butter, cheese, or perhaps the chocolate tart. What would Madame prefer?' he joked.

'All of it. I'm starving, it feels like I haven't eaten for days.'

Before too long we were interrupted by a knock at the door.

'Good morning, Tina. I see you have a visitor,' said Emma as she entered the room pushing a new trolley.

'How 'd you sleep darlin'?' she said as she checked the monitors.

'Best sleep yet. I feel much better, thank you.'

'I took the liberty of bringing in a decent breakfast for you both. I'll leave you in peace to eat. Just buzz me if you need anything.'

We were hungry and devoured the food, eggs, bacon, Danish pastries and hot coffee. It gave us the strength to talk.

'What day is it? How long have I been here?'

'December twenty eighth, almost the end of the year. They found you on Christmas Eve.'

'So I've been gone for almost two months. I left Melbourne at the end of October. How long were we trapped on the island?'

'About two weeks?'

'How long before they found you? How did you get off the island?' I asked.

He told me of the shots that alerted Joe, being found, the search parties. Filling me in on what had been going on until a few days ago. He painted a very different picture to the story Moses had given me.

'But I read the articles, you let Fiona do the talking. Why didn't you defend me?' I pleaded, aware that the story he was telling me bore no resemblance to the few pieces Moses let me read.

'I was sick of them twisting the truth. It was better if I said nothing. The newspapers were pissed off that we weren't talking to them. I directed everyone to your blog. Fiona was the only one who would give the papers what they wanted. Our right of reply was always online, Cindy responded to everything. Even the bullshit Fiona was peddling. In the end Fiona started to look ridiculous and the newspapers stopped calling her.'

He continued to paint a clearer picture of what went on back in Melbourne.

'It was Cindy who got us all together. It was awkward at first, no one knew of our relationship. I had to be careful of what I said, I didn't want to upset your daughter. Cindy arranged for me to talk to Kate. I told her of my feelings toward you. She was surprised, a little bit reticent, thinking I would be like Justin, unsure of whether I could be trusted. Margot really stepped up, taking Kate under her wing. Something Margot said must have changed Kate's attitude and eventually she let me in. I would always speak to Kate first. Filling her in on all we were doing to try to find you, keeping her in the loop, trying to reassure her that we hadn't given up.'

'Do you know much of what happened that day we found you?' asked Adam, tentatively.

'I remember being bundled into the back of his truck, speeding off, gunshots, helicopters and waking up here. The police were in, but didn't really say much. They told me Moses had eventually been found dead.'

'Yeah, he was hit, but managed to escaped into the forest. They found him the following day, he'd bled to death.'

I shuddered to think of what might have transpired if he'd survived. Only Moses knew what actually happened between us. I felt very relieved he wasn't alive to tell the real story.

'What made them come for me, find me after all that time?'

'I was at Joe's.'

'What were you doing at Joe's? The papers said you'd gone overseas and that you weren't alone.'

'Fucking papers! I'm sorry you had to see that photo, I know what it must have looked like. More of the bullshit stories they were making up. It was actually a picture of me dragging Georgina Snelling up the steps to the jet, away from the reporters she and her sister had been blabbing to. That was the last time I saw her. All that stuff about her being my girlfriend was a complete fabrication. It was hard enough losing you. Dealing with the lies being peddled in the press made it all so much worse.'

It had been that picture that had caused my sudden shift in attitude toward Adam. The first of the clippings that Moses had so cleverly let me see. I was shocked to think how easily I had been manipulated, shuddered at what might have happened if I'd stayed. My eyes filled with tears.

'Are you ok?' he asked with a look of panic, as if he had said something to upset me.

'I'm fine. Just very emotional. Everything is still so raw.'

Adam held me, wiped the tears away and continued.

'I felt so helpless being confined to bed. Worked really hard to get walking again and was glad when they finally released me. After I got out of hospital, I realised the police had all but given up. I wasn't convinced you were dead. I got together my own team and we continued to search. The police tried to tell me there was no chance of you still being alive. When your shoe was found washed up on the beach, reluctantly, I had to accept what they were telling me.'

'I went back to Melbourne to try and get on with my life, but I couldn't concentrate, couldn't work, it all seemed so pointless. Each day I would ring Joe. I always hoped he might have some new information. Maybe a local had seen or found something. In the end he asked me to come back down to Lands End. Sam told me I should go. I'd always loved being around Joe when I was a kid and thought it would be good to just do some mindless work down there with him. Get myself together, be closer to you. It was the lead up to the peak tourist season. I knew Joe could do with a bit of help, things had been so disrupted. And quite frankly, I couldn't bear the thought of spending Christmas with my family.'

'Anyway, I'd been there for a few days, just sleeping on his couch, drinking too much whiskey, trying to drown out the overwhelming grief. Eventually Joe had enough and threatened to kick me out if I didn't do something. I started going over the books and was surprised to see Joe had been selling some of those obscure gourmet foods you'd found at my place. At first I was saddened by the reminders of you. I remembered the food you cooked and the meals we'd shared. So I said to Joe, "who's been buying all that stuff, tourist season come early?" and he tells me it's been Moses. Joe thought that maybe he'd developed a bit of a taste for fancy food. Moses had been eating with the search party. Some of the media guys wanted to get his story, took him out to dinner. Joe said he didn't really think much of it. Something wasn't right. I just couldn't imagine Moses, this wild man from the bush, suddenly becoming a cook.'

'Anyway, just as Joe's opening up for the day we see Moses drive in. I went to the back room and watched as he unloaded the dead animals into the cool room, but the man I saw was barely recognisable. He was clean shaven, civilised almost. I kept my distance, didn't feel like socialising and stayed hidden while the two men talked. Moses had some stuff to post, something about a Christmas present to his father, just small talk. Nothing out of the ordinary, until Joe makes this comment, "You got a woman up there Moses? I've never seen you look this good. Didn't know you were a sweet tooth, buying up all this chocolate. Where've you been hiding her?" And it hits me. It could be you. That prick from the bush had been buying the food only someone like you would know how to cook.'

'Moses didn't hang around, in fact he left abruptly, didn't even collect the paperwork for the carcasses he'd delivered. Something wasn't right, he seemed spooked. I quizzed Joe and the more we talked, the more he started to think. It wasn't just the food, but cleaning stuff, strange purchases Moses started making not long after you disappeared. And even on that day he'd bought shampoo, not something a man with a shaved head would need.'

'We had to act quickly. Moses had raced off because he knew we were onto him. We had no idea of what he might do to you. I called my mate, the detective from Melbourne and he pulled out all stops to get a team together from Hobart. I didn't care if they thought it was a ridiculous idea. I told them I would pay whatever it cost and within thirty minutes a chopper had left with a swat team. A ground crew from the nearest town was mobilised and on its way. The local cop who'd taken the call always mistrusted Moses and took little convincing about our need to get to the property fast.'

All along they thought I was dead. Adam held me as I wept. No one had seen the messages I'd been sending, no one but Adam.

'I'd sent Moses out for that food intentionally, the caper berries, all that unusual stuff you and I shared on the island. I'd hoped someone might notice.'

'I know, you were so clever. I'm sorry it took so long to see the signals you were sending. Something in me didn't believe you were dead, I couldn't get you out of my mind. And I was right, you weren't dead. I just didn't know where to look.'

'But you did. You found me, you knew. Adam I love you, I love you so much. Stay with me.'

'I'm not going anywhere, never again without you. I love you too, more than you can possibly imagine.'

We sobbed, his shirt wet from my tears and held each other as if letting go would mean a loss forever.

Over the next few days it was heartening to see all these people together. Adam and Kate joking like old friends, Cindy keeping them in line. My health improved rapidly, my heart was fine and the pain in my shoulder barely noticeable. By New Years Eve I'd been given the all clear and we were free to go home.

Although I was ready to get back to Melbourne, I was sad at having to leave Emma.

'You'll be alright darlin', you don't need me anymore. Look at these people around you, they'll make sure you're ok. They love you very much.'

She gave me a big hug and wiped away my tears.

'I'm only a phone call away,' she said, as we finally parted.

We slipped out quietly, the group had become very good at avoiding the paparazzi. The doctor's had agreed to tell the media I would remain in hospital for a least another seven days. They would give a press conference in one week's time to update everyone on my condition. It would buy us some time.

Adam's jet took us home.

Home

We landed at the small private airport, away from the main terminal at Tullamarine and the gaze of curious onlookers who could easily alert the paparazzi of our arrival. Sam was waiting and quickly got us into the car.

'Welcome back Tina,' said Sam grinning.

'Thanks Sam, can't quite believe I'm actually here.'

'Where to folks?'

It dawned on me I didn't really know where home was. My blank stare was met with Cindy's response.

'Your house is ready. Davina and Raphael have been pulling out all stops to get it just right for your return. You ready to see it?' she quizzed, with an excited look on her face.

I looked at Adam, he just smiled.

'Come on Mum, it's bloody amazing, you'll love it.'

And it was agreed, we would go to my new home.

Riding along the freeway, cutting through the park, past the zoo and into the familiar streets of Fitzroy, filled me with the blanketing warmth of returning home. Back to familiar sights and sounds, to a place where I belonged.

Sam drove us slowly past the simple white facade of the double fronted terrace that was my new house. And when he knew I'd seen enough, he drove down the hill and around the corner, through a series of labyrinthine alleyways, into the back lane and a row of almost identical garage doors. I couldn't tell which one was ours until Kate pointed the remote and we entered the ground floor. Eventually the doors rumbled shut, cocooning us in the sanctuary of my new home. Davina was waiting for us.

'Tina, as much as none of us gave up hope, I was starting to wonder exactly when this day would come,' she said, grinning, holding out her arms, embracing me warmly.

'Lucky we put the lift in!' she joked, very aware I had only just come out of hospital.

Adam took my hand and pressed the buttons, the rest of the group ran up the stairs. Within seconds we reached the first floor. We walked into the main room and I was greeted by the Finestras, crying and smiling all at once.

'Bella, bella,' they chanted, hugging me, kissing me. All of us weeping with the joy of our reunion.

'Mum, do you love it, the house?' interrupted Kate enthusiastically.

'It's gorgeous, thanks Davina, Raphael, it really does feel like home. It's just so good to be here with you all, back in Melbourne, back with the people I love,' I blurted out through the tears, as I looked around the beautiful space.

'Darling we missed you so much. We won't stay long. We know you've been through a lot, but we just had to see you with our own eyes, back here safe with your family, with us,' said Gabriella.

The next hour was a bit of a blur. I sat on the couch, holding court, offering polite conversation to my friends. They told me some of what went on while I was absent. Light conversation, the joy of reunion. No one spoke of the abduction, of Moses. Only Emma knew the full story. Emma and Moses. And dead men don't speak. My secret was safe.

By late afternoon I was beginning to get very tired, the Finestras took this as their cue to leave. Cindy was next to go, mentioning that she had some things to catch up on.

'Surely you're not going to the office?' I quizzed.

'It's New Years Eve, thought I might see what the town has to offer,' she said smiling.

'Come on Cindy, you should tell mum what's really going on,' said Kate.

'What?' I responded curiously.

'She's going on a date,' blurted out Kate.

'Oh shut up you, it's not a date.'

'Yes, it is, you're going out with that young detective, the cute one who was helping out with Mum's case.'

Cindy grinned.

'I'm only being polite, a kind of thank you for all the help he's been over the last couple of months,' she said defensively.

She wasn't fooling anyone and we let her go without any more teasing.

And I was quickly reminded of the resilience of youth when Kate too announced she was going to a party with friends. I gave her my blessing, it would be good for her to get out and have some fun. She and I had spent a lovely few days together, catching up, reconnecting. Kate threw a few things into a bag, gathered from the front bedroom she'd already claimed as her own, and let Sam drive her to her destination. The door clicked shut and finally Adam and I were alone.

'No more partying for you my darling,' said Adam, sensing my tiredness.

He picked me up and carried me to bed. He'd done this before. Contentedly I fell into a deep, satisfying sleep.

I woke, naked and confused in this unfamiliar space. It was still dark. It took a while for me to get my bearings. I was at home in Melbourne and, like that first night when Adam had rescued me from the riots, he'd undressed me and left me to sleep. I reached out to find Adam next to me, fully clothed.

'Hi, how are you feeling?' he whispered.

'A little strange, like I'm in a hotel room, this place is so unfamiliar.'

'Don't worry, you'll get used to it. Davina's done a remarkable job. I'll take you on a proper tour tomorrow, in the daylight. We've got all the time in the world.'

'Speaking of time, is it midnight yet?'

'No, not yet, eleven fifteen. You've been asleep for quite a few hours. Want to go onto the rooftop and watch the fireworks?'

'Yeah, that would be lovely.'

Adam handed me a robe and told me to wait. I heard him clunking around in the kitchen, making a few trips to the top floor.

'Come with me,' he said, taking my hand, leading me to the corridor and into the lift.

The small glass capsule shot quickly to the roof. Keeping the lift had seemed like such an indulgence when Davina first showed me the original plans. A bit unnecessary for a forty year old, and about as sexy as a stair lift. She insisted I might want to consider it if I planned to grow old in this place. And she did mention this house was four stories high, a long way to carry champagne from the cellar to the roof deck. I only agreed when she let me look through a few catalogues and together we found one that was sleek, discreet and modern, hidden in the back wall cavity, not too ostentatious or obvious.

The last time I was up here, nothing had been completed, it was just a windswept barren concrete space that looked like a rooftop car park. Things had changed. We alighted into a large glass room. One side wall of cupboards hid a small, but functional kitchen. Ten black Philippe Starck chairs sat around a simple wooden table in the middle of the room. A long grey Florence Knoll sofa faced the spectacular views of the city. The bi fold glass doors were fully open on all sides. Open in summer or closed in winter, this room would be a great place to be all year round. The air was warm and sultry, beckoning us outside, perfect for watching the fireworks, with views unimpeded by the glass balustrade. On the cheekily astroturfed deck sat two orange Lettini sun lounges, their simple wavelike curves alluding to a day at the beach. The city skyline, the deck, the furniture all looked so beautiful. I liked being up here, it had such a good feel. I couldn't wait to see the fireworks.

'Sit down, I'll get you a drink.'

Adam brought back two glasses and a bottle. The popping of the cork my first reminder of what light hearted whimsy could be, lifting the serious mood of the last week.

I sipped.

'Prosecco, my favorite,' I exclaimed as the bubbles effervesced, teasing my nose as I sipped.

'Yes, I remembered.'

'Thank you.'

Next he presented me with a platter brimming with yummy looking charcuterie.

'When did all this happen? The food, the wine, even my robe,' I asked, curiosity getting the better of me.

'When it looked like you were recovering, I rang Sam. He got together a team from the hotel, housekeepers, cleaners, gardeners, florists, who all worked together to make this somewhere you would want to come home to. Just the basics, a bit of food, sheets on the bed, wine in the fridge. He didn't tell them exactly when you were coming home, just told them it would be some time after the press conference next week. Davina and Raphael worked round the clock to get all the furniture in place, but there's still a bit to do. They knew you would want to add your own finishing touches. When the shops open again I'll take you out for a bit of retail therapy. Until then, Sam is happy to go out and get anything you might want.'

I was so touched at how aware he was of my need to feel that this was my home. He'd done just enough to make the place inviting, without being suffocating. Like the friends who greeted me with love and left before they'd outstayed their welcome. We sat quietly. We would need to learn how to become 'normal' again, have conversations not peppered with the wariness of what could or could not be spoken about.

An explosion in the distance signalled the onset of the pyrotechnic sideshow. We watched like awestruck children.

Kate texted. I wished her much love.

'Happy New Year,' said Adam, delicately kissing my cheek.

'With you,' I said, touching his glass in a gesture of quiet celebration. I snuggled against his chest until the wine and the last of the drugs took effect. He took me downstairs and I crawled back into the bed.

'Should I stay?' he asked tentatively.

'Of course!' I replied, slightly confused as to why he would ask.

'It's just that I want to be respectful of Kate. I'm not so sure how comfortable she is with having me around, sleeping in your bed. I just don't know?'

He was genuine in his concern. I knew Kate understood the depth of his feelings, but he was right not to slap her in the face with it.

'She texted to say she was staying with friends. Won't be home for a few days, something about a music festival. I'll have a talk to her when she gets back.'

'Good,' he said standing at the foot of the bed, dressed and with the furrowed brow expression of concern that had become a regular part of our communication.

'Are you coming to bed?'

'In a minute, I have some work to do. The Chinese never sleep. I won't be long.'

Slightly taken aback by his rebuttal, I realised I knew absolutely nothing about his business and how he operated. I accepted we still had a lot to learn about each other. My weariness took over and sleep came quickly.

The morning light flooded into the gorgeous white bedroom. This time I knew where I was, but the man I expected to find next to me wasn't there. I got up, he wasn't in the bathroom, not on this floor. I grabbed a robe and went down stairs. He was sitting at the table in front of his computer.

'Hey, did you get any sleep?'

'Yeah, but you were dead to the world. I didn't want to wake you.'

His chest was bare. His sweats, hanging temptingly from his lean hips, showed me he'd changed out of the clothes he was wearing when I went to bed. But I had no memory of him beside me. Where had he slept? Surely he hadn't worked all night. He looked rested. That same apprehensive feeling came over me again. I'd felt it last night. Something wasn't right, but I didn't know how to talk to him about it.

'What you doing?' was all I could muster.

'Just reading the newspapers on line. Nothing much happening, just the usual boring bullshit. Babies, parties and stupid resolutions.'

I left him to read and ventured into my gorgeous stainless steel kitchen. After a cursory rummaging I found the coffee.

'Shit, shit, shit! How the fuck do you work this bloody thing?' I swore, exasperated at how difficult it was to use the state of the art coffee machine.

'Here, here let me,' he said getting up, nudging me to one side and efficiently letting the machine hiss away while it produced a cup of coffee.

'Is this what you were after?' he quipped playfully.

'It's a man thing,' I snapped back in frustration and made a mental note to buy a coffee plunger.

We sat and ate breakfast.

'What would you like to do today?' asked Adam.

'You know, I would really love to go for a bit of a walk down Smith Street, perhaps even as far as Gertrude. I feel like I want to get back into things a bit. Wander down those familiar streets I've missed.'

'Sounds good. Why don't you go and have a shower?'

'Why don't you come and join me?' I teased playfully.

'I've already had one, you go, get ready. It's going to be really hot today, let's head out before the sun beats us.'

Don't over think it, I told myself as I walked away, feeling a little rejected.

He was right. A Melbourne summer sun was a bitingly hot assault on my pale skin, I thought, as I waited outside while he grabbed his wallet and keys. The door slammed and I turned to take his hand, but was shocked to see him carrying an ebony cane, a walking stick. He sensed my unease and explained.

'Distances, my leg is still pretty fucked up.'

'I'm so sorry, we don't have to go.'

It had been me who had been the hospitalised wounded. In my own self absorbed way I'd completely forgotten about his leg, the break, and how he'd been affected. He'd helped me to the plane, carried me to bed, given no indication that it was still a problem.

'No, no, I need the exercise. The surgeon said it would be awhile before the bone would knit completely with the steel plate they used to fix the leg. My physio and trainer are always on my back to exercise more. It will do us both good.'

And it did do us good, the familiarity of my old stomping ground was the best welcome home. The streets were almost abandoned, nothing much was open. It was New Years day, a public holiday, no one up this early, and Melbourne was in the middle of its usual holiday season hiatus. It was better for us this way.

I sat to rest on one of the park benches under the cedar trees on Gertrude Street and watched as he crossed the road to buy a paper from the convenience store. He looked sexy. The cane gave him a rather rakish air, like a pirate, devilishly handsome, desirable. My mind and sex connected and I felt the first flickerings of desire. I wanted to be fucked. My breath quickened with the thought of his body against mine. I knew the problem, he was too scared to touch me, frightened of my physical and emotional fragility. But he was misguided. He was the cure and I knew I needed him to make me whole.

First Day

He could barely keep up, I was eager to get home, driven by the possibilities of how I might get this man back into my bed.

It was getting searingly hot and the sanctuary of the house was very welcome. But not quite cool enough. He sat down at the long dining room table, looking out towards the large interior courtyard. The double doors were pushed back, creating one huge indoor outdoor space. The swimming pool sat tantalisingly in the centre. Dark green weeping figs framed the area giving it a shady, oasis like feel.

At first he didn't notice, but eventually he looked up from the paper. I watched the expression on his face as I performed a very slow striptease. When completely undressed, I walked quietly into the pool, then swam under water till I emerged at the other end, to sit, facing him, wondering what would be the next move.

Adam remained still, so I got out and walked towards him. He would need some coaxing. As he sat, I unbuttoned his white linen shirt, running my fingers along his hard broad chest. Then I took his hand, gesturing for him to stand. One by one I released the buttons on his jeans and nudged his pants till they fell to the floor. Now he too was naked. I returned to the pool, dived, and again swam to the far side to watch.

He hesitated at first, then gradually took a few tentative steps till he got to the water's edge. He too dived and I watched as his strong muscular arms ploughed through the water to finally reach me. With great elegance and strength he pulled himself out of the pool and sat on the hard stone edge. I made my way towards him, keeping my head above water staring into his eyes, not breaking contact. I swam up to his legs and rested briefly between them as I caught my breath. Then I lifted his left leg till it was outstretched. I could see the vicious purple scar that tore through his perfect skin. I traced the line of the wound, then kissed it, his chest rose. He slipped easily back into the water, cradling me in his arms, staring intently, apprehension in his eyes.

'It's ok. I'm not fragile. I won't break.'

He paused, then slowly ran his fingers over the scar on my shoulder, just as I had done to him.

'I need you to make love to me, feel you inside of me, make me whole,' I whispered.

His cock stiffened.

My torso bobbed on the surface of the water, my head rested in the crook of his elbow. The weightlessness allowed him to easily hold me, floating in front of him. He gathered me close and kissed with a passion I'd so achingly longed for. His mouth continued its exploration, along my jaw, down my neck, then sucking and biting my nipples till they stood firm and proud.

He carried me out of the water, out of the pool and across the courtyard, to the day bed under the shady trees and placed me gently down. Adam lay beside me, touching the fading bruises on my face. I didn't flinch, they no longer hurt. He ran his hands down my body, across my hips, then to the soft skin of my inner thighs. I eased my legs apart, inviting him to continue. His fingers danced playfully over my swollen sex, his thumb circling my clitoris. I reached for his hand, brushing his knuckles, encouraging him to go deeper. His fingers gently parted my labia and delicately entered me. I arched my back, groaning with desire. I needed more and firmly took his thick rigid cock in my hand, squeezing it, rubbing its length. He raised his body over mine taking his weight as he slowly let his cock slip easily into me, penetrating me, filling me. I wrapped my arms around his back, pulling him hard against me and he responded by thrusting firmly, deeply, my hips locked with his, encouraging the dance. My orgasm and his came quickly.

'I love you,' he pleaded breathlessly, as we lay together.

'I love you, too.'

The ache in my heart was beginning to lessen.

The House Tour

We stayed this way for quite some time. A sense of relief, reacquainted familiarity and post coital satiation made me reluctant to move. The sun was the decider. The black leather sedan inappropriate for a languorous laze, too hot, too sweaty. We both laughed as we peeled ourselves off the couch. Adam picked me up and tossed me into the pool. He followed and swam lazily under water. I watched his muscles ripple as he moved, naturally elegant, like some exquisite marine creature. I forgave his impetuousness. I liked this frivolity, it was hot, the pool was perfect and my man was back. I loved the way the weightlessness made my damaged body feel so much better. Adam seemed to feel the same. He sidled up to me and we both draped ourselves over the steps, semi submerged just enjoying the playful decadence of this naked swim in the middle of the day, together.

'Do you know Ms Maxwell, that this spectacular house, built just for you, would be feeling very sad if it had a soul?'

'Why, what do you mean?'

'Because you've hardly seen any of it. Come on, let me take you on a tour,' he said, grabbing my hand as we got out of the pool.

'Hang on, let me get dressed.'

'No, you're not wearing clothes, we're doing the nude tour, no one will interrupt. I might just have to test some of the surfaces for comfort and durability,' he said, playfully slapping my bottom.

'Ouch, Mr Bossy!'

There were four rooms at the front of the house. The three bedrooms, two up, one down all with ensuites were as I expected. The largest was Kate's, already scattered with her clothes, her things. She had claimed a piece of our home, her home.

But it was the other large room downstairs that held all the surprises. I opened it to find a gym and pulled back the curtains to reveal a view over the courtyard. Then through another door to a large utility room, glass fronted like the gym, with a washer, dryer and ironing board. On the far wall a bench, for the sorting of laundry, long enough to hold my sewing machine, set up and ready to use. Underneath, baskets for both clean and dirty clothes. A linen press filled with sheets and towels, all folded neatly, looking like a hotel storeroom, waiting for an army of guests to arrive. A door on the far side opened to a row of long washing lines. Davina had listened, I'd told her how much I loved the smell of sheets dried outdoors. She'd cleverly snuck this in, hidden from view with a slatted screen, I hadn't noticed it when we were outside. She'd even mounted a television on the wall. I could quite happily spend time here, watching crappy television whilst ironing. It must have seemed such an unglamorous, pedestrian place, but, with her attention to detail, to me it was one of the most delightful rooms in the house.

We crossed the courtyard and looked towards the main room, a massive space, kitchen across the back wall. A hidden butler's pantry to the left, a staircase, on the far right, connecting the three floors above. A wooden refectory table, surrounded by at sixteen of the Starck chairs, made me think of dinners, conviviality and friends. Two more Florence Knoll sofas were positioned in a prime place to sit and contemplate the view of the courtyard and would be wonderful when the glass was in place, northern sun streaming in on a cold winter's day.

Adam told me to sit and wait. He had a surprise. After some time I heard the lift open and saw Adam enter the room, struggling under the weight of a gigantic brown paper package. I tore away the wrapping and was delighted by what I saw. An extraordinary piece, an orange Grant Featherston Contour chair.

'Do you like it? What's wrong?' he said noticing my saddened face.

'It's like the one in the painting.'

'Yes, I know, in my painting of you. I chose the chair, it's my house warming gift.'

'The painting you donated to the National Gallery, I read about it,' I said somberly.

'How could you have known? That article appeared when you were still in America?'

'The hotel, The Regal on Greenwich Street. I was staying there. I recognised the interiors, the furniture. Knew it had to be yours. Started to reconsider what I'd done, leaving you, ignoring your calls. I wanted you back, wanted to make contact. I googled your name and up came that photo of you with the gallery director and Sissy Snelling.'

'You were there at my hotel? When? I flew there after that disastrous time in LA. We could have been there at the same time.'

'It was about a week or so later, you were already back in Australia. That photo and the story about the painting made it very clear to me that a reconciliation was never going to happen.'

He came towards me and took my face in his hands, looked me in the eye and spoke.

'When the time came to mount the exhibition, I couldn't do it. Couldn't bear to part with the painting, with you. The gallery understood. I gave them something else. Your picture's still hanging in my study. I would look at it and wonder how I might possibly get you back. That was at about the same time you rang and asked for an architect. Hearing your voice again made me realise I needed you more than ever, just didn't know how to get you back.'

He kissed me deeply. I kissed him back, smiled lovingly and we held each other, both so aware of how stupid all this game playing had been.

'Thank you. Thank you for so many reasons,' I whispered.

I remembered being invited to the opening of the exhibition, Tim's retrospective at the National Gallery. I'd scheduled a trip to Cambodia so I didn't have to invent some lame excuse for not attending. The truth was I feared seeing that portrait of me hanging so publicly, leaving me exposed, reminding me of Adam's rejection. At the time I had been surprised the press had not made the connection between the subject of the painting, Tina Maxwell, and the blogger Chris Brown. Now I knew the painting had never been exhibited. Adam couldn't let me go.

Eventually the intensity of the moment subsided and Adam playfully squeezed my bum.

'Hey, you should try it out, see if it fits.'

Teasingly I sat down and spread my legs over one arm, just like the pose in the painting.

'Like this I believe Mr Darcy!'

He looked towards me appreciatively, his penis ever so subtly firming. I got up before he reached me.

'Not just yet, I believe you haven't finished taking me on the tour.'

A long raised kitchen bench divided the space, Johannes Anderson stools arranged so my guests might be able to sit and chat to me while I cooked. No overhead cupboards, just deep, under bench, drawers holding what had been unpacked from my meagre old kitchen. Two dishwashers and a massive commercial oven, all stainless steel, camouflaged in the industrial space.

The butler's pantry had been put together just as I had asked. Benches held the electrical appliances. Open shelves, like a small supermarket, were waiting to be filled with groceries. A giant commercial fridge and freezer, glass doors showing empty shelves, reminding me I needed to go shopping, to buy food to share with my family and friends. And at the far end, hidden from sight, the lift. I imagined the convenience of being able to ride up from the carpark, arms laden with shopping, and being delivered straight to the pantry.

'There's something down here I want to show you,' he said, taking me down the lift and into the basement. A wine cellar.

'I got the guys from that great little wine shop on Smith Street to put together some Italian wines, I know you like them. I thought it might also be fun to go on a few wine trips over the next few months, to South Australia, the Barossa, the Coonawarra. I hear the Clare Valley Rieslings are particularly good this year. We could have some fun stocking the cellar.'

'I would love to. Do you think we could take the jet?' I responded cheekily.

'No doubt.'

We returned upstairs to continue the tour.

The splashback across the entire kitchen was an opaque white window, mounted on the back wall, allowing light to shine through, making the kitchen a lovely naturally lit space in which to work. I was feeling hungry just thinking about the possibilities.

Adam took me to the next floor, a vast library, like the original plan, complete with the bespoke timber shelving Davina had designed. A desk against a giant wall of glass overlooked the courtyard. I could imagine doing a bit of writing, quietly, away from the madness of a hectic working week. All the sofas were covered in a soft grey wool, good for curling up in with a good book. The floors were a dark native hardwood, a rich charcoal shag pile rug made me think of what I'd like to do on it with Adam. Didn't Henry mention that all work and no play would make me a very dull woman? Although vast, the space exuded a rich warm cosiness. I would look forward to unpacking my books.

The bedroom above held no surprises. The room was carpeted in a pale neutral wool and apart from two bedside tables, contained only the bed dressed in white linen. The walls were white and the sheer curtains were embossed with a subtle white, almost velvet textured abstract stripe, filtering the harsh summer sun. Heavy light blocking drapes disappeared into a recess in the wall. This would be my sanctuary. The simple functional white bathroom was as I had requested. The walk in wardrobe next to it was the size of my old bedroom. Someone had unpacked and hung my clothes.

Adam was keen to get us out of the bedroom and up to the roof deck.

'What's the hurry, we were there last night?'

'Come and see.'

I wasn't quite sure what he meant. When we alighted into the glass pavilion on the roof, I could see the deck and the city skyline. He took my hand and led me out the front and around a wooden screen to the right of the room. I couldn't believe I had missed it last night. To my utter delight there was another glass room, a beautiful bathroom, just like the one I'd imagined. A giant white stone tub sat close to the windows, all of which opened to a lush tropical garden and high green wall. A long shower extended outdoors, again just as I'd fantasied. Another day bed suggested more of what we had just enjoyed downstairs. A simple open shelf held fluffy white towels and expensive toiletries. Huge glass cylinders were filled with flowers, white Christmas lilies, deliciously scenting the space. Adam turned on the taps to fill the tub, then left the room. I got in and luxuriated at the sheer decadence of bathing in full daylight with magnificent views of Melbourne and the skyscrapers in the distance. He returned, Champagne in hand, French, his favorite and joined me in the bath.

'Cheers my darling, to us.'

I smiled, 'To us.'

He appeared so content, so proud and comfortable.

'You know, I wouldn't let Davina show you anything until I saw it first. Getting this house built was my only connection to you. Working with Davina kept me in touch. Gave me hope that maybe one day things would change. I can't believe how much time I've wasted with my pig headed stubbornness, this idiotic pride that kept me angry and alone, without you, for so long.'

'Me too, I was just as stupid, I was just as guilty. I promise it will never happen again.'

We spent at least an hour in the tub, just sitting quietly, comforted by the sound of his beating heart as I lay against his chest.

'You know I'm feeling really tired, I might just go back down stairs. I didn't get much sleep last night. Do you want to come?' said Adam, climbing out of the tub.

'No, not just yet, you go. I'll be along later.'

It was good he didn't feel the need to watch over me like a hawk, his fear was abating.

I sat back, feeling a lot more hopeful, confident even, that I could get over the ordeal of the last six weeks. That maybe all I needed to do was think about the future Emma had spoken of, one that did not include Moses. The future Adam and I had talked about on the island. A future together, in this house, his love letter to me.

Sweet Dreams

My skin was beginning to wrinkle, I had no idea how long I had spent daydreaming. I padded down the stairs and into the bedroom. Adam was sprawled out on the bed, fast asleep, his chest rising rhythmically. He looked completely serene, relaxed. I stood and stared. He looked magnificent, he had the body of a young Adonis, his tan showed me he had an obvious predilection for swimming naked. His dark tousled hair fell across his eyes, his strong jaw darkened by the stubble of his unshaven face, his lips slightly parted, begging to be kissed. I quietly lay next to him propping my head on a pillow, just lying there mesmerised by his sexy masculinity.

He looked so utterly fuckable.

Carefully I lifted the sheet loosely draped over his torso. I didn't want to wake him. His cock was hanging languidly against his groin. Tentatively, I reached out and touched the soft velvety skin. It was beautifully formed, as if its smooth head was designed perfectly to enter me. I loved him being inside me. Just the thought awakened my senses, I breathed deeply. Not yet.

Without disturbing him, I eased my way down the bed to continue this voyeuristic curiosity, my face now close enough to his penis that I could see every detail. I became even more inquisitive. Leaning in, moving closer, I let my tongue reach out, cautiously touching the tip, probing the slit at the very end, a slight taste of saltiness. I was curious to see what he felt like soft, innocently asleep, unaware of my intentions. I opened my lips and let his flaccid cock fill my mouth, it felt wonderful and I just lay there transfixed by the intimacy of the gesture, my head nestled in his groin, not wanting him to wake.

My tongue pushed him to the roof of my mouth and ever so delicately I began to suck. Magically I felt the faint stirrings of his arousal. I increased the pressure and marvelled at how much bigger his cock became. I breathed deeply and swallowed, relaxing the muscles so that I could take him further into my throat. He was still asleep and my goal was to have him come before he was fully conscious. I now needed to work quickly, sucking hard, working my lips along his huge length, taking him deeper than I ever thought possible, increasing the pace till I tasted the first droplets telling me he was close. Faster I worked till I felt his thick vein pulsate, then erupt, pumping the rich salty nectar of his orgasm into my mouth. I swallowed, licking him to ensure that not a drop escaped. Then relaxed as his erection eased, delighting in feeling him soften, just like he'd been when I started. My head sank back against his thighs and I felt his hand sweep the hair from my forehead, caressing my face. I released him from my mouth and moved up his torso, greeted by his open arms that lovingly wrapped me up and held me close. He had not even opened his eyes. I felt the slowing beat of his heart and together we went back to sleep.

Once, I had found dusk a depressing melancholic time of day. Today was different. Waking, slowly, I now felt happy. Delighted in the feel of his strong body holding me, skin on skin, in our bed, for the first time since our reunion. He lifted my chin and greeted me with a kiss. Hugging me vigorously, no longer afraid I would break. New hope, new beginnings after our shaky start. I was bursting with happiness. He looked at me lovingly with the faint smirk of a questioning smile. I knew he wasn't exactly sure of what had just happened. I smiled back, it could remain a pleasant mystery. His very sweet dream.

It was another hot night, a late afternoon storm had left the air moist and steamy. Adam got up and surveyed the sky. Heavy purple clouds illuminated by flickerings of distant lightning.

'I love this weather,' he said.

'Me too, pity we can't open the windows, I love the smells and sounds of this tropical weather.'

Adam looked back at me mischievously as I lay draped over the messed up white sheets. He walked over to the wall and pressed a button, the low hum of a motor signalled the movement of the windows. Like magic the top panes folded away into the cavity wall and the lower pane was now a glass balcony stretching across the entire front of the bedroom. The smell of warm rain filled the air.

'Is this to your liking?' he said, grinning like a schoolboy.

'Very much,' I said and joined him, leaning out, filling my lungs with that sultry air. Looking out to the brooding clouds, expectant, about to erupt into a summer storm.

'This is amazing, did you think of this?'

'Yes, I did.'

'Boys and their toys.'

'My intentions weren't all that pure.'

'How so?'

'Davina told me about the bathroom on the roof deck and I started to think about you, naked, lying there in the tub. I fantasied about having hot steamy sex with you in the bedroom and thought these windows, opened wide, would be perfect to cool off afterwards.'

'You are so naughty! Poor Davina, she must have wondered about your intense interest in this project?'

'I told her that I was also sick of doing such large scale work and was interested to see what she would come up with. She told me you were a very easy client to work for and that you had both joked about designing dream houses when you were young kids. She loved coming up with ideas that referenced that same type of playfulness.'

'Before Tasmania I was thinking of ways I might chance upon you again. I'd hoped that maybe this house would help break down the barrier we'd both put up. I was planning all sorts of schemes that would see me 'accidentally' be on site, turn up instead of Davina, bump into you, making some lame excuse as to why Davina couldn't be there. Then, just as the project was finishing, she sent you away. I freaked out knowing the keys would be in your hands when you returned and I would no longer have this chance again,' he said, running his hands through his hair, in a somewhat exasperated manner.

'Well, I think I should come clean. I went to Lands End Lagoon to see your place because I too couldn't get you out of my head. I was frustrated when I couldn't look into those images at the exhibition. That I couldn't look inside and get closer to you.'

'What idiots we've both been. I'm so sorry about what this all led to.'

'You know the last bit was pretty fucked up, but imagine if I'd made it to the road? We'd be looking back at that time, reminiscing about the island and what we'd done there. About how much fun we'd had. It's been the only way I've been able to deal with what happened. It was Emma who taught me to think that way.'

He took me in his arms and held me close.

'You are amazing, so strong. I love you very much.'

'And I love you and how you didn't give up hope. That is what gives me strength about us and our future.'

He touched my face, tracing my lips, kissing me, groaning at the intensity of the emotions we had both just stirred.

'Come, there's still one thing I need to do,' he said, leading me back to the bed.

'What?'

And ever so tenderly we made passionate love.

The Streets I Love

He looked so beautiful, just fucked, his handsome body stretched across the bed.

We woke occasionally to watch the storm, to touch and luxuriate in the pleasure of each other's company. Making love at sunrise. Our first morning waking up together contented, without fear. We lay there for a long while.

'Do you have any plans today?' I asked.

'Only plans to be with you.'

'Have you ever been to Victoria Street?'

'In Richmond?'

'Yeah.'

'Well, I know where it is, but I don't usually stop. It's on the way to my mother's house and I'm usually just driving through.'

Victoria Street was often dubbed 'Little Saigon'. This buzzing commercial strip was lined with Vietnamese cafes, supermarkets, butchers, bakeries and two dollar joints. The high rise towers behind housed the immigrants when they first arrived as refugees after the Vietnam war. Some of them opened up businesses, taking over from the post war Greek migrants who had previously occupied the suburb. Many of the Vietnamese people had prospered and chose to live further out in the more affluent eastern suburbs. Luckily Melbournians fell in love with their food and the businesses remained.

'I'm surprised you've never stopped. Lots of Cambodians use the strip, to eat, buy food. Didn't you ever have a sense of curiosity about what was going on in that bustling road? Crave the food you'd eaten in Asia?'

'Not really. You have to understand that I loathed going back to the family home. I tried to get in and out as quickly as possible. And I guess I just don't have your curiosity about food. And anyway, what's this got to do with anything?' he asked, puzzled by the cryptic nature of my questioning.

'The thing that always drives me, hunger. Do you realise we've barely eaten since breakfast yesterday.'

'We've been a bit busy,' he said, smiling seductively, reaching for my breast, circling an erect nipple.

'And I don't believe hunger is the only thing that drives you.'

His fingers travelled down my belly, resting between my thighs.

'Stop! We have to eat, or I won't have any energy left,' I said, playfully chastising him, pushing away his hand.

'There's a famous noodle soup, Pho, traditionally served in the morning. I want to take you there for breakfast.'

'Soup, for breakfast?'

'Yeah, for breakfast, good for stamina. Don't think I've finished with you yet,' I said, slapping him on the bum.

'Come on, let's try out the roof shower first, it's made for two, I need someone to scrub my back.'

Although Victoria Street was not far away, we decided to drive. His leg probably wouldn't make the distance and I would need more than a few bags to carry the groceries I intended to buy. We were greeted at my favorite restaurant by the same wacky guy who seemed to always be doing a shift, no matter what time of day or night I arrived. It felt good to be welcomed back. I often wondered what history his happy demeanour masked.

There were many places that sold the famous soup, the secret was in the beef stock. I had tried other restaurants, only to be served up an inferior broth, more often than not, spoilt by the flavour of powdered chicken stock. This restaurant was the best, the one I always returned to. Not only for their 'soup number two', but their crispy quail, salt and pepper squid, betel leaf beef rolls and Vietnamese coleslaw. Food I didn't cook for myself, but food I always craved.

I had become a bit of a food snob and often wanted to chastise diners for selecting the dishes such as lemon chicken or sweet or sour pork that had been concocted to suit Western tastes. This was not authentic Vietnamese food. But perhaps I shouldn't judge so harshly. Maybe it was enough that they at least ventured out. Food was always a good way to break down barriers and at least they came. I could just imagine how awkward my late husband Paul would have been, sitting here, completely out of his comfort zone. My world had changed so much since his death. It had been nearly two years.

I signalled to the waiter and gave him our order. And then I was completely shocked out of my smugness. Adam had begun to speak fluently to the waiter in a language I didn't understand. They chatted, laughed and seemed to be sharing a few friendly jokes.

'What the hell was that about?'

'I heard him talking to the guy at the bar, his accent sounded familiar, so I spoke to him in Khmer. He comes from an area of southern Cambodia near the Vietnamese border, near Kep. He learnt to speak their language in a refugee camp after the liberation.'

This was meant to be my chance to show Adam something of my everyday life, and just like that, he had taken complete ownership of the situation. His physical presence often commanded the room, but now I saw this other side, an intellectual integrity, an ability to speak to a complete stranger in that man's own language. A charm which had my smiling waiter completely captivated

It was ridiculously sexy.

'Compliments of the house,' declared our new friend, as he presented us with a plate of delicate little spring rolls.

I slipped my sandal off and stretched out my leg till my foot reached his crutch and playfully rubbed against the mound in his trousers, quietly letting him know how sexy I thought his performance was.

'Ms Maxwell, we'll never get your shopping done if you keep that up,' he declared, coughing as he attempted to slurp his soup.

My playfulness was stopped when the waiter returned to ask if the soup was ok. I took a deep breath and withdrew my foot. Adam tried to answer without seeming too distracted. We would not be able to leave until his erection subsided.

'Hey, I'd completely forgotten about Kep. How are your family there, have you finished the house?'

'They're great, we try to Skype at least once a week. They knew about what had happened, were very worried, sad for me. I called them when you were found. I'd love you to meet my little sister and her mother,' his eyes lit up as he spoke.

'The villa is amazing. We finished it a while ago, but I haven't had the chance to stay there yet. I'd always hoped it might be somewhere we could go together.'

'We can now. I'd love to see it, to meet your family. Maybe we can go soon. I feel the need to get over there and talk to Chenda and the women at the factory. We should go before it gets too hot, April can be stifling.'

Although Cindy would have kept Chenda informed, I realised I'd need to get back to the office soon. I had no idea what state the business was really in. Cindy had assured me everything was under control. That world in which I'd previously operated seemed a million miles away. Right now I was content to laze around with Adam all day and he too didn't seem too keen to return to work. Both of our offices were closed for the Christmas break. We wouldn't have to go back just yet.

'Penny for your thoughts?' he asked.

'Sorry, just thinking about work. What were we talking about?'

'You were saying we should go to Cambodia before it gets too hot.'

'Yes, I miss it. Although after the many trips I did last year, I began to dread seeing the inside of a plane again.'

'Not if we take mine.'

'I can't believe you have your own jet?'

'It's convenient, it saves time and I can afford it. I don't have kids or an expensive trophy wife,' he responded.

'Do you ever wish you had?'

'What, a trophy wife or kids?'

'Both.'

'Not really. I've always been too busy, it just hasn't been a priority.'

'So you've never been driven to continue the dynasty?'

'No, my fucked up family put me right off.'

'I think that's really sad.'

'Which one of my relatives would you put up as a role model?'

Suddenly the image of my husband being sodomised by Fiona and Justin came into my head and I realised there was probably a lot of truth in that statement.

'My father has spread his seed widely enough for both of us. I know of at least four siblings I've never met. And anyway I have a little sister who needs looking after, and even then I don't get to see her as often as I would like.'

'Yeah, but you're not your father, I think you'd make a great dad.'

'Look, even so, you're forgetting that we blokes can't just go out and get pregnant and I've never felt any of the women I've been with would make great mothers.'

'I'm actually surprised that none of them has ever 'accidentally' fallen pregnant. You know, you are a very good catch.'

'Without sounding too arrogant, I have never left that to chance.'

'What do you mean?'

'After seeing the results of my father's cavalier attitude to contraception, I've always used condoms and they have the added advantage of letting me have a sex life without catching some nasty little disease.'

At first I was taken aback by his rather cold practicality until it occurred to me that we had never used contraception. I knew I couldn't get pregnant, but he didn't.

My mind raced at the thought of what this could mean.

'And you, why didn't you have more? You had the good husband, the nice house, a beautiful daughter. Why didn't you fill that rambling old mansion with kids?'

'We tried, nothing seemed to work. My periods were irregular, I had no idea when I was fertile. None of the doctors could give us an answer. Kate was my miracle child. I would have loved more kids. In the end we just gave up.'

Tears welled in my eyes, as I was reminded of what that life had been. He reached over and took my hand.

'I'm sorry, I didn't mean to upset you,' he said, sadness reflected in his eyes.

'It's ok, I seem to be a bit more emotional these days.'

The waiter interrupted, presenting us with the bill. Adam paid and we headed out the door to the bustling street. Shopping was a good distraction.

We used the lift and I unpacked the groceries straight onto the pantry shelves.

Our conversation would not leave my mind.

Adam made us a coffee and we sat at the kitchen bench, staring silently into our cups. I sensed something was wrong. The mood was sombre, he was distracted, melancholic.

'Adam, that thing you said before, about not wanting to be a father. You didn't know I couldn't get pregnant, you never asked whether I was on the pill. You, we, have never used condoms. I don't understand?'

'You're not like those other women I'd been unable to love. I'd waited for you for so long. With you it was different, being with you was about making love, not fucking. I needed to feel you, I loved being inside you. Perhaps I was subconsciously hoping you would get pregnant, I only ever wanted you to be the mother of my children. And today I found out it may never be. It feels raw and painful, like a little death.'

He wanted to be a father to our children and I couldn't give that to him. I held him close. Neither of us spoke. I felt cold.

'You don't have to stay,' I whispered.

'I could never leave.'

A grey mood shrouded us, neither of us knew how to deal with the sadness. We both moped around the house. I sat in the library trying to read, but couldn't concentrate. I stood and watched as he swam lap after lap in the pool, his body mindlessly thrashing through the water. At sunset we sat on the roof deck, watching the city lights begin to twinkle like stars. The silence was deafening.

I opened a bottle of Soave and poured us each a glass. The wine helped.

'I'm sorry about this, I just didn't see it coming. I feel confused that I'm mourning something I never really lost,' said Adam, at last opening up, talking to me.

'I'm touched by the depth of your emotions. We could try to do something about it?'

Adam took my hand and looked me straight in the eye.

'No, my darling, you really are all I need. There's so much we have to do together. I think nearly losing you has affected me more than I thought. We have each other, that's enough.'

The mood lifted as the wine flowed.

'I've got an idea,' I said.

'What?'

'Why don't we pretend?'

'Pretend what?' said Adam puzzled by the riddle.

'I would like to pretend you were trying to impregnate me. That you have been away for a very long time. That you need to claim me back,' I said suggestively.

'And who am I, this man of your fantasy?'

'You are a tall, dark, arrogant, but very handsome, warlord who has been away fighting, expanding your empire. You have not been with a woman for months, your cock is hard with the thought of the fucking you need.'

'And what type of fucking would you reward me with?'

'I too am hungry with desire and want you to fuck me hard, from behind, on top, underneath, in my mouth. Anywhere you want, I am open to receive you, to fill me with your seed.'

Adam pulled me to my feet, grabbed the hem of my dress with his two hands and with one almighty pull ripped my dress apart, threw me over his shoulder and raced me off to bed.

And that night, covered in sweat and cum and tears, we fucked like animals, till our bodies could take no more, till every ounce of energy was spent, till our reunion was complete.

Back to Sydney Road.

We still had a few more days alone together, before Kate returned, before the press conference, before work.

In all the time that had passed since Paul's death, there was one place I had not revisited, Sydney Road. It wasn't far away, it was time to go back.

I sat dangling my toes in the pool as I watched him swim. He came up from under the water, resting between my legs, taking my foot, sucking on my toes. I giggled like a schoolgirl at the playful tickling.

'So Ms Maxwell, what adventure have you got planned for us today?'

'Well, it's nearly lunchtime and I thought I might take you to a place that was a favourite when I was a student in Brunswick.'

'Brunswick? Sounds interesting.'

The trip only took ten minutes by car, it really was very close. I hadn't been back for twenty years. When I lived there, Paul could never understand the attraction, he felt uncomfortable with the people, the shabby old shops, my flat. Once he'd moved me out, there was no encouragement to return.

Sydney Road was changing. There was still the mismatched rabble of shops, although upon closer inspection some of the traditional old places had been transformed into hip little coffee joints, wine bars and vintage clothing stores. A large number of apartment towers were rising above the old industrial landscape. Its gentrification was well and truly in place. We pulled up in front of the Lebanese bakery. Some things never change.

'You hungry?' I asked.

'Starving.'

We walked inside and instantly the smell of freshly baked manoush transported me to a time long past. I went to the counter, looking around to see if Fatima was still here. A beautiful young woman took my order, perhaps she was Fatima's daughter. Adam found a table near the window.

'I know this place.'

'How so?' I quizzed.

'Across the road, that flat above the shops, you lived there.'

'You remember?'

61

'How could I forget.'

'I don't understand?'

'I remember taking Paul to your place. He encouraged me to come up with him, I think he just wanted to show you off, I knew he was pretty keen. When you opened the door, I couldn't believe what I saw. It was as if you had been transformed, you looked amazing, so sophisticated, so sexy, nothing like the wild young punk you'd been at university, you had become a woman. Your house was decorated so simply, just a few perfect pieces, it told me so much about who you really were. I wanted to take you in my arms and fuck you there and then.'

My body heated at his suggestion, my heart wished he had acted.

'Why didn't you?' I said teasingly.

'It wouldn't have been appropriate. I thought you and Paul had something going on. And anyway I had to leave, I had an appointment with a real estate agent.'

It hit me like a blow to my head. Had he acted, things would have been so different. I told him about what happened after he left, the dinner, the clumsy sex.

'Why did you let him touch you?'

'I was drunk, lonely, I had no one. I let it happen, never considered the possible consequences. I had no intention of starting a relationship.'

'Why did you continue with the pregnancy?'

'Because I had no one else, no family, my parents were dead. The baby represented a connection to life and to me, someone to love. And anyway, I'd always been fiercely independent, I thought I could do it all on my own.'

'So why didn't you?'

'I lost my job, couldn't afford the rent and got really sick. Paul was very kind, declared that he loved me, offered a way out and I said yes. And I tried to persuade myself I could make it work.'

Adam was silent, his brow furrowed, as I revealed my secret.

'Did you ever love him?'

'For a while I convinced myself I did. He was a kind man, a good provider and a loving father. But as the years went by, we grew more distant, he worked long hours, was barely home, the company was his life. We stopped sleeping together, he didn't touch me, we lived like brother and sister. I was not desired. I gave up hope and lost myself in a domestic fantasy land. On the outside I was the perfect housewife, I cooked, cleaned, sewed and had a beautiful child. For a long time I convinced myself it was enough. I didn't know what else I needed, what to ask for.'

'Why didn't you leave?'

'It was all I knew. We didn't hate each other, we just lived with workable indifference. Neither of us cared enough to change.'

'I remember seeing you at the funeral. I was shocked. My memories were still from that night, your apartment, that dress. I didn't understand what had happened. You had lost your husband, but it wasn't sadness or grief I saw. It was a soullessness. Where had that bright young woman gone? It troubled me, now I know.'

Adam could not believe what he was hearing. He should've gone out with them that night. Paul had asked if he wanted to come along, but he'd politely declined, not wanting to get in the way of his friend's romantic pursuits. If he had gone he could've seen that Tina was not interested in his friend. He could've driven Paul home and maybe even have called Tina the following day. She'd had a loveless marriage, he'd had a loveless life. He had no time to waste, he loved her and wanted to make it up to her.

Adam reached for my hand and squeezed it. The food arrived, we ate silently. We had so much to find out about each other, both of us only had bits of the story. We needed to talk about something other than my pathetic life, I hated the pity. What had happened, my past, was new to him, but I had moved on. Eventually I spoke.

'Remember you said that you had to see a real estate agent, that was why you were in Brunswick that night? What was it that you were looking at?'

'It was an old industrial site and I was looking at starting up a property portfolio. People thought I was nuts paying what I did, but I'd done my homework and knew the whole suburb was undervalued. Developers from the eastern suburbs still saw the north as a less than desirable wasteland. Thought no one would ever want to live there, with its migrants, housing commission flats and rundown factories. It was the class war that had always divided this city and those that didn't see Brunswick's potential would be left behind in their Toorak mansions.'

His eyes came alive with excitement as he talked about this first project.

'It's not far from here, do you want to have a look?'

The street was very familiar, but it had completely changed. Standing where the old clothing factory once stood was a stylish multi storey apartment block. Adam looked excitedly out the window. I didn't share his enthusiasm.

'What's wrong?'

'I used to know this street really well, there was an old factory, JD Dresses. I told you I lost my job, couldn't support myself, this was where I worked.'

'God Tina, I'm sorry. I had no idea,' said Adam, dragging his hands through his hair.

'It's not your fault, the company was struggling. Lots of factories were closing down, not just this one.'

Neither of us spoke on the drive back home. I could almost hear his mind ticking over, both of us thinking about what could have been.

First Date

Unlike the previous night, there was no ferocious fucking. Adam held me, as if I was wounded, fragile and broken, like he did when I had first been found. I didn't like waking up to this mood of pity.

'Please Adam, it's not your fault, I hate feeling like the victim here.'

'Rationally I know, but it's not so much that I feel responsible, but that both of us have paid such a high price for not following our instincts.'

'I know, but at least we have each other now. And anyway who says I would've fallen for your charms. Can't you remember the cold reception I gave you that night? I thought you were an arrogant asshole.'

'And you were a smart mouthed girl,' he returned somewhat defensively, but with a broad grin.

The mood lightened immediately.

'So you never had any thoughts about me, when we'd had those heated discussions in the bar. I always found you quite sexy when your mouth was on fire,' he said teasingly.

'Sexy you say? You never showed it. I always thought you were very good at putting me in my place.'

'I was just hoping you'd bite back, I liked sparring with you.'

I grabbed his arm and bit hard into his muscled shoulder, and jumped off the bed, away from any retaliatory attack.

'Fuck, that hurt,' he yelped.

'I thought you wanted me to bite back?' I said grinning.

He leapt up and before I could run, grabbed me and whacked me hard on the backside.

'Ow! That really hurt you bastard!'

'It was meant to, you've been very naughty, look!'

I could see the tooth marks forming on his skin. This was going to get interesting, but I was no easy target. I wriggled out of his grasp and headed for the door. He followed, wincing as he sprinted on his damaged leg. I tore down the stairs and into the study, slamming the door behind me, leaning hard, trying to stop him from forcing it open, but he was too strong. I staggered backwards and he came tumbling down on top of me, right in the middle of the soft rug.

'Don't think you can escape me so easily Madame, you need to be disciplined.'

I couldn't move, he was lying on top of me and quickly pulled out the cord of the sweats he'd been wearing and tied my wrists together.

'You know what I do to naughty girls like you?'

I feigned horror, daring him to continue. He rolled me onto my belly and pulled my arse into the air, my heart was beating wildly, I liked this game. His hand roughly parted my legs and touched the warm wetness of my highly aroused sex.

'This is what I do.'

And instantly he rammed his rock hard cock into me. I groaned at the lustful agony it incited.

'Harder,' I yelled and he slammed back with a ferocity that caused my breasts to slide across the pile.

'Ah, you feel so fucking amazing,' he groaned as he ramped up the assault.

He forced his palm against my clitoris pulling me harder into him, his fingers circling, working his magic. Wave after wave of pleasure pulsed through my body as he forced one climax after another, until I felt the full force of his cock pulsating with the cum he pumped into me. Panting, hot and sweaty we collapsed onto the floor.

'Not so fragile, Mr Darcy?'

'Not at all, Ms Maxwell!'

We both staggered down stairs and dived straight into the pool to cool off. He kept swimming and I got out and made us a hearty breakfast, all this brutish sex had given me a monstrous appetite. He walked into the kitchen, naked and dripping wet.

'Mmm bacon, I'm starving!'

He made us coffees and we sat and ate.

'Tina, I've got to go into the office for a little while today.'

'Really, I didn't think you were going back till Monday,' I responded with obvious disappointment.

'It's the bloody Chinese, they expect me to be on call 24/7. I need to get some stuff organised before I take a conference call at three. I'm sorry, I can't get out of it, but I have an idea.'

'What?'

'I want to take you to dinner. Somewhere special, on a proper date. I want you to pamper yourself. I rang Sam and he's sending the spa team over from the hotel.'

'Really, you've organised that for me?'

'Nothing but the best.'

He was gone within the hour and for the first time I was alone in my big beautiful house, happily contemplating what the night might hold. I too had a surprise planned for him.

The cupboard above the sewing machine was filled with tubs of fabrics, cotton, patterns, dresses that needed a bit work, half finished ideas and old favorites. I frantically tore through each tub till eventually I found what I had been looking for. The dress, the beautiful little black dress I had worn on that fateful night almost twenty one years ago, the night that had changed the rest of our lives.

I'd kept it because I'd always loved its timeless sixties design, a simple sheath with a daring low back. Tentatively I slipped it on and miraculously it still fitted, all it needed was a wash and pressing and it would look brand new

After lunch the spa team from the hotel turned up.

I remembered the first time I'd been pampered like this. Of the wondrous gift Raphael had given me and the sensuous sex that had brought my body back to life.

Lying on the massage table, every part of my body was being awakened, alive with the expectation of what the night might hold. I felt like a new bride, ready for Adam and for the heady world of pleasure that awaited me.

The body hair was stripped, I felt the naked smoothness of my legs, armpits and groin. Fingernails and toes were given a simple treatment, nothing too garish or overstated. It had been months since I had attended to these things. Lastly my hair, swept up into a simple elegant French twist, emphasising the sweep of flesh from the nape of my neck to my bare back. A light application of makeup, some foundation to cover the fading bruises, some eye-liner, mascara and a smear of red lipstick, just enough to highlight what was there. I slipped on the dress and the killer heels, the team applauded, then disappeared.

I was ready and sat waiting for the sound of the garage doors opening and for Adam to dash up the stairs. Instead the front doorbell rang, startling me. Who could that be? Very few people knew we were back in Melbourne. I glanced at my reflection in the hallway mirror, very Audrey, very pleased.

Standing before me was Adam. He looked so fucking sexy, like a model in his dark Italian suit, a huge bouquet of green goddess lilies in his arms. My eyes welled with tears, he knew I loved these flowers, he had sent them to me for my birthday, long before I even knew he was interested.

'They're beautiful,' I exclaimed.

'Not as beautiful as you,' he said, holding my hand and stepping back to admire what he saw.

'You found it, the dress. Turn around.'

He ran his finger down my spine, my nipples sprang to attention.

'I remember when you turned to lead us into the room, your flat, I saw your back, I wanted to do that then,' he paused, pulling me towards him, holding me close, my back against his chest, the faint stirrings of his erection telling me he liked what he saw.

'And then I wanted to fuck you,' he whispered huskily into my ear.

'Like I want to now.'

My back arched as he nuzzled my neck, nipped my ear lobe. I turned and kissed him passionately on the mouth.

The driver of the sleek black Mercedes, politely coughed, reminding us that we were not alone, holding the door of the car open ready to whisk us away.

'Where did you find this, him?'

'I don't always do my own driving,' he said with a wry grin.

The driver took the flowers from me as we got into the car.

'Where are we going?'

'You'll see.'

The drive was short, along Brunswick Street till the road veered right and became Saint Georges Road. We pulled up in front of Tavola, my favourite Italian restaurant.

'How did you know?'

'What other Italian restaurant is there?' he said, all cool and confident.

The interior was dark and stylish, club-like, tasteful, a far cry from that shabby place with Paul. The restaurant was completely empty. We were greeted by the Maitre'd who took us to a smaller, more intimate room. The sommelier opened a bottle of Prosecco and poured.

'To you my darling, to our first proper date, to a new beginning.'

'And to you, this is so perfect, I can't believe you've done this, where are the other diners?'

'There are none, the restaurant was still closed for the summer break, the owner opened it especially for you, for us tonight.'

'I love you.'

'I love you, too.'

No menu appeared, instead we were fed a series of delicious small plates of Italian delicacies, I lost count of all the courses. Maria Callas sang her deep, sexy, guttural arias discreetly in the background. And yes, there were charming, handsome and flirtatious Italian waiters, but tonight I almost didn't notice they were there.

We stepped back into the car and headed north to Lygon Street. Not the tacky tourist strip in Carlton, but the much more exciting part, further out, in Brunswick. This was where the clever young restaurateurs and retailers were setting up. Where rents weren't as high as in places like Gertrude Street. The driver stopped out front of Gelissimo, the gelati bar that looked like something straight from fifties Rome.

'How did you know?'

'Sam helped me out.'

We strolled arm in arm finishing our gelati, window shopping, calling into the hip little bars that peppered this vital street.

'Look, over there, the furniture,' I said pointing to the brightly lit shop front displaying mid century modern European furniture in the window.

We crossed the road, and pointed to some of our favorites, talking about how fashionable these once discarded pieces had become.

'I remember seeing your flat, the way you furnished it with those few beautiful pieces, furniture like this. It spoke so much of who you were.'

'Part of the thrill was in finding the treasure on the street, it doesn't seem quite the same just being able to step into a shop and buy them.'

I gasped at the price tags and wondered who could actually afford to pay thousands of dollars for a chair and then remembered the house warming gift Adam had given me. People like him, like me could easily find the dollars.

'You know, I remember that time as if it were yesterday. Paul called me the next day, bragging of his conquest, I knew I had lost you and kept away.'

'But not anymore,' I responded quickly, not wanting our night to be spoiled by regret.

Adam took me in his arms and kissed me lovingly.

'Not anymore,' he whispered huskily into my ear.

The driver had followed us at a discreet distance.

It was getting quite late and I was surprised when we drove back down Lygon Street and straight into the city. We pulled up at the Tsar, a brand new boutique hotel on Spring Street overlooking the Treasury Gardens. It was the hippest and most desired place to stay in Melbourne. The driver opened the doors, we were greeted by the concierge who sent the bell boy to retrieve two bags from the trunk of the car.

I looked questioningly at Adam.

'I packed them while you were in the shower this morning.'

I smiled, shaking my head in disbelief at his clever and romantic planning.

We didn't stop to register, Adam walked straight to the lift, swiped a card and we sped up to the top floor, the penthouse.

'I thought you might like to have a sleepover at my new place.'

We stepped into a magnificent grand room, decorated like the palace that Catherine the Great would have lived in if Andy Warhol had been her decorator. A very strange eclectic mix of elegant, but reworked antiques and ultra contemporary design. Midnight blue walls, modern art, vases filled with long stemmed green and purple artichokes, chairs and sofas upholstered in luscious yellow striped fabrics, bowls of pomegranates, some split open displaying their sweet ruby jewels. A look smartly put together, hard to describe without sounding like a clashing cacophony of colour, one that had to be seen to be believed. It was stunning, a clever mind fuck, like great abstract art, that worked absolutely perfectly.

'Adam, this place is amazing. I remember reading about it in one of the architectural magazines. I had no idea it was yours.'

'I am a very private man.'

He took me to see the rest of the suite and I couldn't wait to get him into the bed. We were interrupted by his phone. He took the call, I heard him say he would ring back.

'God Tina, I'm sorry, it's the fucking guys in China. I need to talk to them, clear up some stuff we were discussing earlier today.'

'It's ok, I understand, how long do you think you'll be?'

'I have no idea, I thought we were done, but obviously not. This is bound to take ages, nothing is ever simple about doing business in China.'

'I have an idea. Remember that day on the island when I asked you to surprise me, to take me whenever you desired?'

'God yeah, how could I forget.'

'Well, I want the same tonight. I'll go to bed. I don't want you to wake me, I want you to take me, without me knowing you've returned. I want to wake with you inside me, filling me, then we can make love. That is what I want from you tonight.'

'Fuck Tina, I won't be able to concentrate,' he groaned.

'You will, because you have to. Now ring those bastards, I'm going to bed!'

He heaved a frustrated sigh and walked out of the room.

I wondered, my cunt wet with arousal, how I was going to calm myself enough to sleep.

I heard the muffled tones of a heated discussion and got up. I had remembered seeing a bottle of vodka sitting in an ice slurry, next to a tin of caviar. Neither of us needed to eat, but the drink might calm us down. I poured us both a glass, he looked up and smiled, acknowledging my interception, clinked my glass and winked at me. He had the situation under control and so did I. Quietly I returned to the bedroom, shut the door and crawled into the enormous bed.

The vodka did it's work.

And my wish did come true. I woke to the gentle embrace of my lover, nestled against my back, skin on skin, his cock filling me. His heart pounding with erotic intent. This was what I wanted, passionate, physical love from a man I desired, not the feeble fumblings of someone I pitied. I secretly fantasied about it having been Adam in my bed all those years ago, not Paul.

'I'm here for you, I will never leave,' he whispered into my ear.

Anna Buckley

His embrace was all encompassing, holding me close, fearful of letting go. Slowly he began to push more deeply, harder than I had ever felt before, then withdrawing and back again, faster, more urgently with each new thrust, letting me feel his full glorious length, each penetration delivered with more brutal force, pounding the very neck of my womb. This was what I desired, needed and responded with an equal urgency as my body awoke to the full force of his lovemaking.

'I so fucking need to be in you. To feel you, to love you,' he groaned, as we both became overwhelmed by the emotional and physical intensity of the connection our bodies, our very souls, were making.

My orgasm came over me like a drug entering a vein, slowly at first then building till my mind could barely comprehend the shattering pleasure exploding through me. He cried out at his own release, burying himself in me, breathing hard until his orgasm stilled. We remained in this position, cocooned together and I felt truly loved, protected, safe.

I woke with his arms wrapped around me, he had barely moved, his rhythmic breathing told me he was still asleep. I wriggled my bum against his groin and delighted in feeling the innate response of his penis. The luscious slipperiness of my cum soaked vagina meant that his firming cock easily found its way back inside and I relished the feel of its slow thickening begin to fill me once again. What a delicious sensation. This time it was me who moved deftly against his firm belly till I found that sweet spot letting me bring us both to a delightful morning orgasm.

What a wonderful way to wake.

What a perfect end to a perfect new beginning.

The Last Days of Christmas

It was the last Saturday before Kate went back to Canberra and we would be returning to work. The hospital was scheduled to give its press conference tomorrow night. We had bought ourselves a week of freedom and by Monday morning we all knew the media circus would begin again.

Kate reminded me we had missed Christmas and both thought it might be fun to gather our friends around to have a belated celebration. We had so much to be thankful for. It was nice to have my daughter back home. Adam had gone back to his apartment at The Imperial so Kate and I could have a bit of 'mother daughter' time. He had been concerned that his presence in the morning might be a bit sudden for Kate. Sam probably was also glad to have his boss to himself. It was the first night Adam and I had spent apart since our reunion in the hospital and I slept a fitful lonely sleep.

Another gorgeous clear blue January day greeted me. I took full advantage of the pool and swam a few laps to clear the cobwebs of a restless night. To my surprise I heard a splash and was delighted to see Kate gracefully swimming towards me.

'Hey mum, nice pool.'

'Very. Can't believe you're up so early.'

'Thought you might like a hand with all the Christmas stuff.'

After a few laps we both got out. I volunteered to make breakfast and she elected to tackle the coffee machine. We sat around the table I'd set by the pool, under the shade of the weeping figs. I knew she wanted to talk.

'Mum, I was just wondering who would be coming this afternoon?'

'The Finestras, Cindy, Adam, you, me... just family really. Is that ok with you or is there someone else you would like to invite?'

I wondered whether that horrible boy, Will, might be in town.

'Well, while you were gone there was someone who really looked after me and I would love it if they were to come.'

'Sure, who?'

'Margot.'

I was a bit taken aback. We had both always tolerated her and quite frankly Christmases had always been such tedious formal affairs. She wasn't the 'family' I had in mind.

'It's just that she's changed, I feel like I've really gotten to know her.'

Kate talked about how kind and protective Margot had been.

'She thinks what you're doing is really great.'

I remembered the unexpected praise last Christmas and was not entirely surprised at her change of attitude.

'Kate, that would be fine, I would love to have her over. Why don't you give her a call?'

'Another coffee?' she asked, while texting her grandmother.

'Thanks, more toast?'

'Please.'

Margot called back immediately and said she would love to come over.

'Is there anyone else you would like to invite? Will perhaps?' I said, thinking I should at least ask.

'Will? That slimy little prick! I dumped him after he started mouthing off to the papers. He was just using me and my money. That stuff he said about you and your company was so he could further his own political aspirations. I kicked him out of the house. He's gone back to live with his parents. I hope I never see him again.'

Kate was getting back to her old self and I was glad we wouldn't see a repeat of that dreadful time in Canberra.

The weekend papers were spread out and we both laughed at the pictures of Fiona and Justin trying to look fabulous at some party down in Brighton.

'Jesus, I hate those two!'

I wondered where she was headed with this conversation.

'He was always so creepy around you and Dad. And that bitch Fiona, after the way she blabbed to the press, I wanted to kill her.'

'Well, you know I only ever tolerated them and, quite frankly, after seeing some of those clippings I felt pretty much the same way.'

'Adam, he's so different from his brother. Margot told me they were twins. I could hardly believe it. Adam was so good to us while you were missing. He reminded me of Dad, had a similar way of saying things, told bad 'Dad' jokes. It was really good to have him around. Where is he? Sleeping in?'

And in a few short sentences she had given me the approval I'd been wanting.

'No, he's at his place, he thought you and I might like to spend some time alone together before you go back to Canberra.'

'Mum, you don't have to pretend around me, give him a call, tell him to come over. I'll make us some lunch. He can help decorate the tree.'

'What tree?'

'I rang Sam yesterday, asked him if he knew where I could get a tree and he said they had a big old potted pine in the courtyard of the hotel. Their delivery guy is bringing it around this morning.'

'Seems like you and Sam are great mates. I had no idea you even knew him.'

'Sam's been brilliant. When Adam was looking after Margot and me, Sam was always in the background making sure everything was alright. He'd send over meals, check whether we needed anything. He looked after all of us, especially when things were looking really shitty, when they found that shoe. He too wouldn't let us give up hope.'

'Well, my gorgeous girl, you'd better give him a call and tell him to come along, as well.'

She was texting before I could blink.

Within a very short time Sam and Adam arrived, looking like labourers, shirtless, unloading the tree from the truck.

'That was quick.'

'Couldn't bear being away. How was last night?'

'Lonely without you. Kate wondered why you weren't here?'

'So she's cool about us?'

'Seems to be, said you remind her of her dad.'

'Really, that's nice,' said Adam smiling contently.

The men set up the table under umbrellas in the courtyard. I delighted in rummaging through the cupboards to find the crockery, cutlery and linen to set the table, objects chosen from catalogues before the house was finished, small details giving life to this interior design photo shoot. The tree, decorated in plump ripe cherries, looked invitingly delicious, perhaps this would be dessert?

The guests would be arriving at four, very late lunch, very early dinner. Eating would be over so we could watch the telly together, get a feel for the response from the media.

Margot was first to arrive and Kate grabbed her by the hand, racing her off on a tour of the house before we had a chance to talk. Kate seemed to have lost the eye rolling contempt that had plagued our relationship for the last year. It was more than just the relief of my return, she had gained a new confidence, a more positive exuberance for life. I went up to the roof deck to meet them. Kate disappeared, leaving me alone with Margot.

'It's beautiful, Christina.'

Margot used my full name, I'd always hated being called Chris.

'Thanks, although I can hardly take any credit for it, it was mostly Davina's work.'

'Ah yes, but I'm sure, after living in that mausoleum on the other side of town, you couldn't wait to have something that was actually designed to be used this century. Something that was yours, not a shrine to a family whose past was not your own,' said Margot with a wry grin, the sarcasm in her voice quite a surprise.

I'd always thought she felt disenfranchised when we took over the mansion, resented being ousted from her seat of power. Perhaps she found it just as odious a chore as I did. Perhaps I knew very little about Margot at all.

'I never thought about it that way, but you're right. It was fun having the chance to put it all together, my own little dream house.'

'What's Kate going to do with the Toorak house? Don't let it be a noose around her neck. Do you ever think she'll live in it?'

'I'm not sure, it's part of her history, a connection with her father. We have tenants in it at the moment, she's living off the income. I thought it would be a good way for her to learn to manage money. She saves most of it. It's quite a considerable sum.'

'That's good, I wish someone had given me that type of advice. You know financial dependence is a trap. Women like me were always trained to be someone's wife, still are. When Paul's father died I had nothing of my own, nothing saved for a rainy day. He handled all the financial affairs and thought he'd made provision for me in the will. Charles died so young, the money was nowhere near enough.'

'God Margot, I had no idea you felt this way. How are you coping financially now?'

'I'm doing what I've always done. I have a gentleman friend, he looks after me and I pretend to be grateful. It's all I know.'

I was shocked by her candour, her revelation that painted the picture of the aging courtesan, doing what she knew best in order to survive.

'Christina, what you've done has been extraordinary. My stupid son left you with nothing, I was so ashamed, didn't know how to help.'

'It's ok Margot, we all do what we have to do to survive. And I believe you really stepped up when I was missing, looking after Kate.'

'You have no idea how much I loved being with my granddaughter. It gave me the chance to redeem myself, to love someone who was so frightened of being left alone. She had been brought up by you to feel loved, something I had rarely experienced, given or received. Her loss was so profound. I felt privileged to be given this chance of redemption.'

Kate came up the stairs, bottle of Prosecco in hand.

'Sam couldn't get this to fit in the fridge, said we should open it, have a drink, what do you think?'

'What a good idea,' said Margot, as I grabbed the glasses.

'To family,' I toasted.

'Family,' we all responded.

The table groaned under the weight of the shared feast. I had bought Chinese roast ducks from Victoria street, made colourful mountains of Vietnamese red cabbage, chilli and coriander salad. Massimo had cooked a suckling pig and Gabriella had brought platters laden with antipasto. Sam and Adam had procured exquisite pastries baked in the hotel kitchen. Lola and Raphael had raided their cellars and found some great Italian wine. Cindy had found a confectioner who had made nougat, glace fruits and chocolate truffles. A bit of a multicultural mish mash, but none of us cared. Everyone around the table was relaxed, happy, joyful. Adam would grab my hand occasionally giving it a squeeze, to let me know he was there, smiling at me and our friends, happy to be able to celebrate together.

The six pm news saw us head to the library. The press conference was brief. The hospital spokesperson told the packed room that I was well, would make a full recovery and would be back in Melbourne tomorrow. He asked that our privacy be respected and despite the pesterings of the journalists, no further comments would be made. And with that it was over. Adam turned off the television, he didn't want to hear the speculations of some talking head news reader. We all agreed the hospital chief had been a good sport to play along with our ruse. I knew Adam's donation had been very helpful.

Prosecco on the roof deck at sunset was a fitting end to a wonderful day. Adam's driver had taken Kate to the airport. She had missed so much time and the university had allowed her to catch up before the new term started. We had already booked a number of flights so she could come home more frequently. Neither of us wanted to spend such long stretches apart anymore.

Tomorrow things would start to return to normal.

Part 2

Private No Longer

The press conference passed without fuss. Our guests had left us by eight thirty.

The cleaning up together was such a pleasant exercise in normality. Adam looked so endearing attempting to load the dishwasher, clear the mess, round up the bottles. He helped without prompting, my shoulder was still a bit sore, he felt at ease in this house. He did these chores efficiently but, with an army of cleaners and staff back at the hotel he called home, I knew this was pretty unfamiliar territory. I remembered that first night we spent at his place, Sam, the cleaners and chefs, all being present at some stage running his household like a well oiled machine. Why was seeing him at my kitchen sink so sexy?

'Thanks,' I said.

'Thanks for what?'

'For being so amazing, for looking after Kate while I was gone, for letting me celebrate Christmas with my closest friends. For not giving up. For being you.'

He turned and took me in his arms, kissed my temple, my cheeks, my lips, breathing deeply as if I gave him life.

'Our relationship, us, it's something special, precious. I almost lost you and now I have you back, here, just the two of us together. It's what I've wanted for so long.'

I kissed him passionately, with a longing twenty loveless years had fuelled.

'Let's leave this,' he whispered into my ear.

He picked me up, his erection pushing against my groin as I wrapped my legs around his waist.

We made gentle, deeply connected love, reclaiming small parts of ourselves that had been taken away, holding each other all night, bound by the unbearable thought of what that separation might have meant. The unspoken desperation in our thoughts was beginning to lose its intensity. Soon the voices in my head would quieten.

The alarm at six thirty was a rude awakening to this new Monday. Both of us knew the magical week was over and now we would be thrown slap bang into the reality of our working lives.

'Are you ready for this?' he said sleepily.

'Do we have to? Couldn't I tempt you to spend the day in bed with me?'

'Come on, get in the shower, I'll help you wash your hair.'

He lovingly soaped my back, washed my hair, and wrapped me up in the big white fluffy towel when we had finished. By the time I had dressed and ventured downstairs he had made coffee and breakfast.

'I'll get the papers.'

Now that Kate had left, I would have almost no need to venture across the courtyard to the front of the house. If it wasn't for the laundry, I could just about shut this part of the house up completely. I padded, barefoot up the hallway, surprised by the hum of traffic noise so early in the morning. I guessed, like us, most people would be returning to work today after the Christmas break. I wondered if there would be anything about the press conference in the papers?

'CHRISTINA, WHAT'S IT LIKE TO BE BACK?'

'DID HE TREAT YOU BADLY?'

I slammed the door behind me, trying to comprehend what I had just experienced. I fumbled with the security bolt, heart pounding with fear, scared they were trying to force their way in. Shaken, I walked back through the hallway, past the pool and into the kitchen.

'What's the matter? You look terrible, like you've seen a ghost?'

'Outside... it's crazy.'

Adam ran to the front bedroom to see what I was talking about and came back just as shattered.

'There must be hundreds of people out there, reporters, cameras, onlookers, the street is packed.'

'What are we going to do?' I said, panicked by the invasion.

'I'll check that everything is locked and secure, curtains closed.'

Adam dashed around the house, returning when he knew all was safe.

'I had no idea so many would be out there. How are we going to leave the house?'

'Jesus Tina, I feel like such a fuckwit. I should've known this would happen. Should've been prepared. I'll ring Sam, he can get a team of security guys to come over from the hotel.'

'It's not your fault, you weren't to know.'

'No, I should have known. It was exactly like this when you were missing, they didn't leave us alone. I guess we'd been lulled into a false sense of security over the last week.'

Within thirty minutes Sam and two big Maori guys, Abel and Jacob, had arrived. Sam knew the pass code and entered through the rear basement garage without alerting the reporters.

'How is it out there?' asked Adam, furious at this new intrusion.

'We drove past, the street is absolutely choked with vans, reporters, cameramen, people. They haven't worked out there is a back entrance, we snuck in unnoticed.'

Adam went into command mode, I could sense his brain ticking over. I saw him transform into a hard core decision maker and leader. His demeanour changed from just fucked lover to menacing overlord.

'OK. This is how it's going to work. I'm going to go out front and make a quick statement. I'll tell them you are still recovering and that we ask for some privacy.'

'Jacob, you'll accompany Ms. Maxwell wherever she needs to go, be her driver, never let her out of your sight, use my car.'

'Adam, I'm only going a few streets away to work. Jacob doesn't need to wait around all day. Why don't I call him when I'm ready to come home?'

'As long as you don't take any risks. You've got no idea what this is going to be like.'

Adam hadn't been around after Paul's company had gone broke, I knew exactly what this was going to be like. At least this time I could respond through my blog. Jacob took Adam's Range Rover, it was big, the windows were tinted and I felt shielded from the world outside. We pulled up out front of my office and the crowd there was just as bad. I rang Cindy and she said she would make sure the door was unlocked. Jacob parked right next to the entrance and whisked me inside.

Back to Work

WELCOME HOME TINA, said the banner in the foyer. The staff were all waiting in the main body of the office, cheering and clapping as I entered. The tears flowed, it really did feel like home. I had forgotten how much I loved this place, the people and what we all did, it felt very good to be back.

Once things had quietened down, I went through the loading dock at the rear to the other building and was greeted with an equally warm welcome from the tenants. I felt it was important to let them know I was ok. It must have been an uncertain time for everyone, assuming that I was never coming back, wondering what this might mean for their careers, their futures? It was my job to let everyone know it was business as usual.

Next I Skyped Chenda and I could hear the relief in her voice. The women, their children, the factory, so much was at stake. I reassured her I would come over in a few weeks just to see how things were going, talk to the women, thank them for their unflagging support.

Cindy got me up to speed on the business and all that had happened in my absence. The second edition of 'Escape Money' had outsold all other publications and had remained, quite perversely, on top of the bestseller lists throughout the entire time of my disappearance. A new peak was reached when I was rescued and the same publishers were itching for the story of my capture.

'You should see these,' said Cindy, pointing to a stack of printouts from publishers, all making ridiculous offers for my story.

'Thank God I'm here to write it. Imagine the stories that would've been concocted in my absence? Did you see the shit that bitch Fiona was saying?'

'Yeah, we always responded to her crap on the blog, it pissed the papers right off, none of us would talk to them. You know we are getting millions of hits, our advertising revenue is through the roof. Seems like your popularity worldwide turned this into a much bigger thing than we ever expected. I've gotta say, it was really hard trying to deal with this when we thought you'd never be coming home.'

I couldn't believe the figures. I was an extremely wealthy woman and could stop working right now. But I couldn't. Just being here reignited my passion for what I loved doing. How could I have ever contemplated a life playing the peasant wife, living off the land with that wild maniac? Why had I so naively thought it would be enough?

Cindy and I walked around to each of the departments. Lana showed me the upcoming styles the designers had been working on. The range had been put on hold and I told them to get everything out as soon as the IT guys had all the systems in place. What better way to celebrate than with a new dress? The increase in business would give Chenda all the reassurance she needed.

Next came a meeting with Jane, our chief editor. She gave me an outline of how she thought we should deal with my homecoming and I agreed to write something today.

By five pm the piece had been completed and I was ready to call Jacob. Adam rang to say that he was already at home waiting. The media were still out front. I decided I would talk to them now. Whatever I said would satisfy the six pm news bulletins and hopefully give us some peace tonight. I got Jacob to pull up in front of the house, took a deep breath and stepped into the fray.

The whole experience was completely daunting. I could barely string two words together, but hoped I made enough sense to give them what they wanted. I finished by letting them know an extended version was available on my blog, they could use this as a press release, and after some jostling, was finally able to get through the front door.

Palace or Prison

'What the hell are you doing coming in that way? Where's Jacob?' screamed Adam, as he saw me walking across the courtyard.

'I spoke to them, wanted to get them off our backs for a while. Jacob has gone the long way round to park the car. I wanted to enter from the front, so they didn't discover the rear entrance.'

Adam was furious at not being kept in the loop and I kind of resented him taking control. I was not a child and handling the media was something I knew how to do well.

'Jesus Tina, you should've told me, I would have made sure Abel was out the front to protect you.'

'I'm fine, look come and see, they're packing up,' I said taking his hand and leading him into the front bedroom where we could easily see most of the camera crews leaving.

'You've got to remember this is how I started my own career, you've got to trust me. I appreciate your concern, but I'm a big girl and can look after myself.'

He looked at me, hurt that I had chastised him for his concern, but I was too tired to stroke his wounded ego. As we left the front room I noticed a bag and a computer had been set up on the desk.

'Have we got guests?' I enquired.

'I've installed Abel here to keep an eye on things. He has everything he needs and won't be coming over to the main house.'

'Do you think it's really necessary?'

'Someone tried to get in through the bedroom window, he had a camera, was shooting pictures, attempting to get into the back of the house.'

'Alright, I agree, but you have to let me know what's going on. Don't assume I can't handle it, I need to be kept informed.

The kitchen was back in pristine condition, this is not how I had left it this morning.

'Did you finish cleaning after I left?'

'No, I got Sam to send over a team from housekeeping.'

I was a bit pissed off. My life was being micro managed. Returning to work had given me back control, reinvigorated my drive and ambition. Yet here at home, what should have been my sanctuary, was feeling more like a prison. I was being guarded, someone was being paid to clean, people were making decisions about my life without consulting me. Adam's intentions were good, but he didn't understand how undermining it felt. I said nothing, he had already been told off by me once today, he didn't need to be slapped again. He was tired and angry and I didn't need to antagonise the situation further. It had been a difficult day. Things would ease off and return to normal eventually. I would have to give it, and Adam, time. He was my ally not my enemy.

The bi-fold doors had been closed and the airconditioning had been pumped up, making the house feel cold and claustrophobic. I went to the fridge to get a glass of wine only to discover it had been filled with food. I bit my tongue and took out the Riesling. It was only temporary, everyone was acting in good faith, doing their best.

'How was your day?' I enquired hoping to break the ice.

'Just the usual, putting out the spotfires, keeping the staff up to date, reassuring investors that everything is ok. How about you?'

'Great, my team has everything under control. A bidding war has started for the rights to the book.'

'What are you going to do about it? Are you sure you want to go down that path?'

'If I don't write it, someone else will. Don't worry, I won't publish anything unless you've seen it, I understand your need for privacy. And anyway when I went into work today I realised I'd almost made myself redundant, they were all managing quite well without me. Writing might give me something productive to do.'

That night Adam held me close, protectively, we did not make love.

The media had been satisfied with the doorstop interview and over the next few days they left us in peace.

A few shots of the interior courtyard of my house appeared in one of the tabloids and we realised some unscrupulous neighbor had been bought off. The glass roof was put in place over the courtyard, to provide a bit more security, but on this hot January evening it only added to the stifling atmosphere.

Adam was incensed at this violation of our privacy and insisted we move to his penthouse in the hotel. I agreed reluctantly and after packing some things, we returned to the place where we spent that first night together. His sanctuary, his territory.

Over the next week, I got a feeling for what our life together would be like. Most nights I returned to an empty apartment, feeling alone and somewhat lost in the cavernous space. I had forgotten that his business interests all over the world meant many late nights, but I guess it was the compromise he made so that he could be here in Melbourne with me. I often went to bed alone, falling asleep before he came to the bedroom. And sometimes he was gone before I woke up. We did not make love, he seemed to be showing the same type of reluctance as when we were first reunited. I was mentally and physically exhausted and didn't push the point.

And when he was at home, there were the frequent phone calls from his brother, taken in his study, away from me. This was still an unresolved problem.

Things would get better when our lives returned to normal. Just when that would be, I didn't know.

Sweat Shop

The media had enough information to keep them happy, but a new shit storm had just erupted.

Overnight a clothing factory in Bangladesh had collapsed killing hundreds of the workers trapped inside. The situation had been made more tragic because the owner had forced his employees to get back to work even after they expressed their fear of entering the dangerous building. Factories like this make the clothes that fill the shops and online stores. Well known brands, produced in horrendous conditions, at low cost, in places where life is cheap.

The UDressU site and the blog were being swamped with vitriolic diatribes about this very subject. Accusing us of being equally to blame, of feeding this insatiable desire for cheap consumer goods at any price. The press had found a good scapegoat and it was me.

All that we had worked so hard to achieve at the factory in Cambodia was at risk. We were being tarred with the same brush as those in charge of these third world sweatshops. The 'Victim or Villain' headline of that day's paper gave its readers someone to point the finger at. The gutter press were having a field day. The Australian media loved cutting down a tall poppy and were obviously fed up with the small bits of the kidnapping story we were drip feeding them. One particular journalist lead the charge. Geoffrey Kinane was an old school writer who mourned the glory days of investigative journalism when newspapers were king. He had written a particularly scathing attack on 'dumb blondes' fronting the cameras, claiming they knew nothing about their subject matter and all they needed to get these jobs was a pretty face. He made a point of saying that all this shallow reporting was compounded by the influx of electronic news sites made up of amateurs and mummy bloggers who, he claimed, had no idea what they were talking about.

Men like him were a dying breed. They resented change and were desperately trying to hang on to some glorified ideal of the good old days.

They were also the type of men who'd made it difficult for cadet journalists like my editor, Jane Smith. As an ex columnist from one of Australia's leading national newspapers, she told us many stories of the work place bullying endured at the hands of men like Mr Kinane. Jane also talked about the sexual harassment suffered in a work environment hostile to women. My blog now employed many women who'd lost their jobs on these dinosaur publications. These women had learnt their survival skills very early on and were now equipped to forge careers in the new media environment. It seems Geoffrey had a bone to pick and I was the perfect target.

We called a crisis meeting early that morning and it was agreed that I should immediately take a film crew to our factory to document the good work being done in Phnom Penh. One of my tenants was a film-maker and she rose to the challenge. Adam agreed to take his jet and by late that afternoon we were heading to Cambodia. I had intended to travel there in the next few weeks, this just brought the trip forward and quite frankly I was glad to be away from Melbourne and the constant intrusions into my life.

We arrived without any hassles at immigration and customs, Adam knew who to pay to expedite the process, and drove straight to the factory. Chenda was waiting for us, upset they were being so wrongly accused. I told her of our plan and asked that she arrange the most fluent English speakers to front the camera. This was easy, all the kids were learning English as a second language at the factory school.

Adam flew off to China to attend to his more pressing business needs. He knew if he went there personally he could tie up some of the loose ends that had been stalling his development projects. It was good to have him gone, not hovering around, micromanaging everything, undermining my confidence.

The crew and I spent the next two days filming, interviewing the women and their kids. Showing the viewers what financial empowerment and education could do to end generational poverty. The crew worked tirelessly, editing into the small hours of the night, no time for overwrought, over thought ideas. Every minute we delayed in telling our story was costing us so much more than money. I could sense the fear in the women at the factory because it was them who had everything to lose.

In the early hours of day three we released the video, the documentary went viral and the real story of our clothing business was finally told. The volatile market responded instantaneously and sales again started to come back. We had averted this near disaster.

Farewelling the film crew on the tarmac, Adam and I had decided we would distance ourselves from the story. The director could handle all the publicity, the film spoke for itself, and quite frankly we were both reluctant to return to Melbourne just yet. Adam's trip to China had bought him some time. Here in Cambodia we could both be free. Tomorrow we would drive to Kep, to meet up with Adam's sister and get our first look at the restored house.

Having barely slept for three days Adam and I both collapsed into bed, too tired for sex. I reflected on a different time I'd been in this hotel, in this bed, with Philippe. An experience which had left me crying and lonely, longing for more. Then that fateful following day when I'd accidentally bumped into Adam on the building site in Kep. So much had changed in such a short time. Tomorrow I would wake up in my lover's arms, content I had found something once so longed for.

Return to Kep

It was beautiful. The villa was complete and sat proudly in the lush tropical gardens on the seashore at Kep. Adam raced around excitedly, looking into all the rooms, proudly checking out the workmanship of the men he'd trained. It had been restored back into its sixties Riviera glamour, a glorious testament to a different era of happier times past. Brigitte Bardot would surely fit perfectly into this stylish re-creation. I almost expected to see her descending the stairs to the tune of 'Girl From Ipanema'.

Each room had just the right amount of minimalist furniture, some familiar, other newer pieces probably sourced from the Finestra's latest collection. A comfortable mix, all perfectly appropriate for this superb space.

The weight of the world had lifted from Adam's shoulders, gone was the stressed out, angry man. I had never seen him this light hearted and carefree before. So much of our time together had been fraught with some ridiculous level of drama, compounded even more so by the events of the last few weeks.

I found my way to our bedroom and unpacked as he made a few phone calls. It was hot and humid and I quickly changed into a bikini and sarong. The ground floor had been built of stone and the floor was paved in the same mosaic tiles I'd seen at our hotel in Phnom Penh. A colonnaded verandah sheltered the front of the house from the blistering heat. Ceiling fans kept the moist air circulating and a faint breeze from the ocean was a refreshing change from the claustrophobic air conditioned interiors we'd been forced to endure at home.

Adam had a few errands to run. Meeting up with his foreman Saimlan in town, checking out some of the new projects they had been working on. He asked if I wanted to join him, but I politely refused, relishing the luxury of a few hours of quiet solitude.

In Adam's usual ordered manner the fridges had been filled with food and drink. The yacht club next door had a fully staffed kitchen and he'd left a note to say I could order anything I liked from its restaurant menu if I didn't feel like cooking. Within thirty minutes a waiter delivered to my poolside table a bowl of hot and sour soup along with a pitcher of some exotic drink laced with alcohol, limes and mint. Refreshed and hungry after my swim, I devoured the hot spicy soup and thirstily guzzled the cool punch. Relaxed at long last I eventually succumbed to the lulling powers of the rum and took myself off for a decadent afternoon nap.

A drizzle of warmed liquid, coconut oil perhaps? What a lovely way to be roused from sleep. Strong hands massaging my back and shoulders, rubbing in the unctuous oil, kneading out the stress of the last week. I knew his touch, Adam had returned.

Kneeling behind me I felt his soft cock and balls nestled against my backside as his fingers worked their magic, up my spine, along my arms to the tips of my fingers, touch reconnecting us. He was back, my sensual man, not afraid to feel. Wordlessly acknowledging his desire.

I wondered how this time away from the madness of business, of family and the intrusions of our private life would play out. Whenever Adam had seen my vulnerability he seemed to want to shroud me protectively, but it caused him to withdraw from me sexually. A confusion which left me feeling safe yet somehow bereft.

My breath quickened, his actions stirred the core of my sensual being. How I needed his touch.

After some time he knelt back and, with two strong arms, lifted my hips and spread my legs. He had full access to my swelling cunt from behind. I supported myself on my elbows and knees, my head resting on the soft down pillow, curious to know where this might lead. The oil trickled down between my cheeks, his hands spreading me apart exposing my anus to his deft fingers, circling then teasing, pushing firmly with his thumbs, arousing a sensuality that had barely been explored. More oil and ever so gently I felt his index finger take the lead. With a gentle force he push beyond the tight ring of muscle, awakening a new pleasure zone. I was surprised at the intense carnality of the gesture and wanted him to continue his exploration. More oil and a knuckle opened me wider, preparing me for his next daring manoeuvre. He leaned into my back, his mouth nipping, biting at my neck and I stretched, feline like, signalling my pleasure and approval.

'I love you,' he whispered huskily.

'I want you,' I replied.

'I will be gentle.'

I was eager to shed this new virginity. Excited by what might be explored with my experienced, adept lover and eager to let go of any inhibitions I might have once held.

I felt his hard cock against my anus, teasing me with its slick head, trying to enter. He knew I was not yet ready so he eased two fingers in, massaging gently as he opened me further, preparing me for him.

When he could sense my tenseness had abated he tried again. I breathed deeply to relax. He pushed firmly till the tip of his cock began its invasion. He stopped as I let my body become used to this slight confusion of pleasure and pain. A hand reached for my breast and he brutally twisted a nipple, sending an electric charge deep into my core, a strange but pleasurable distribution of this sensual pain. I breathed deeply, my back arched, I was ready. He responded with a slow push that sent shivers down my spine. This was a brand new sensation and I wanted more. He paused momentarily, sucking in his breath, trying to control the effect this was having on him, of the orgasm that simmered. And when his breathing quieted he thrust a little further and I thought I would explode with this most intimate of fuckings. And again he stilled as my heart beat wildly against my chest. These short intervals of containment teasingly leading my mind to wonder just how much more erotic this could be. As one hand tugged my nipple the other ventured down my belly over my pubis, circling my clitoris then sliding his fingers into my wet throbbing sex, filling me. I groaned at the intensity of our coupling and let his cock sink further into me, deeper, beyond the fullness of pain and into the sanctuary of uninhibited pleasure. I rocked aggressively against him and he responded by slamming harder inside me, plunging, then almost withdrawing, only to ram back into me with an increased ferocity. Slick sweat dripped between our heated bodies as we thrashed together, groaning like animals, releasing all that pent up energy that had been building for so long. He moaned loudly, grunting with every explosive thrust until finally I could control my body no longer. Wave after wave of indescribable ecstasy pulsed over me, through every vein and every nerve ending, like no other force I'd ever experienced before. And when I thought the sensation was beginning to wane he expertly found my clitoris and coaxed another orgasm till I felt I would die from the torment of so much pleasurable agony. And when he knew I was completely spent he let himself come with one final brutal assault until I felt his cock throbbing as he pumped, pulsating, filling me with his seed. As our breathing slowed I held his hand against my sex, needing to feel his fingers deep inside me. His cock softened but the tight muscle held him in place, gripping his quelling erection, reluctant to let go. We collapsed together, hot, exhausted, and connected more profoundly than ever before.

He was back.

We had spent most of January imprisoned in our homes, locking out the intrusion of the media, the curiosity of complete strangers, the constant scrutiny of our private lives. Even the freedom of the balcony and outdoor spaces had become fair game for the all seeing lenses. Trapped inside breathless summer rooms, air conditioned for comfort, but completely and utterly stifling. But at last, here in Kep, we were free. I walked naked in the delicious humid heat. Overhead fans moving the air, just the right amount of breeze to let my skin breathe. In the secret garden to one side of the bedroom, the cool outdoor shower washed the sweat, the sperm and oil away.

Adam lay stretched out across the bed, tangled in the fine white sheets, watching as I performed the almost ritual like cleansing. My wet hair was combed and twisted into a simple knot. My body rubbed all over with moisturiser, plumping my still tingling skin. I sat on the divan facing the bed, looking at his beautiful body, thinking about how much I loved what this retreat meant for both of us.

'I love your house, I love you, I love being here,' I said, as I crawled back beside him.

The view from the bed was magical. Over the water, bright turquoise fishermen's boats were heading out to sea to catch the shellfish we might soon eat. I could see the sun, a red orb slowly setting into the gulf of Thailand. An exquisite farewell to a perfect day.

'What shall we do tonight?'

'More of what we just did,' he responded lustfully, kicking off the sheet and propping himself on the pillows.

'We have all the time in the world for that, but actually I believe last time we arranged to meet here, you stood me up. You have some amends to make and I'm starving.'

He smiled at the playfulness and I thought about all that had happened after that somewhat disarming meeting all that time ago.

'I know I owe you, but I already have other plans for tonight... for us,' he quickly corrected.

'Dara, Nary's mum has planned a welcome feast for you. I hope you don't mind, but I've already said yes. They are all dying to meet you, I could barely keep Nary away. I told her we would come tonight. That was the only way I was able to come back to our bed this afternoon, so we are kind of stuck.'

'I would love that, love to meet them. It's not a problem at all.

We strolled the short distance into the main part of town to the school Adam and his team of tradesmen had built. The buildings were surrounded by a high whitewashed stone wall slowly being overtaken by bright purple bougainvillea. The little compound contained a group of open classrooms, some dormitories and, to one side, an elegant traditional teak pole house where the little family lived. Green lawns, lush ferns and ancient shade trees made this a truly beautiful sanctuary.

I could see tables set in the garden. The trees were festooned with decorative paper lamps. The smells of delicious food wafted through the air and mingled with the scent of blooming frangipani.

'Adam, Adam,' came the excited calls from the little girl running toward us. He held his arms open and she let him pick her up and giggled with exuberant delight as he effortlessly lifted her onto his shoulders. We walked together towards the smiling woman waiting, at the bottom of the steps.

Dara held out her hands and warmly embraced me.

'Welcome Tina, welcome to our home, we are very pleased to meet you. Nary have you given Tina her gift?'

Nary ran inside to quickly return with a parcel made from woven palm fronds and tied with brightly dyed raffia. This packaging was used extensively for many things from floor mats to the most dexterously folded jewellery boxes. I carefully unwrapped the gift to find a traditional Krama, hand woven in exotic silk. The Krama is a type of large scarf that can be used for a sarong, a baby sling or a head covering. The one I had been given was obviously something very special, not for the everyday. I unfurled it then artfully draped it around my shoulders.

Anna Buckley

'Thank you, Nary, it's gorgeous,' I said, kneeling down and hugging the slightly apprehensive child. She responded with an infectious grin and took both mine and Adam's hands and dragged us toward a pair of seats. We sat before a small, makeshift stage decorated with garlands of bougainvillea. Many others were also seated, teachers, friends and proud parents.

'Sorry Adam, but Nary and the children have been so excited by your visit and have been waiting all day to show you what they have been practising. I hope you can wait a little longer before we eat.'

Adam smiled and took my hand in his as we sat. Quickly the children came on to the stage, dressed in brightly coloured traditional clothing. Behind them another group carried an array of unfamiliar instruments. Under the instructions of a smiling teacher we were treated to a short display of classical Apsara dance and music. I was reminded that these children's education was so much more than reading and writing. There were many traditions and customs being brought back to life, nearly gone, but not forgotten after the brutal regime of the Khmer Rouge. We applauded wildly when they finished.

Nary quickly jumped off the stage and once again took our hands, this time taking us to the now groaning tables, set with plates full of Cambodian delicacies. Again we sat and Nary plonked herself on Adam's lap. Dara explained each dish as it was presented to us. Crispy taro spring rolls, fish cakes, banana blossom salad, pomelo with dried shrimp, sizzling beef lok lak, amok fish curry, red champour seed chicken curry. Plates piled high with the freshest barbequed seafood, stir fried water spinach, steaming bowls of rice and icy cold bottles of Angkor beer to quench our thirst. And when I thought I could eat no more, platters of tropical fruit and French patisserie were presented to complete this sumptuous feast.

After much protest and a promise to return tomorrow, we staggered home.

It had been a long day for Adam. He'd been at the building sites for most of the day and not been afforded the luxury of an afternoon sleep. I sent him to bed and wandered out to the pool, set in the gardens near the sea wall. I luxuriated in the warm water on this hot tropical night. The inky moonlit sky was peppered with distant lightning, the night air filled with a chorus of cicadas. I thought about the man who I observed doting on his little sister, content and happy with his extended family, at peace. He seemed whole and I felt a deep sense of sadness that a family was the one thing I could never give him.

The following morning Adam had organised a bit of pampering and we were both treated to a long massage and pedicure. I tried to convince Adam to paint his toenails, but he said he didn't think he wanted to have to explain that to his workmen. I conceded his point and let him off the hook. His playfulness did not extend quite that far.

As promised, we returned to the school later in the morning and saw how keenly the children spent their time in the classroom. No bored indolent kids, their enthusiasm for learning seemed infectious. Adam said many of the teachers were former students and Dara told me Adam paid all the university fees. We knew the value of education, especially for the girls and women.

Next, Adam took me to the building sites where Samlain, the worker who had been injured and caused Adam to miss our dinner date, showed us the projects they were working on. A new eco lodge for high paying western tourists, an extension to the hospital and new worker accommodation being built to house the increasing number of people needed to meet the ever growing demands of the tourist industry. And again I witnessed a man deeply fulfilled by what he had helped to realise around him.

By two o'clock we were done and made our way to the crab shack where Adam could finally make up for his missed dinner date. The restaurant was almost empty, the lunch rush over. We chose to sit in a secluded corner at one of the tables right on the water. I looked out to the view of men and women cleaning their catch, the crab sellers haggling with the restaurant owners and little kids frolicking playfully in the warm tropical waters.

Kep was still a relatively unsullied place, not over run with garish tourist hotels and music throbbing backpacker hostels. The drug trade and sex tourism had stayed away. Kep remained a simple fishing village and market town. It didn't have the white sandy beaches of nearby Sihanoukville, perhaps this would keep the ugly side of tourism away for just that little bit longer.

The owner greeted Adam like a long lost friend and told us to ignore the menu and that his chefs would cook us something special. While they spoke, I looked at the wine list, all French and completely unfamiliar to me. I took a guess and hoped it would be ok. I made a note to do further research and convinced myself it was time to perhaps venture away from my familiar and much loved Italian wines, broaden my bacchanalian horizons a bit further.

It occurred to me how much my life had changed. Nothing in my world bore any resemblance to the life lived by the shy, frumpy housewife I'd left behind in Melbourne's leafy conservative eastern suburbs almost two years ago. I looked over at the handsome man sitting across from me, once my nemesis, now my adept lover, speaking fluent Khmer, smiling as he talked. That in itself was very sexy, my core warmed with thoughts of him.

The service was impeccable and just as the wine arrived, so did the food. Grilled squid, chilli prawns and the famous green pepper crab, and as before my dress and mouth became spattered with the red sauce from the delicious lunch. Adam reached over and wiped the errant juices from my chin.

'Drop your napkin under the table,' I whispered.

He looked at me, puzzled, I repeated my request.

He reached down, under the tablecloth, and I ran my foot along the length of his arm. When he sat back up he smiled, but was still a little perplexed. I stretched out my leg again and let my foot rest against his crotch, playfully rubbing the fabric separating me from his stiffening cock. He breathed deeply and smiled.

'Is this what I missed out on when I stood you up for dinner?'

To think I'd been angered by his intrusion, stumbling upon him at the building site of the half finished villa, when I'd first visited Cambodia. Completely ignorant of his feelings for me, of his long held dream that one day we would be together. Feelings that had held him back from forming any long term commitments with other women. I'd misread him as some cold hearted bastard whose first love was business, a rich and aloof man.

'Kick off your shoe,' I said.

I heard the shoe slip to the ground and my foot toyed with his, encouraging him to play some more. Slowly I felt him run his foot along my leg, higher, until he reached the soft skin of my inner thighs. I separated my knees and he went further. I watched his face as he realised I wore nothing under my dress and knew he understood exactly what I needed as he delicately placed his newly manicured toes at the warm wet entry of my hungry sex.

'You are very very naughty, Ms Maxwell,' he playfully growled, not missing a stroke.

I looked him in the eye and smiled even more seductively and used the finger bowl to meticulously clean my hands, then discreetly place my right hand into my lap then under the tablecloth to find his foot. My back arched, I breathed deeply as my hand guided his foot, using it as my own personal pleasure toy. The table cloth masking my sinful transgressions.

'Tina!' he quietly gasped, but I looked out to sea, pretending to ignore his faint protestation. Very soon I found that sweet spot and quietly brought myself to a very pleasant and hummingly delicious orgasm.

Adam called for the bill. He left a wad of cash and almost marched me out, holding me close against his chest hiding his swollen erection. The tuk tuk driver could not understand why we didn't want a tour of the beachfront. Adam was insistent that we get home, quickly!

We satisfied what seemed to be our insatiable sexual appetites, spending the entire afternoon in bed. Our decadent playing was interrupted by the unmistakable sounds of the excited squeals of young girls, an apologetic text from Dara telling us that she could no longer keep Nary away. Adam smiled, he didn't mind, and got up, pulling on the clothes that had been so frantically tossed to the floor.

The girls begged to be allowed to stay and without any hesitation, Adam took them out to the pool. I slipped on a clean dress then gathered up an armful of neatly rolled towels and joined him.

'Does your father ever make contact with his daughter?'

'Never. I'm sure he just sees her as someone else's problem.'

'Do you ever see him?'

'Not if I can help it. We don't get on, he has his own life and I'm not at all interested in how he lives it. He means nothing to me.'

My mind raced back to the conversation I'd had with Moses about the acrimony between father and son. And although the story he had given me was distorted, I couldn't easily dismiss what my kidnapper had said, because it contained an element of truth. Another trigger, bringing back the black emotions of my kidnapping and betrayal. Feelings of guilt, hovered like a dark storm cloud waiting to be unleashed. It was difficult being with this man who so obviously adored me, who had such high hopes of a future together, but who knew nothing of what had really happened with Moses and the choices I'd made. The voices of guilt, of my conscience were getting louder. I had refused the help of the psychiatrist at the hospital. Perhaps now it was time to consider talking to someone about the thoughts that were weighing so heavily on my mind. I would speak to my doctor when we returned to Melbourne.

I retreated to the kitchen, needing to distract myself. Adam found me.

'You ok?'

'Yeah, fine, just putting some food together for the girls. Here, could you help me take these out?' I said, gesturing towards a large platter of fruit and jug of iced water.

It was surprisingly easy to fit back into the maternal role that had filled my life for eighteen years. The hungry children wolfed down the offerings and I knew we would have to feed them something more substantial before long. Adam looked at me fondly while he tended to the kids. I could almost read his mind, sensing the longing looks of someone who would make a great father.

The children were still hungry and the kitchen didn't come with a supply of kid friendly food, so we gathered up the girls and walked down the drive to the yacht club next door. The sunset crowd had not yet gathered for happy hour, so there were plenty of tables for our little group of girls. Apart from Nary, none of the other children would ever have been to a place like this. The yacht club, although not an exclusive members only institution, was not the kind of establishment the families of the girls could afford, let alone feel comfortable in. They all sat quietly, not knowing how to proceed in this foreign environment. Jugs of bright coloured fizzy drinks, french fries and satays eased the impasse and very soon their excited chatter and giggling filled the room. Their innocent appreciation of something so simple was delightful and we had a wonderful time being pretend parents to this happy little bunch.

Samlain arrived at nightfall, in the school bus, ready to take his charges home. Nary waved them all goodbye. Tonight she would stay with us. Adam had set aside a special room just for her, a princess's palace festooned with pastel pinks and purples, the universal colour of little girls. Adam read her a story and we both tucked her in.

We retreated to bed, holding each other closely, contemplating what might have been.

I woke early, the heat and insomnia forcing me from my bed. A cooling swim helped clear my mind. Adam and Nary interrupted my solitude and dived in together. Nary paddling like a puppy, then clinging to me when she reached the middle of the pool. We ganged up on Adam trying to pull him under. He responded by playfully flinging Nary into the air, he was too strong for us to subdue. Nary continued her taunting and he continued to toss her back into the water, she loved this game.

Eventually we coaxed her out of the pool, convincing her to eat some breakfast before the school bus arrived. Her protestations fell on deaf ears. Dara was adamant that not a minute of school be missed. We agreed and, after some skilled negotiations involving bribery and lollies, we waved goodbye as she grumpily left us.

The next few days were a blissful haze of precious time together. Neither of us spoke of our reluctance to leave. Did we fear what the future, what returning to Melbourne, might hold?

Leaving on a Jet Plane

Having the luxury of Adam's private jet made the homeward journey much less tedious.

'I still can't get used to this, the jet, it seems like such an indulgence?'

'I do most of my business in the northern hemisphere. It's just easier for me to set my own time table and actually it was you that persuaded me I needed one.'

'I don't understand.

'If I'd been able to follow you to LA after that fuck up with my brother, things might have turned out differently for us. It took me a day or two to come to my senses, to realise what had happened. I'd abandoned you and feared I might never see you again. I couldn't contact you and you weren't taking my calls.'

I was hesitant about him continuing.

'It was Sam who told me what a fuckwit I'd been. He said I should follow you, apologise, try to get you back. Cindy wouldn't give me your details, she was protecting you, wouldn't even tell me where you were staying. I found out who your publisher was and was able to coax the information out of some disgruntled secretary, but by that time the earliest available flight only arrived Sunday morning.'

I understood immediately. I knew he'd seen me kiss Dan goodnight, he must have been shattered.

'God, I'm sorry things ended that way,' I responded, flooded with shame at how quickly I'd found myself in another man's arms. Sorry Adam had witnessed it.

'Don't apologise, it was my fault. I treated you badly. I should never have let my brother speak to you that way. I should've been there to protect you from his abuse, instead I ran after him and left you alone. I still feel pissed off at my behavior. Anyway it got me thinking, I'd always resisted the urge to buy a jet, saw it as a rich man's indulgence. Had I been able to reach you earlier, I would never have lost you, and that's how I justified it to myself. Truth be told, it also meant that I could travel alone, not have to engage in the forced niceties of travelling with strangers on commercial flights. After you left I became even more of a recluse.'

I thought about the role fate had played in our turbulent relationship and wondered if fate would ease up a bit in the future. I craved a simpler life with this man.

We had been sitting in the comfortable leather recliners for takeoff and the seat belt sign was now off, the attendant had disappeared to the galley. I got up and sat snugly in his lap. Kissing him, lovingly letting him know of my happiness that we had finally found each other.

'I love your jet, but you seem to be forgetting the one major advantage of travelling this way,' I said.

'What would that be?' he responded, his mood lifting.

I took him by the hand and we walked to the rear of the jet, to the private bedroom suite.

'Eight hours till we land, I have an idea,' I said, pushing him back as he sat on the bed.

First I slipped off his shoes, then undid the buttons on his shirt, then his belt and unzipped his trousers. He helped me pull them off. I went to the door, putting the 'do not disturb' sign out, checking it was locked and returned to the bed.

'But you're still dressed,' he said.

'Yes, I know, but that won't stop me from what I'm going to do next. I need to thank you for providing me with such excellent transport.'

And with that I crawled across the bed and took his silky soft cock into my mouth, teasing the velvety skin, inserting my tongue, delicately, into the sensitive tip, then sucking it hard to bring it back to life. Very quickly he was ready. I lifted my dress and he was surprised to see that once again I wore nothing underneath. I rose to accommodate him and groaned as I came to rest, impaled on his long, thick cock, filled with the pleasure and pain of this deep penetration. He held my backside and rose up, tilting at my womb till he could push no further. We fucked slowly, indulgently like this for ages, relishing the decadence of the location and the luxury of the time we had together with no one but each other to entertain.

It made the return so much more bearable. I could imagine becoming accustomed to this life and as long as we could escape like this every so often, was sure we could cope with anything that fate could throw at us.

Reality Strikes

The media storm seemed to have died down, our Prime Minister's leadership woes had become a much more interesting news story and, quite frankly, I was very happy to pass that baton to Julia.

I was getting used to coming back to an office that didn't really need me. My next project would be to start on the book, to tell the story of my kidnapping in an attempt to stop the gossip and speculation. My editor, Jane Smith and I had decided to write from two angles, my account of what had happened in Tasmania, interspersed with the recollections of the people back at home. Our goal was to give a broad perspective of the drama that unfolded, to show how everyone had been affected, the cops, the team at the office, my friends and family.

I decided to do my writing away from the office and work from my study at home in Fitzroy, away from any distractions. But once seated at my desk in the study, I realised I didn't know how to begin. Full scaled procrastination took control. I cleaned every room, baked cakes, reorganised the linen press, was busy every day. Perhaps being at home wasn't such a good idea? Then it occurred to me the reason for my delaying tactics was I'd never fully addressed the enormity of my experience. I had to face up to the guilty thoughts plaguing me. I didn't want to write a sanitised account. The problem was, I didn't know just how much of the truth could be told.

The postman's visit was another distraction. I even opened the junk mail and read it cover to cover, as if it had some great significance, couldn't throw it out just in case it was important. I received a lot of mail, I wasted a lot of time.

On Thursday a letter arrived from my gynaecologist, Dr Anthea Scott. I was due for a checkup, the appointment was a month away. That was too long to wait, I really needed to talk to someone I could trust about the things weighing heavily on my mind. Anthea would know who I should contact. When I telephoned her office, she said I could call in at six that evening, when the waiting room would be empty and the staff had gone home. She was sympathetic to my need for privacy.

Anthea hadn't always been my doctor. The person who had been my obstetrician with Kate was the same man who'd delivered Paul. Dr Lambeth was a close family friend of the Browns, who I'm sure told Margot all about my failed attempts to produce a son and heir.

Anthea had prescribed the pill in an attempt to regulate my periods. She had given me advice on protection from STDs when I had become sexually active. She had been my confidante when I'd told her about the unprotected sex with Dan and had made sure he hadn't left me with any lasting reminders of that unfortunate little incident. Today I would ask for her advice again. Not only for a recommendation of a therapist, but also to see if I could have more tests, find out more about my infertility, see if it would be possible to give Adam the child he wanted. Many new breakthroughs had developed in the science of conception in the past two decades, maybe now they could find a cure for me.

When we opened the medical facilities in our second office building, she'd taken up a part time tenancy. She only consulted from our building two afternoons a week. We had both agreed it was better that we meet at her main practice, away from staff and gossip. Her rooms were in an elegant old Victorian terrace in East Melbourne, not far from my house in Fitzroy.

Anthea was a grey haired woman in her late forties. She sat behind a stately antique desk, the examination couch discreetly hidden behind a carved oriental screen. Pictures of her family sat in small silver frames beside her computer, documents on the walls boasted her many qualifications and medical specialities.

'Christina, it's lovely to see you again. How can I help?'

I explained I was due for a pap test and Anthea suggested we get that out of the way first.

'I understand you've had a bit of a trying time,' said Anthea.

'That's an understatement,' I replied, trying to make light of the absurdity of the last few months.

I climbed on the couch and the uncomfortable process began. Anthea appeared to be taking much longer with the internal examination, she had a worried look on her brow.

'Is there anything wrong?' I asked, my heartbeat quickening with fear.

'Um, I'm not sure, something not quite right, it feels like your uterus is enlarged. If I didn't know your history, I'd say you were pregnant, but that would be highly unlikely given you've been on the pill.'

Her words hit me like a sledgehammer, this was not a conversation I ever expected to have. I got dressed and shakily sat back down at her desk.

'I stopped taking the pill when I was stuck in Tasmania. Apart from the clothes I was wearing, everything else was left back in my hotel room. I didn't expect to be away for more than a few hours. And I couldn't see the point in taking it when I got back home, my periods had stopped. I wondered whether I was starting menopause,' I said weakly.

Anthea ripped open a pregnancy testing kit, handed me the stick and told me to go to the bathroom down the hall. We both waited impatiently for the result. I felt sick as we observed the two very distinct lines appearing, confirming Anthea's suspicion.

'How far along am I? How many weeks?'

'From the way your uterus felt, very early.'

Fear overtook my thoughts, I needed to know exactly how pregnant I really was. She wheeled over the ultrasound machine, telling me this would give a more accurate date. And to my horror she told me I was probably about six or seven weeks. Seven weeks ago I had taken Moses to bed, six weeks ago Adam and I had memorably made love. Either of these men could be the father. I burst into tears and poured my heart out to Anthea, revealing the whole sorry story. Facing the manifestation of the guilt that had been eating me up for so long.

'But I don't understand. I thought I was infertile?'

'You're not the first woman to have thought she couldn't get pregnant. Do you know the reason for your supposed infertility?'

'No, not really, my obstetrician, Dr Lambeth, told me it was something to do with my irregular periods and weight gain.'

'Let me check your old files again. Could you just wait for a few minutes while I retrieve them?'

I'd arranged for my files to be sent from Dr Lambeth's office when I started seeing Anthea. She came back with a thick folder and began to flick through the pages.

'Christina, it seems the problem was not solely yours. According to this, Paul had a very low sperm count. It was your husband who had the problem, not you.'

'But how could I have conceived Kate and then not been able to get pregnant after she'd been born.'

'You were young when you got pregnant and would I be right in assuming you were quite a normal weight?'

'Yes.'

'Your body would have been at its most optimum for conception. And as for Paul, I said he had a low sperm count, not no sperm count. I guess it was just good luck. As you got older and gained weight your chances of conceiving decreased.'

I was furious at Doctor Lambeth for not giving me the full story. I'd carried so much guilt and shame at not being able to give that family the much hoped for son. Paul would surely have known, as he had spoken privately to the doctor on many occasions. It now came as no surprise that the Brown family had only ever produced one child per generation. It was the problem of those impotent males all along.

And now I carried a child, accidentally pregnant again. This time I would take control and not let another unplanned pregnancy dictate my destiny.

'I don't want this baby, not like this, not with this doubt.'

Anthea understood. She said were a number of options, but would like me to spend some time thinking about it before a final decision was made. She gave me her private cell number and said I could call any time.

I sat in the car thinking about what I'd just been told and the possible solutions to this problem. Anthea said the pregnancy was still early enough that I could take the abortion pill, a tablet, followed a couple of days later by another drug, administered at home, away from hospital and gossipy staff. It would be more like a very heavy period. She told me I had to make a decision within the next few days, as this method was only suitable up to nine weeks. It seemed this might be the answer, the quickest and simplest solution.

I don't know how I made it home and was upset to see Adam's car already in the garage. I paused, took a few calming breaths before I went upstairs. We'd hardly seen each other in the week since Cambodia and tonight was not a good time for a reunion.

'Tina, where have you been? Your phone has been going straight to voicemail.'

'I'm sorry. It was turned off. I didn't think you were coming over tonight?'

'Neither did I, but the stuff in China I've been working on is nearly done and I was sitting at my desk thinking about you, missing you, so I left the office,' he said, walking towards me with an armful of green goddess lilies and a bottle of Prosecco.

I took the flowers only to have him take them back again and put them on the bench.

'And I missed this,' he said, as he swept me up in his arms and kissed me with a hunger the abstinence of the last few days had created.

'And also this,' as he ran his hand down my back cupping my backside, pulling me towards his hardening groin.

And immediately I was back in his spell. His love, his desire, making me feel cherished, connected, safe. He was here for me, I didn't have to ask. I loved him deeply, my fear was abating. He picked me up and took me to the bedroom.

'Tina Maxwell, I can't bear to be away from you,' he whispered, as he gently placed me on the bed and removed my clothes.

'I'm not going anywhere,' I said, silencing him with a kiss.

Our lovemaking was slow and passionate, we needed this to reconnect, make ourselves whole. When we finished I lay with my head on his chest. I loved hearing his heart beat as we tenderly breathed each other in. Adam got up from the bed and went down stairs, I could hear him gathering some glasses and the bottle of Prosecco. He knew it was my favorite, he knew me, I loved him and wanted to give something back.

He poured us each a glass and came back to bed. I thirstily drank the sparkling wine in one quick go and lay back, the alcohol calming me. Adam stroked my back as I lay against his chest.

'So where were you tonight when I tried to call?'

'Doctor's appointment.'

'This late, are you ok?' he asked, his voice unsettled.

'Yeah, I'm fine, in fact I'm more than fine,' I responded.

'So what kind of doctor sees patients after hours? What was so important that it couldn't wait?'

'Obstetrician.'

'Obstetrician? Don't you mean gynaecologist? Obstetricians look after pregnant women.'

'You're very astute.'

I felt his heart start to race. In that split second I had begun to reveal something there would be no going back from. He sat me up and looked me in the eye as he began to process my response.

'Are you telling me something?' he asked, looking at me, wide eyed with expectation.

'Are you, we, pregnant?'

'Yes, I, we, are.'

He bundled me up in his arms and held me so close and tight I could hardly breath, repeatedly telling me he loved me so much. Instantly I was swept up by his adoring mantra. This was the right thing to do, this was the best gift I could ever give him. I had made the right choice.

When he finally let me go the questions came.

'So how did this happen, I thought you couldn't get pregnant?'

I told him about the new information I'd found out about Paul and the way I'd been deceived into believing it was my problem.

'Looks like I just needed the right man,' I said playfully, watching his chest fill with pride.

'And so when is our baby due?'

'I haven't calculated the exact date, but the doctor seems to think I'm about six weeks. I think this baby was conceived in that magical week we spent together when you first brought me back home. Maybe that night, when I fantasied about you being my dark knight, cast a lucky spell.'

I was surprised by how easily the words tumbled out of my mouth, the lies had already begun.

'We should celebrate, I feel like another drink.'

'Not with this. From now on I'll be watching you like a hawk. I will let nothing harm you or this baby and that means no alcohol!'

I smiled at his concern and was quite happy to be cocooned in his love.

The Story

The voices kept me awake. By five in the morning I realised sleep would never come. Adam, sleeping contentedly, was blissfully unaware of the enormity of my decision. I extricated myself from the bed, threw on a robe and went to the study.

I had an answer. I would write my own version of the truth. Moses was dead, only Anthea and Emma knew the full complicated story. My account of what happened in Tasmania would be a new history created for Adam and the child inside me. The computer hummed into life and very quickly I began typing. After the procrastination of the last few days it was cathartic to start writing. The words just tumbled out, a tall tale obliterating the truth, attempting to mask the guilt that had plagued me.

'Hey, what are you doing up? Shouldn't you be resting?' said Adam, surprised to see me in the study.

'I'm pregnant, not sick,' smiling at his concern.

He embraced me.

'Pregnant,' he whispered, nuzzling my neck, words tempered with joy and love.

'What are you working on?'

'The book.'

He knew I had asked to be left alone to start the process and laughed when he'd phoned only to be told of my days of procrastination and fucking about.

'So, what's changed?'

'I need to get it written. I've been mapping it out in my head, but the story didn't have an ending. Last night changed that, I know how I want it to finish up. Now leave me alone so I don't forget my train of thought,' I said, smiling back at him with mock indignation.

But he couldn't leave me alone and it wasn't long before he walked back up the stairs with a tray full of food, eggs, bacon, toast, fruit, juice, bagels, tea. I rolled my chair back, stood and took the tray from him.

'Come on my darling, let's have breakfast together.'

Since the media pressure had backed off, we had much more freedom. We had dismissed the security guys and could open up the house, retract the skylights, let the fresh air in and breathe again. It was going to be another hot February day and it was good not to feel like a prisoner trapped in my own home.

'What have you got planned for today?' I asked.

'More of the same old shit, it's pretty unrelenting,' Adam replied, pausing before he continued.

'And I don't like it, I don't want to be so tied to the business any more. What you told me last night changed things.'

'How do you mean?'

'I don't want to be like my old man, a distant father who always put business first.'

'Don't do anything you'll regret, it's early days yet and anything could happen.'

'I know, I know all of that. But I've watched the way you've run your business, seen how you've been able to delegate, give responsibility to the team around you, watch it thrive in your absence. I want that, I want to be able to relinquish control, not live this 24 hour a day existence. I've lost interest.'

'Adam, I had no idea. Your business has been your life, it's what's made you get up in the morning, given you success beyond anything your father ever achieved. What would you do to replace it?'

'I could float the company, leave it in the hands of a board of directors, extricate myself from the minutiae of running it, step away and do the things I really want to do.'

'Like what?' I asked, amused by this sudden change.

'Like be with you, be with our child, get out of the city, spend more time in Cambodia. Be an architect again, do what I love with the people I love.'

I was surprised by this sudden change of heart, but upon reflection remembered the difference I had seen in him when we were in Tasmania, in Cambodia, away from the pressures of his family and business.

This moment of dreaming was interrupted by his phone.

'Sorry about that, have to get to the office,' he said, looking at his watch, reluctantly leaving to get dressed, knowing that his day should've already begun.

Today there was a noticeable change in his demeanor and the normally driven man looked different. I would often watch the transformation in the morning, from sexy just fucked lover, to arrogant businessman, as he prepared to get ready for work. The process would begin with the donning of one of his immaculately tailored suits, throwing back a coffee, a deep breath, the aggressive stance and the persona was complete. Sometimes I barely recognised the man who walked out the door.

I heard him start his car, the engine idled and then he ran back up the stairs. He grabbed me, lifting me in his arms, a long lingering kiss.

'I won't be late, stay like this,' he said, as he cheekily undid the ties on my robe, exposing my breasts, my legs, then bent down and kissed my belly.

'See you tonight, beautiful baby.'

He got up, kissed me again, then was off. What I had just witnessed was all I needed to let me know this was so right, that sometimes things happen for a reason.

Writing was easy, the words flowed.

Adam came home early that night and he continued his pampering, bags full of my favorite treats, a scented bath on the roof deck, never ending adoration in the bedroom, right through to the next day,

Saturday. We swam and slept, decadently wasting away this glorious summer afternoon.

'What are you doing? Did we have plans?' asked Adam, as I put the finishing touches on my make-up.

'Lola, remember. I'm catching up with her tonight. She's only in town for a few days and we arranged to meet at Civita for dinner.'

'Does 'we' mean me?'

'Well, it could if you want to sit and listen to stories about Lola's love life.'

'So I guess you're politely telling me this is a girls' night,' he said, slightly crestfallen at his exclusion.

'Oh, don't give me that look! You'd be bored within minutes and anyway we've spent most of the afternoon together, you haven't exactly missed out.'

'So what will I do without you?'

'Why don't I meet you in the city, the restaurant is just up the road from The Imperial. We'll stay at your place tonight. You could wait for me, think about what you might do to me when I return.'

'Like what?' Adam replied.

'Like anything you want Mr. Darcy!' I responded teasingly.

I could tell he wasn't too pleased about me going without him, but he had to understand that sometimes I needed space. Since the kidnapping and the media storm, Adam had become quite possessive and I knew I needed to wean him off this behavior if our relationship was to survive.

We drove into the city, parked in the underground carpark and took the elevator to his penthouse where I dropped off my things. Living in two houses wasn't quite working, we would have to eventually decide which one would be our home. There was still a feeling of temporariness, when either of us stayed at each other's house. Like that feeling when you're travelling, living out of a suitcase, always packing and unpacking, leaving some important little thing at home. And with such a big change to our lives, who knew where home might be this time next year?

As I sat and waited for Lola, late as usual, I did start to feel slightly guilty about leaving Adam at home on his own. I noticed he never went out with friends and apart from the odd gallery opening and charity event, Adam was usually preoccupied with work or with me. It occurred to me his arrogant exterior probably masked not only his shyness but loneliness as well. When Kate was little so much of my social life was centred around her and her friends, their families and all the activities associated with kids. Adam did not have this and maybe all his male friends were caught up with their own family commitments as well. This was most definitely going to change, a baby would make a huge difference to his life.

'Cara, mia, sorry I'm late,' said Lola, turning heads with her vivacity as she made her entrance, greeting me with kisses and hugs.

'Look at you. You look amazing. That break in Cambodia has done you good.'

'Thank you Lola, but the last time you saw me I was a little bit worse for wear.'

'Kidnapping, bullet wound to the shoulder, I believe. All in a day's work...' she joked.

I loved this about her. No mournful silences about the kidnapping, just a bit of mood lightening humour.

'And you too, you look radiant. Who are you keeping hidden from me back in Italy?'

Lola had hinted at a man, inferred that it was far easier to have a relationship away from her adorable, but demanding parents.

'His name is Dario, he's a painter.'

'Sounds very exotic. When are we going to meet him?' I quizzed.

'That's the problem. I'm sure my parents would never approve. He's as poor as hell, in fact I'm supporting him. They would die if they knew who I'd chosen.'

'But your mother loves artists...'

'Yeah, only if they're as successful as the people she represents. Not struggling artists like Dario. You'd be quite surprised at how contradictory she can be.'

'I find that hard to believe, especially because I know of her own romantic love story with your Dad.'

'Christina, people are different when it's their own child.'

The menus came, Lola handed them back and told the waiter to choose for us. She called him by his first name, she was such a charmer and he melted at her request.

'Drinks?'

'Vermentino, thanks. Tina, you too?'

'Actually nothing for me, just a water.'

'What's wrong with you?' said Lola, shocked at my new sobriety.

I had to think quickly, it was too soon to tell of the real reason.

'Something I picked up in Cambodia. Still on antibiotics, no alcohol, doctor's orders,' the lies came easily.

'You're no fun,' she replied, not questioning my excuse.

We had a great night catching up on all the gossip, eating good food, being in Melbourne, just hanging out with each other.

Lola's phone rang, there was a problem with a shipment of furniture. Many calls later and the issue would not go away. Lola apologised profusely, she would have to get back to the office to get to her computer to sort this thing out. We kissed and departed having made promises to catch up again soon, maybe in Italy, maybe meet the man.

Oh Brother

I entered through the foyer of the hotel. Sam was doing the night shift and greeted me warmly as I walked past.

'Hey Tina, nice to see you. How's the book going?' enquired Sam.

'Brilliantly thanks. Have stopped fucking around. Feels like I've been attached to my keyboard for the past 24 hours, can't seem to type fast enough.'

'Yeah, Jeanie said you were busy when she went around there the other day.'

Adam had insisted the housekeeper, a very trusted employee, should still come over to clean.

'Yeah, procrastination and writer's block had kept me pretty preoccupied. I knew it was getting bad when I reorganised the linen press!'

'That bad, what changed?'

'A few things. I got a clearer picture of how the story might go. I had a beginning and a middle, but not an end.'

'So you've found your happy ending I take it?'

'Yeah, I think I have,' I said with a slight grin.

'And anything you'd like to share with me girlfriend?' he quizzed cheekily.

'I can't give anything away, that would spoil it!'

'I can't loosen your tongue with a little Pedro Ximenez?'

'No, you can not, you wicked man!' I responded, surprised at how often I would have to give excuses to refuse alcohol.

'Is he in?'

'Yeah, he came down here, moping about, said you were having dinner with Lola. I'm surprised you're back so soon.'

'She had to go, some problem with a shipping container.'

'Adam will be pleased, he's such a sook these days when you're not around.'

My mind was awash with the pleasant memories of that night I ventured upstairs with Sam to check out Adam's place. Sam had thought his boss had left the country. I'd been out with Lola to a fundraiser for Cambodian schools when I'd heard Adam talk about the work he was doing there and was completely taken aback by the humble and compassionate man who had spoken. I'd called into his hotel, had a drink with Sam, who was on night duty, and talked to him about what I'd just discovered about his boss. The sherry had made me game enough to go upstairs with Sam to check out Adam's penthouse, but was shocked when a naked Adam Darcy emerged from the pool. Adam's plane had been cancelled, neither of us expected him to be home.

'Penny for your thoughts?' he asked.

'Just thinking about that night you took me upstairs and the things that brought Adam and me together,' she replied.

'I'm pleased I took you up there. It's strange how fate works.'

Sam liked Tina a great deal, he liked her warmth and easy going nature, but most of all he liked what she had done for his once lonely boss. She was good for him and he hoped their relationship would finally be given the chance to work.

As I rode the elevator I thought about how much I was looking forward to seeing Adam, my changed man, in love with me and blissfully happy at the prospect of becoming a father. I snuck quietly through the front door to surprise him but was stopped in my tracks. I could hear loud voices, yelling, and knew immediately who had paid Adam a visit.

'Jesus, you're such a fuck wit! I can't believe you've gotten yourself into this situation.'

It was Justin.

'First Paul, then you. She's had you in her sights for some time. She's unstoppable. You didn't see what Paul had to put up with. That fat lazy bitch did nothing to help. If it wasn't for me and Fiona that business would have gone down the gurgler much sooner.'

'Can't you see what she's doing? She's driving a wedge between us. We've always looked out for each other, remember when we were kids? You'd better be careful or she'll make you choose, her or me, you don't want to be doing that.'

I didn't need to hear anymore of this, of Adam just standing there being yelled at, not speaking up in my defence, succumbing to his asshole of a brother once again. The lift took me quickly to the ground floor and I ran out the door not bothering with niceties, too furious to even acknowledge Sam as I made my escape. I stormed up the road, attempting to hail a cab. Not one would stop, it was Saturday night and they were all busy. The walk would do me good, give me some time to think, clear my head.

Adam had said he was going to cut back on work, disengage from his company, turn over a new leaf to be the type of man his father never was. Or was he? Adam, the golden child, still carried around a sense of responsibility for the way his father had treated his brother. It left him with a sense of guilt that Justin knew how to manipulate to his best advantage. Adam seemed to have no ability to control this destructive symbiosis. I was a threat to this fucked up relationship and the longer I stayed the more difficult Justin would become. It was not me that was asking Adam to choose, it was Justin. I had kept away, never asked Adam to disenfranchise himself from his brother, hoping that we could all somehow sort this out. But tonight was different. I had listened to enough of the abuse and was no longer prepared to tolerate it. If we had this baby, if we had a future together, would Adam always be under the spell of his brother? Who would come first? Me and the baby or Justin? Adam's brother was a problem that would not go away and as long as Justin had a hold on him, there would be no future for our relationship. Cutting through the park and back alleys, the normally thirty minute walk, was stormed home quickly in fifteen. I slammed the front door behind me, a picture fell from the wall. I ripped off the heels that burned my feet and threw them into the pool. My blood was boiling, I was furious.

Sam had seen her tear out of the lift, fuming, bumping into a guest, not stopping to apologise. Something was very wrong. His boss was upstairs and knew he should ring, not caring whether Adam would think of this as overstepping the mark. Sam didn't want the same miscommunication to happen again.

'FUCK!' I howled like a she-wolf into the empty courtyard of my home. I fell into a heap on the couch, beat the cushions with my fists, and wept.

I felt his arms around me. Adam had beaten me home. I pushed him away like an impetuous child.

'It's too fucking hard!' I screamed.

'I hate your brother and what he makes you become. I can't live with the poison he spits out about me. Why do you keep letting him control you? He's not that same little boy any more, you don't need to rescue him,' I yelled, as I ran to the study, not letting him get in a response.

I rifled through the top drawer of the desk and found what I was looking for. Adam had followed me up the stairs and before he could speak, I fed the disc into the computer.

'Don't say a thing!' I spat.

'Just sit down and look at the screen.'

The images were as sickening now as they had been then, but it was important that Adam see them.

'This is the kind of 'man' your brother really is. Look at what he was doing to my husband. Paul was a weak bastard. Look at the control they had over him. Are you just as pathetic?' I screamed, holding his head forcing him to look at the screen as he sat at my desk.

Adam looked shattered, but I was in no mood to console him. I'd put up with Justin's undermining and intimidation for years.

'Paul and I did not have the perfect marriage, but with your brother around what hope did it ever have?'

It was a low blow, Justin was only part of the reason, but tonight I didn't care. Adam needed to see those images, stuck in my head, that best portrayed the evil bastard Justin really was.

'And so now I choose. I choose to no longer be part of your fucked up family. GET OUT AND GO BACK TO YOUR BROTHER!'

I stood there, arms folded defiantly, trembling with rage.

Adam slowly rose, he looked broken, but instead of walking away he came towards me, tilted my chin and held my face firmly between his hands.

'I choose you,' his voice quiet, sombre.

'I've told him to get out, to never speak to me, come into my home or contact me again.'

I stared at him, silent, my eyes brimming with tears. He held me close and I felt his heart beating heavily.

'Sam rang me when he saw you run out. I jumped straight in my car, I couldn't find you, I came straight here. You are my family, my love, my life, you make me whole. I will never let him intrude on our lives again.'

Silently I contemplated what Adam just said. He'd made a momentous decision and I wondered what had changed.

'He came up to my apartment,' said Adam, as if he had read my mind.

'Wanting money, more money for another one of his fucked up business schemes and I told him 'no', that he would have to go it alone. He was a bit confused at first, so I told him I was getting out of the game, selling up, floating the company, starting a new life. He still couldn't understand why, so I told about him the baby, told him I wanted to be a good father to this child. He went crazy, it was as if I had already replaced him, let him go. He went into a rant about me deserting him, that I was a traitor and I would be no better a parent than our father. By this time he was turning completely insane and I tried to calm him down, tell him that he could still be part of my life, an uncle to our child. But he would have none of it. He went into a tailspin of rage, spewing out a whole lot of bullshit about you, accusing you of trying to split up the family.'

'I know, I heard it all,' I said, completely unnerved by the fact that Justin now knew of the baby, fearing him as some kind of threat.

'I had no idea you were even there. But that was it, I'd had enough, I told him to get out. He tried to throw a few punches and I threatened to call my security guys if he didn't go. Finally he left, screaming abuse. I told him I never wanted to see him again. The lift was closing when Sam rang. I asked him which way you went, drove along Victoria Street, but I couldn't find you. I was so scared of losing you again. I thought you'd never come through that door.'

Finally the enormity of what he said hit me and I burst into tears and cried out all the sadness of the last few years, decades. He sat down and cradled me in his lap until my sobbing stopped. Slowly I looked up at him and saw the fear still in his eyes.

'It's ok, I'm not going anywhere, I choose you too. I love you. We are our own little family now.'

Adam slept fitfully, the events of the night must have weighed heavily on him. I would have to give him time. I slipped out of bed early and went across to the bakery to buy fresh bread and pastries. My man had made big changes in his life, changes for me. I needed to nurture him. Feeding him would help. It had been a hot night and we barely needed the sheet I found Adam's naked body tangled up in. I rested the tray on the bedside table and kissed him awake. He breathed deeply, sucking in the early morning air, rolling onto his back, stretching his arms, revealing his body and his magnificent morning erection. He grabbed me and pulled me close.

'What's this?' he groaned, tugging at my sweats, wondering why I was clothed.

'I got up, cooked you breakfast, thought you needed a little bit of loving.'

'I do,' he said, grabbing my hand and placing it on his cock.

'You'll have to wait, I can't bear to see good food go to waste. I bet you didn't eat anything for dinner last night?' I said, removing my hand, extricating myself from his grasp.

'You make things difficult woman, I want both,' he joked, caveman style.

'I didn't say you couldn't have both, I just want you to have something to eat first. You'll need all the energy you can get, my hormones are raging. Now eat!'

He wolfed down the food and I sat in bed next to him, stealing a piece of bacon, watching contentedly as he devoured the breakfast.

'What shall we do today? The weather is perfect. Let's get out of the city. Daylesford, Trentham, there are some great places to eat, what do you think?'

'To tell you the honest truth, I've never actually been to either of those towns, but I've heard that Daylesford is amazing. Lola was only talking about it last night. Said there was a big Italian community up there as well. Great food, great farmers market. I think I'd really love to do that. But first I've got some things to attend to.'

'Like what?' he said, as if I was about to abandon him and head off to the office.

'Like this,' I said, as I took the tray from him, slipped off my clothes and crawled down the bed where I took him in my mouth and treated him to a different kind of delectable feasting.

Unwelcome Stranger

A day spent in the countryside should have been a relaxing, cathartic escape. I should've felt better. After all, Adam had banished his brother from our lives. Instead my mind raced. No wine to silence the voices that were demanding answers. I realised just how much I'd been using alcohol to dull the incessant chatter of guilt since my return to Melbourne.

Another sleepless night meant an early start to the day. Adam had an early meeting in Sydney and had flown out late last night. Something related to the China deal I presumed. He would be there at the end of the week and had much preparation to do if the deal was going to be a successful one. Slowly I was getting some insight into his working life and understood why he craved something different.

The sun had not yet risen when I wandered downstairs at 4.00 am and started to write. At least while he was away, I would have no distractions, free to tell the story of my reinvented history.

I had fallen asleep at my desk and was startled awake by the incessant pounding on my front door. Who could that be, it was still only 6 in the morning? They were back, an army of reporters, blinding flashes, cameras rolling, questions being thrown at me.

'CHRISTINA, DID YOU KNOW ABOUT THE DIARIES?'

'DID ADAM KNOW ABOUT YOUR RELATIONSHIP WITH THE KIDNAPPER?'

'WERE YOU PLANNING ON ABANDONING YOUR BUSINESS, YOUR FAMILY?'

I slammed the door, blinded by the flashes, ears ringing from the screeching of demanding reporters, aware that some new storm had erupted. I went on line hoping for answers and felt mortally wounded by what I read. Moses had kept diaries? I remembered seeing him writing in his notebooks what I thought were records of his kill, notes about where the best hunting sites were, how many carcasses he'd landed. I knew he kept newspaper clippings, telling his side of the story and revealing things about Adam I had conveniently chosen to ignore.

My eyes scanned the pages of the tabloid and very quickly I was hit by the killer avalanche that was the story unfolding before me. There was a photo showing the ragged, manhandled and re addressed package that finally found itself in the hands of the one person who could spread the news very quickly and effectively. Geoffrey Kinane, the disgruntled old journalist who tried to discredit me with the article about sweatshops, now had his prize and I was powerless to do anything about it. From what I began to read, it was Moses' father who had contacted Kinane and sent him the diaries. He wanted the truth to be told about his dead son.

It was far worse than I could ever have imagined. All that went on in Moses' mind, all that had happened during my kidnapping was documented in graphic detail. The first sexual encounter I had initiated. The cleaning of the shack, the food I'd cooked, the garden I'd planted, the creation of our own slice of paradise. He wrote of the truths I'd told about my marriage, about not fitting in, about looking for something that had eluded me. About my seduction of him, then submission to the fantasy I had described to Moses. Of a new life we could share together by escaping from a world that did not understand. Of the choice I'd made to abandon my daughter, my lover and go willingly to the bed of Moses Smith.

Adam, I needed to talk to him, they would be hounding him. The phone was dead. As I plugged it into the charger its screen lit up with texts and missed calls. Everybody now knew the truth, I had been exposed. I tried to ring Adam, but the calls went straight to voicemail. I shut down the computer, turned off the phones and buried myself under the covers of my bed.

The blankets were ripped off, I blinked at the harshness of the light. Adam stood next to the bed, seething with rage. I didn't want to face him, I stared into the distance, trembling. No comforting embrace, just the cold hardness of a broken man.

'Is this true?' he asked, speaking in measured tones.

I couldn't answer.

'Is this the real you? Am I just another one of the men you need in the desperate search to find yourself? Like Paul, like that Californian, like Raphael and the countless others you so casually persuade are the 'right ones'?' he spat, tossing the newspaper at me.

'I feel like such a fuckwit, reading that bullshit about you playing house, cooking for him, finding a soulmate. You don't even keep a toothbrush at my place! Were you afraid of getting too settled, just in case someone better came along?'

'And Paul, what really happened there, was my brother right? How does your daughter feel about your 'true confessions', discussing your loveless marriage with a complete stranger. Did your daughter know how you felt about her father? Kate was beside herself while you were gone, I wonder how she feels now that she knows you were planning on abandoning her in favour of a life with your psycho kidnapper... easy choice!' he sneered.

These were statements, not questions, and there was nothing I could say to calm him, or ease his sense of betrayal, because he was right.

'And that child, it's his, isn't it!'

His words cut like ice. I buried my head in my hands.

'I don't know,' I feebly replied, my voice barely audible.

This was the answer that confirmed his deepest fears, all trust had been broken. He left the room, the house, and drove off.

I lay there in a state of numbness for what seemed like ages. After a while my mood shifted. I needed to take control. I unfurled myself from the foetal position, got out of bed, showered and dressed. I would no longer allow fate to play roulette with my life.

First I rang Kate. We had been through this type of intrusion before. I reassured her she was not to take seriously the ravings of a delusional madman. The fact that she was in Canberra slightly shielded her from the immediacy of the situation. I asked her if she would like me to go up and see her, but she said she would be fine and reminded me that this was not the first time her mother had been in the headlines. She had learned to be suspicious of what she saw on television and read in the papers. And despite her stoicism I sensed a tiredness in her voice, a frustration at having to deal with another of her mother's media shitstorms. She said she would head north to Byron Bay for a week, till the story quietened down. When I asked about her studies, she said she could do it all on line. I wondered how much more of this she could take.

Then I rang Cindy and persuaded her to give me some space, that I couldn't begin to face anyone at this stage and I just needed time alone to gather my thoughts.

Immediately I knew I had to secure the house and went to the front bedroom to check the windows were shut and the blinds drawn. I hardly ever went to this part of the house. Adam had taken over the guest bedroom as a kind of temporary office. He could work here late at night and not interrupt me. His stuff was still on the desk, a computer, folders, a Chinese language dictionary, boxes of paperwork and files. He would have to come back and pick these things up.

I wondered if any of it was important. I began to look through the folders to try and discover a bit more about Adam and his business. Mostly old notes on the redevelopment of land for the Beijing Olympics. Adam's company had built a lot of the iconic stadiums, apartment blocks and shopping centres.

None of it was of much interest until I got to a folder, deep down in one of the boxes, marked 'Tasmania'. So much of it was familiar. Names of places, Lands End Lagoon, photos of the shipping containers, that beautiful patch of paradise we had once shared. I rummaged further and found the title to the land at Moon Bay, the land I'd read he'd bought to remember me by. My eyes filled with tears, we hadn't even talked about that yet. We hadn't spoken much about what happened in Tasmania at all. It was a subject we avoided, still too raw.

And then I saw it, a mining survey and a report. It pre-dated the protests, was at least ten years old. The report said the area of Moon Bay was rich in rare earth minerals, vital elements needed in the manufacture of mobile phones and electronics equipment. It said China had the monopoly on the mining of these minerals. With a growing demand all over the world, new sources of these materials would need to be found. Another page showed Southern Timber Holdings, the company that originally logged the site, was a subsidiary of G D Industries. Graham Darcy, Adam's father. Then a clearly notated plan on how to get Graham Darcy to sell the land. Setting up a shelf company to buy it, knowing Graham would never sell to his son. And when Graham Darcy showed no interest in selling the land, it got even more underhanded. Written notes from a lawyer laying out the plan to tie up the forest in a long legal dispute, that would make it unprofitable, forcing the owner to sell. I could just imagine the joy Adam felt when his father made true his threat to clear fell the lot. By destroying the land, Adam's plan to mine it would be so much easier. He would eventually be seen as the hero who bought the town and the area back to life.

Everything Moses talked about was true. Adam had always intended to mine the area. On the pages before me was a clearly spelt out and elaborate plan to take the land from right under Graham Darcy's nose. The document from the lawyer said it all, it outlined the strategy Moses had speculated on in uncanny detail.

Remarkably, I remained clear headed as I dialled Anthea's number, and although it was early she came over quickly. She too, had read the papers. I gave her the entry code to the garage and she eluded the mob outside. I spoke clearly and succinctly about our conversation in her office and she agreed it was not the right time to be bringing a child into this world. I didn't tell her that Adam knew and was ashamed to think just how long I'd let this 'true romance' charade fester. It was a relatively simple thing to do, she handed me the pill and I swallowed. She would be back in two days to administer the final dose. Then I closed the skylight, shut all the windows, pulled the curtains, found a bottle of vodka and went back to bed. The next two days were a blur.

I sobered up enough so that Anthea had no doubts about my state of mind. She handed me the medication. And with the taking of another pill the procedure was almost complete. Within about four hours I started to bleed. A surreal calmness overtook me. I had made the right decision.

I heard him enter the room. He still had keys. He spoke, his voice raspy with despair.

'I'm sorry, you're not to blame. I've read about women who fall for their captors.'

And with that simple statement my blood boiled. He had quantified this into one simple cliché. This time I found the words.

'Yeah, kidnapped by a man seeking revenge. And you're right, I'm not to blame, I just accidentally got caught up in the idiotic game played by you in the name of business. Moses was as much a victim as me.'

'I know all about you. Of the shelf company you hid behind in an attempt to buy that land from your father. And when that didn't work you pretended to save the forest. Getting some bullshit report written about a species of wallaby that was not really under threat and tying the land up while your lawyers battled it out in court. Did you ever think about what your little game was doing to those innocent people of Lands End who watched their town die? The loggers whose only sin was to do a hard day's work like the generations that preceded them, or the idealistic young kids who believed in your 'big green adventure'. You even promised that tourism was the way forward, but did little more than buy the service station, a relatively cheap way to show these unwitting fools that you were on their side.'

'When you lost the court battle to save that piece of forest, your father clear felled the lot, just to show you who had won. But this wasn't a tragedy, he played straight into your hands. You needed him to destroy it before you came along and made it so much worse. Clear felling would be a picnic compared to the mining you were eventually planning to do. And I'm sure you were pleased that even then, your father didn't sell to you, because if you waited long enough you could ride in on your white stallion and save the town with the promise of the new boom that mining would bring. Long after the timber industry had shut down and long enough for people to forget about your campaign to save the forest. You would play into the hands of a community desperate for any type of investment that might bring back prosperity to the area. And what did you do to put things right with those who had lost so much? Absolutely nothing, because you needed the people who had lost their jobs to be gone, loggers weren't miners. You knew no one was investing in timber anymore, you were quite happy to wait until the land was almost given away.'

'It must have been so inconvenient to have all that attention when I disappeared. You must have been dreading someone else might find out about the untold riches the land had secretly held for so many years. And then your most brilliant move was to be seen to buy it in remembrance of me, that would've thrown them for a while. Stupidly I believed you'd been up working all night trying to get building projects completed before Beijing shut down over Chinese New Year. It was all bullshit. What nobody knew was you had been secretly negotiating with that Chinese mining magnate who was prepared to pay you vast sums NOT to mine the land, so that his company could continue its monopoly on the market of rare earth minerals. I found the documents, copies of the contract. The whole memorial thing was a brilliant way to hide the fact you would never ever be mining that land while the Chinese were paying vast sums for you to leave it alone. Millions and millions of dollars straight into your greedy pockets for doing absolutely nothing.'

'Oh yes, Adam, you cover it well, you build schools for kids in Cambodia and train the young men and women needed for the hotels you are constructing. You pretend you're doing it for them, but you need their labour. Without those workers you could never staff your hotels. Their slave wages keeping them poor, desperate for any meagre handout you throw their way. And the schools are cheap child care centres, so the women are freed up to work for you. You are making a killing on those sites. I don't buy any of that philanthropic bullshit you spin.'

'Your deals in China, you made a fortune out of the Beijing building boom. But did you ever think about the people who were forcibly removed from their homes to make way for your award winning stadiums and luxury apartment blocks?'

'You dare to comment on my motivation for marrying Paul, but fail to see that even there you disrupted my life. Moses told me of the building you first bought, the one in Brunswick, snatched from right under your father's nose. I read the claims of you being a 'self made man', of not accepting handouts from your father. People loved that story of your success. What they didn't know was that you merely spent part of the trust fund left to you by your rich grandparents.'

My heart was pounding, my mouth dry, I paused and took a drink.

'That factory was where I worked. The brothers who lost their leasehold, who ran the clothing business, were forced to sack all their workers. Some had known no other way of life. I was just starting out, they let me use their facilities to produce my own range of clothing, I could barely keep up demand and worked hard, after hours, to fill orders. Then suddenly my world was turned upside down, my parents were killed. Paul was a good friend and helped me through the endless days of loneliness and grief. The boundaries of our relationship blurred and I let him sleep with me. It was my own carelessness that led to my pregnancy, but I was determined to go it alone. I never lied to Paul about my feelings toward him and told him I needed this baby, I needed to replace the family I'd lost. I never deceived him. I told him I would do it alone. I was employed, my business was taking off, it wasn't going to be easy, but I knew I could make it work.'

'Then you bought the factory. I lost my job, my business, couldn't afford to pay my rent and lost my home. I was hospitalised with chronic morning sickness and it was Paul who stepped up. He declared his love for me and after I said 'yes' I took our vows seriously and although it was no fairytale, I did everything in my power to make our marriage work. Then your prick of a brother and his cunt of a wife showed up and did everything in their power to undermine me and seduce Paul.'

'You saw that brutal shit on the DVD they were blackmailing him with. He was addicted to them, what they offered and was prepared to sacrifice everything to keep his addiction going. He was at their place when he died. And after his death I was left with nothing, they had tried to take it all.'

'And as for that bullshit about you buying Paul's company and saving my house, you just wanted to protect your brother from the inconvenience of bankruptcy. If Justin had lost his right to practise as an accountant, or lost his ability to be a company director, then he couldn't do your dirty work with the mine, talking to the unions with promises of jobs. I saw Justin's name on the papers, Moses told me he was the man to talk to about the mining deal. Justin must have been really pissed off when your sentimental gesture put that plan on hold for a few more years. When were you going to tell him what was really going on? Or was he in on it too, your 'numbers man'? How much of a cut were you giving him?'

Adam looked shell shocked after my rant. I didn't care, he needed to know.

'I was part of that collateral damage your business caused, one of the many faceless victims of your success. But it hurts, doesn't it, because it's not nice to be confronted with the reality of your actions.'

'And two days ago when this shit was hitting the fan, you had to confront another truth. The woman you had fantasied about, me, no longer existed. The story you'd been telling yourself of what your life might have been with her, was all a lie. I was your excuse for not committing to relationships, for treating women badly, for choosing to live a hollow life. It wasn't my fault I couldn't live up to those expectations. I wasn't the one who had created the myth.'

'I'm sorry, what can I do?' he pleaded.

I paused before I replied.

'Nothing, it's too late.'

He saw the sanitary napkins, the pain killers and the bloodied soiled underwear.

He got up, ashen, and walked out.

Finally the truth had been told and the lying was over.

I needed to get on with my life.

151

Part 3

Where do I Belong?

My house, this city, was becoming a prison. I tried to write, but was distracted by the emails and gossip filling my inbox. I couldn't go out into the street, the journalists were baying for blood. People couldn't get enough of the story of the fallen woman who'd betrayed them all.

The only break from my own personal witch hunt was when the real story of Adam's involvement with the land in Tasmania was exposed. Moses' diaries had hinted at it. It didn't take much investigative journalism to uncover the whole ugly truth. When the election was over and the unions no longer had to keep quiet about the so-called mining deal, they too spoke out. They felt cheated that they had been so cleverly silenced. Felt their workers had been betrayed when they discovered that the mining was never going to happen and the jobs would never eventuate. And when they learnt Adam was being paid tens of millions of dollars not to mine the land, they went ballistic and called for strike action on all of Adam's building sites. They would make him pay. I felt vindicated and was happy to see 'Saint Adam' feel the sting of retribution. Adam was finally outed as the hardnosed sociopath he really was.

But of course this was only a minor distraction and within a day or two the press wanted to know how I felt about the lies Adam had told. I needed to get out, to escape to a place where I could be left in peace.

With just a suitcase I got in the car and, as if on autopilot, hit the highway west. On this early February morning, heading out of Melbourne before the sun rose, the roads were very quiet. In contrast I watched as the freeway into town was almost at a standstill filled with commuters making their tedious daily trip to the jobs they needed to meet the mortgage repayments on that dream house in suburbia. I wondered if they ever felt like turning around and escaping, just as I was doing today.

I don't know why I was even on this road, it seemed almost a hard wired response. What I did know was I hadn't travelled along it for at least twenty years.

It all looked so familiar. The Mallee scrub, the dried out yellowed wheat stubble, the deserted small towns, the CLOSED sign on an abandoned petrol station, the weeds growing in the grounds of a deconsecrated church.

I was heading home.

It was a typical summer's day. The heat shimmered off the black road surface. Sheep, surrounded by barren fields, gathered around the last of the water in almost empty dams. Crows, momentarily disturbed as I sped past, picked over the dried and desiccated carcasses of kangaroo road-kill. I was in a big hurry to get to nowhere, for what reason? There was no loving family waiting, no friends to catch up with, no place to even call home. I really didn't have anywhere else I could run to.

My mobile phone lost coverage about two hours out of Melbourne. I would have to ring Cindy from a phone booth. Were there still pay phones?

The drive would normally have taken about four hours, but I had been slowed to a crawl, stuck behind a huge truck carrying an old weatherboard house. The road was too narrow for me to overtake so I just sat there patiently waiting for an opportunity to pass. The banner draped across the back said HOLMES HOUSE REMOVALS, and I laughed quietly at the appropriateness of the name. I recognised the prefix on the phone number, a Greenhope number, similar to my parents, the digits etched permanently on my brain like a sing along jingle from times past. I wondered who would answer if I rang home now.

Eventually the road cleared and it was safe for me to pass and I sped ahead desperate to end my journey.

It hit me with an unexpected jolt. There ahead was a very familiar sight, my old house, about ten kilometres out of Greenhope. I slowed and turned into the driveway, red sand and weeds caught in the wire mesh gate, held permanently open. The old weatherboard house looked unloved, the paint was peeling, flyscreens rusted, dirty windows, the garden nothing more than dead bushes and dried grass. I drove around the back, doors falling off hinges revealing empty sheds. I was surprised to see the gnarled old peppercorn tree still standing, alive, its vast green weeping foliage shading the barren backyard. The back door was locked so I walked around to the front door jiggling the handle hoping to be able to look inside, but it wouldn't budge. As I sat on the steps, wondering what I was doing here and wondering what I would do next, I noticed a flat piece of timber lying on the porch. I kicked it over with my foot and saw the handwritten sign HOUSE FOR RENT, RING GEORGE. I picked up my phone, still no service, so I wrote down the number, curious as to whether George was still around. The bank had sold the farm. Had George purchased it? Right now the house was giving up none of its secrets. It was getting very hot, I was thirsty and should at least let Cindy know where I was.

The town was far worse than I'd expected, most of the shops were empty, the main street virtually deserted. I was tired, sleep had been almost impossible after the scandal had surfaced and I desperately needed somewhere to rest. Surprisingly the 'Greenhope Gardens Motel' was still in business. I rang the bell at reception and within seconds a man in his early sixties, wearing neatly pressed shorts, polo shirt, long socks and shiny lace up shoes presented himself at the desk. The badge told me his name was Malcolm.

'How may I be of assistance Ma'am?' he asked in a friendly and efficient manner.

'I'd like a room. Do you have anything available?'

He opened up a ledger and pored over it as if he was struggling to find a vacancy and only after quite some time, looked up.

'You're in luck, room number one, right next to the office. How long will you be staying with us?'

'Not too sure, one, maybe two nights?' I replied, not really knowing the answer myself.

'Not a problem. Just fill out this form and I'll show you to your room.'

Briefly I thought about what name I would write, and decided against an alias, my days of lying were done.

It was exactly like so many motels built in the seventies, dark green paintwork contrasting gaudily with the cream brick. A car space right out the front. He opened the door then handed me the keys. A faded floral bedspread, pine bedside tables held the brass reading lamps and the digital clock flashed the wrong time. A pine table and a vinyl covered chair sat in front of a window hung with sheer white nylon curtains, drapes on either side the same fabric as the bed. A feature cream brick wall ran the length of the room and the built in desk bench and wardrobe were in matching pine as well.

'I'll leave you now, Ms Maxwell. Don't hesitate to sing out if you need anything.'

'Thanks Malcolm, I will.'

He shut the door behind him and left me to explore. The bathroom was a shrine to salmon pink, tiles, laminate vanity and porcelain basin. The step through shower was enclosed by a brass and meshed safety glass screen. A large mirror reflected my rather ragged image, made even more dazzling by the bright humming fluorescent light above. The vanity held a supply of cheap toiletries neatly stored in a woven cane basket, the towels a contrasting dark green. I wondered if Malcolm's wife had done the decorating?

I still had no service, so I made the call from the phone in the room.

Cindy sounded a bit pissed off at my sudden departure, annoyed at my inaccessibility, no phone, no internet. She had put up with a lot over the last few months and I understood her weariness. I appeased her by saying I would go to Smithfield that afternoon and get a new phone and new provider that could give me access to all the services I needed.

'So how's the writing going?'

'It's been hopeless, I really don't know how to tell this story now. That's why I've left Melbourne. I need to be far away, to clear my head, to try to get some perspective.'

'Yeah, I know boss and I'm not really mad. I guess I wish things were more like they used to be, a bit simpler, like when we were just starting out.'

'Yeah, I get it. Me too.'

'Everything ok at the office?'

'Running like clockwork, busy as hell. You know what happens when you hit the headlines, the site goes crazy, the advertisers spend more dollars and we all get richer. Chenda said the women have been working overtime to keep up with demand. You might want to give her a call when you get the phone hooked up. You know how she worries.'

'Yep, good idea, will do. Now I should let you get back to work. Bye.'

'Bye.'

Where Greenhope had withered, Smithfield had thrived. A bustling main street was filled with many shops. A homeware store crammed with reproduction shabby chic nic-nacs. Wooden letters arranged to form obvious words, EAT, LOVE, HOME, just in case someone needed to have this spelled out. Gourmet deli's and cafes selling local produce and real coffee, even a bakery selling 'home-made' goods, although the bread looked not unlike the factory loaves of any other franchise. Dress shops displaying smart casual clothing for country women of a 'certain age', statement jewellery and pashmina scarves. This town displayed many signs of prosperity, restored, grand old Victorian buildings and houses, shiny new four wheel drives parked in the main street, even a big regional art gallery overlooking the river. The drought had broken, wheat prices were good, the canola harvest bounteous. A new crop, wine grapes, added to the successful agricultural mix.

I fixed up my phone problem and was now connected to the outside world. I didn't like the thought of any of my incoming calls going through Malcolm's front office. He could know my name, but he didn't need to know everything about me.

Strolling along the pedestrian mall I picked up a decent supply of food. With the wine industry came the 'gourmet' food industry, fuelled by jaded city folk, venturing out to find the next authentic regional food experience. A wine bar, a boutique brewery, opera in the vineyard and a music festival in March might be worth a visit if I decided to stay longer.

By the time I eventually returned to Greenhope, I was quite exhausted. I showered, put together a meal, turned on the television and just as I was about to sit down, there was a knock at the door.

'Sorry to impose, Ms Maxwell, but I thought I'd better let you know I had a call from someone looking for you, said they were from some newspaper. Told 'em you'd decided not to stay and that you were heading to Adelaide. Think I got rid of them, your secret's safe with me.'

I felt ashamed at my initial annoyance with his intrusion, ashamed at my snide thoughts about the motel and it's decor. Malcolm was a good man.

'Thanks Malcolm, I appreciate it. I came here to get away from them. Can't believe they tracked me down. Thanks for thinking so quickly.'

'No problems, have a good night.'

'You too, and thanks again.'

Watching the local news brought back many memories, familiar places and names. Even some of the old family run businesses were still advertising with the same jingles and slogans. I took my food and a glass of wine and propped myself up on the bed. Tomorrow I would try to ring George, but tonight I was glad to be drinking again, away from the rat race, back in Greenhope and watching crap TV.

It was so familiar and yet so foreign, this once thriving town was all but abandoned, only a few shops remained opened. The church run second hand shop, the grain and feed store, the garage that sold petrol and the pharmacy which now only opened on Mondays and Tuesdays.

The pub was still operating, the smell of beer soaked carpet and cigarette smoke wafting from the dark interior as I walked past. A not altogether unpleasant smell, reminding me of the times when my father would take us into town for a pub meal on special occasions, giving Mum a night off on her birthday. Chicken in a basket, seafood platter, schnitzels, steaks. An all you can eat, self serve bain marie piled high with overcooked vegetables, tinned pineapple, beetroot, fried rice, scalloped potatoes and pasta. A selection of salads on ice popular with those women wanting to cut back on the calories. I was always uncomfortable when Dad went back and refilled his plate, worried that it wasn't quite the right thing to do, failing to notice that just about everyone else was doing exactly the same thing.

The hospital, built to cope with a post war baby boom, was now an aged care home. The sign telling the sick and injured that the nearest emergency facility was at the new regional hospital in Smithfield.

Some of the vacated shops still had posters stuck in their front windows advertising a 'Save Our School' rally. I looked across the road at the rusted playground equipment and saw the plea had been ignored. The only people out on the street were old, the new school at Smithfield had claimed the young families as well.

The train line had been closed for years, the politicians deciding this was a service no longer needed since the construction of that new bypass. The station had been converted to a cheery looking cafe, but its dusty interior and empty tables told me it had only managed a brief run, that it needed those commuters the government had redirected elsewhere.

Smithfield was in a marginal seat. They had lobbied harder and had kept their train. It brought in many tourists who stayed in town but without a car, they were unable to make the thirty minute drive west to Greenhope.

Empty shops everywhere. Sharolyn Snips and Clips closed, I remembered those girls, Sharon and Lynne, slightly scary netball playing sisters who had left school early to start their hairdressing apprenticeships. The real estate agent's window filled with photos of houses 'priced to sell', where $50,000 was still more than anyone was prepared to pay.

The general store had become the post office, newsagent and takeaway. The meagre offerings on the shelves told me that most people did their grocery shopping in Smithfield where the big supermarkets felt it was imperative to wipe out all competition.

'You staying at the motel?' asked the woman behind the counter, her face somewhat familiar.

'Yeah.'

'You're Edward and Mary Maxwell's daughter, Christina aren't you?'

'Word gets round.'

'It's a small place. Malcolm tells me those reporters have been sniffing around. Don't worry love, you'll be ok here, we're all looking out for you.'

I was touched by her words.

'Yes, haven't been home in ages.'

'Shirley Goodchild, Malcolm's wife. Terrible thing that happened to your mum and dad, they were a truly decent couple,' she said, reaching out a hand for me to shake.

I remembered now, although the woman across from me had aged beyond her years and I barely recognised her. Shirley was one of those salt of the earth country women who was on every committee, attended church, helped out the less fortunate and was capable of doing any job thrown at her. I remembered seeing her serving morning tea at the funeral.

She didn't need to say, but I knew most of the remaining townspeople had been alerted to my presence, and even though I hadn't lived here since I was seventeen, I was still one of them and during this crisis they would protect me.

'Hang on a minute, I've forgotten a couple of things,' I said, taking my empty basket and filling it with unnecessary treats. This little shop needed patronage much more than the supermarket in Smithfield.

I returned to the motel room hot from my walk and despondent about what I had just seen. At least the noisy old air conditioner provided me with some respite from the blistering Australian heat.

I was upset by what I had seen and did not feel inspired to write. What would I do all day? Why was I even here? The number on the scrap of paper. I would call George, see if he could let me into the farmhouse.

To my surprise the call connected.

'Cameron Pastoral Holdings, Andrew Cameron speaking,'

'Ah yes, I was wondering if I could speak to George please?'

'George?'

'Yes, I was driving past the old Maxwell place on the bypass, just out of Greenhope and saw the FOR RENT sign. It said to ring George.'

'George hasn't worked here for years. That house is pretty run down. I wasn't even aware it was still available for rent. Why do you ask?'

'My family used to own the farm, I was just driving through, passed the old place and wondered if it would be possible to have a look inside? But it's ok, it doesn't matter, it's not that important.'

'Listen, I'm heading out that way later this afternoon, need to do a soil check. I could meet you there, about four, if you like. What was your name again?'

'Sorry, Christina, Christina Maxwell and that would be great, thanks, I'll see you at four.'

The peppercorn tree provided some respite from what had turned into a blazing forty degree day. I had arrived at the farm house a bit earlier, anxious not to miss the opportunity that had been offered. After waiting thirty minutes, he eventually pulled up. I turned off the engine and got out of my air conditioned cocoon and stepped into a wall of stultifying heat. He got out of his truck, company logo painted on the door and walked over. Tall, with the swagger of a rider, light brown hair, blue eyes, skin of a man who worked under a harsh sun. Jeans, dark blue work shirt, rolled up sleeves, boots, ruggedly handsome.

'Andrew Cameron.'

'Christina Maxwell,' I responded and shook his hard calloused hand. He was obviously a man who got out of the farm office once in awhile.

'Sorry I'm late, had to pick up the kids. Follow me.'

We stood on the back veranda, he pulled out a large batch of keys, sorting through till he found the one the right one.

'How long since you've been back?'

'A long time, at least twenty years.'

With a bit of force and a nudge from his shoulder he was able to push open the heavy old wooden door.

'Ladies first,' he said, gesturing for me to enter.

Faintly amused by his gentlemanly charm I stepped inside and was instantly transported back to a time many years ago. My body responded viscerally to the overwhelming familiarity, my eyes welled with tears.

'I'll leave you to have a look round, got a bit of stuff to do outside, take your time.'

'Thanks.'

It was so small. People always said that returning to places of your childhood was often underwhelming. Had the years of living in the big mansion in Toorak and now in my own beautiful modern, minimalist home dulled the reality of the humble house in which I grew up? I knew my parents had been poor, but coming home for the first time in twenty years and looking inside this most basic house, was confronting.

How had my mother felt when she first walked through the door of a house that had changed little since it had been built in the late eighteen hundreds? She was a young bride from a city where each house had running water, electric stoves and heating. It took ten years before they got connected to water and electricity She must have had a deep and profound love for my father to put up with such primitive conditions for so long.

Although the house was devoid of furniture and the other things that filled the small rooms when we lived there, it was still so unmistakably mine. Its ghosts faintly whispering a welcome home. The kitchen still had the same built in cupboards, the old wood stove sat under the brick chimney and I could faintly smell the odour of coals in the fire box. Mum had produced many a great meal from this oven. I was reminded of just how hot this kitchen would get if she cooked a roast in Summer, but also fondly remembered the welcoming red glow on a cold winters night. The kitchen was the heart of this house and most of our time here was spent around the old table that occupied most of the space in the room. The lounge still had its fireplace with a simple wooden surround. The two bedrooms off the main hallway had no adornments, no ornate cornices or ceiling roses. My room was tiny, it would only just have held my small single bed. When I was a kid I covered the walls with posters and pictures torn out of magazines, projecting the fantasy life I hoped I would someday find.

And as I was about to walk out, I spied the markings on the door frame where Dad had drawn lines with dates showing just how much I'd grown. My eyes filled with tears and I longed for them to be here to comfort me. I walked back through each room looking for other evidence of my life here and although there was almost nothing tangible, I felt a great sense of calm and belonging, the noises in my head quieting, finally at peace, at home.

When I finished I sat on the steps of the back veranda and waited for Andrew to return. I watched as he drove in from a distant paddock, a cloud of dust following the truck. He got out and grabbed something from the back before coming to join me on the step.

'Beer?' he said, assuming a yes, handing me a bottle.

'Thanks,' I said, twisting the top, guzzling the icy cold liquid inside.

'Thirsty?' he observed, with a wry grin.

We sat silent for awhile, strangers looking into the distance awkwardly wondering what there was to be said.

'I know who you are. Had a bit of trouble down there in Melbourne?'

'God, no where's safe. So much for getting away from it all,' I said, exasperated by the way this sordid tale followed me.

'Surely you didn't think you could hide out here. Country towns are the last place you could disappear to. Everybody knows everyone's business. The locals can always spot a new face, not much else happening, gives them something to talk about.'

'Could we please not talk about me?' I groaned.

'So who owns the farm now?' I asked, quickly changing the subject.

'My father bought it years ago. Bought up lots of these small holdings in the area. Could see we had to get much bigger if we were going to survive.'

'And do you work for him?'

'No, not any longer, he died a while ago. George was one of the farm managers who worked for Dad. Was still here when I got back from uni.'

'Where'd you go.'

'Roseworthy in Adelaide, completely changed my ideas about farming.'

'Like what?'

'Like not making the same mistakes as our fathers, about diversifying. We were one of the first farms to plant canola, that's what I want to put in here. Came to check the nitrogen levels of the soil, see how much we'd have to add when planting. Some of the land around here is pretty depleted, farming the same stuff for too long, fucks up the soil.'

'What else do you do?'

'Wine grapes near Smithfield and sheep and wheat further north.'

'Do you live around here, your name is unfamiliar, can't remember you from school?' I asked.

'We lived on another bigger property near Horsham, moved there when I was a baby. Grandparent's farm, Dad took over from my mother's family. Like a lot of kids in the area I was shunted off to boarding school in Ballarat when I was six. Didn't move back here until I finished uni. I now live about twenty minutes east, pretty much halfway between Smithfield and Greenhope, on my Dads original farm.'

'And you?'

'Born and educated here, went to MIT when I finished high school. Dad's family were third generation farmers, but it was a shit of a life, barely enough to keep the wolf from the door. Bank sold it when my parents died. I haven't been back since.'

'So what are you going to do while you're here?' he said, assuming I was staying.

'Funny you should ask. Up until now, I didn't really know. I walked around Greenhope and was shocked at what a ghost town it had become and was convinced there was no reason to stay. But today, after coming here, I was wondering if you'd let me rent the place. I need somewhere to write, away from Melbourne. This place feels safe, it feels right. I've been surprised by how emotionally connected I still am. It feels like home.'

Before he could answer his phone started ringing.

'Yeah baby, I'm sorry, Dad won't be long, get your homework started. Mrs Goodchild has left something in the fridge, I'm just leaving now.'

'Kids?' I asked.

'Yeah, completely forgot about them, gotta go. I'll have a think about the house, call you tomorrow. See ya,' he yelled, as he headed for his truck.

I flipped the lock, pulled the back door shut and followed him out the drive. He turned left and I turned right.

The shower washed away the dust and the sweat. I sat on the bed wrapped in my towel, contemplating whether the treats I'd bought, chocolate, chips and Tim Tams, were actually classed as food, let alone dinner. My phone started to buzz. The caller I.D. said George and for a brief moment I wondered who the hell it was.

'Christina speaking.'

'Christina, Andrew, Andrew Cameron.'

My brain was a bit vague and it took me a few seconds to work out who was calling.

'Andrew, Farm Andrew, sorry, my phone said George, how are you?' surprised at how pleased I was to hear his voice, once I finally worked out who was making the call.

'I'm fine, thanks, and you? Are you surviving the heat? Have they got air conditioning where you're staying?'

'Yeah, it's not too bad, I'm at the Greenhope Gardens Motel.'

'Bloody hell, that old place, I'd thought you'd be staying in Smithfield. Has old Malcolm been knocking on your door?'

'Smithfield isn't home and Malcolm has been really kind. Do you know him?'

'They call him the Mayor of Greenhope, but anyway that's not what I'm calling about. I've been thinking about your request and I can't see any reason why you can't use the old place, it's just standing there empty.'

'Brilliant, thanks Andrew. How much do you want for it?'

'Nothing.'

'But I have to pay something. It wouldn't feel right.'

'To tell you the honest truth, I was thinking about knocking it down, it would get in the way of the canola planting. We wouldn't be seeding the crop till late autumn, so you can have it till then.'

'Well, I'd better get a move on. When can I get the keys?'

'Tomorrow, I'll meet you there at ten, after I've dropped the kids at school.'

I put down the phone with mixed emotions, glad to have the house, but disturbed by the fact that Andrew wanted to pull it down. I looked at the pile of food on the table and decided I needed something more. A hamburger from Shirley's shop.

'You been out to your old place today?' she said, making small talk as my burger cooked.

'Yeah, it was really good to see the farm again.'

'That Andrew Cameron's a bit of a catch. Show you round did he?'

'Yeah, in fact I'm going to rent the house for a few weeks. Got some writing to do, thought it might be a good place to escape to. Do you know Mr. Cameron.'

'Lovely man, I clean his house, cook for him, do a bit of babysitting occasionally.'

'So he's not married?'

'No, not anymore. She lives in Smithfield, has the kids one week on, one week off. Bloody stupid arrangement if you ask me.'

My hamburger was ready, I paid and said good night.

Greenhope just got that little bit smaller, having that house, away from the centre of town would be a very good idea.

Return Home

His truck and a ute were already parked under the peppercorn tree when I arrived at the farmhouse. I was a bit late as it had taken me a little longer to find the cleaning supplies I needed. Detergent, sponges from Shirley's, a broom from the grain store, mop, bucket and rags from a very curious, but keen to help, Malcolm. I unloaded, looking like a hotel housekeeper.

'Knock, knock,' I called out, as I entered the back door, trying to be heard above the sounds of power tools and hammering.

The house was buzzing with activity, a young man tinkering with the taps in the sink, another shaving off a warped sticking door. Andrew was in the hallway looking at the meter box, calling out to someone up a ladder outside.

'Hi.'

'Hi, how are you this morning?' said Andrew, pausing to welcome me.

'Good, thank you. Just a bit surprised to see so much going on.'

'Couldn't let you live in the old place in the condition it was in. Thought I'd get you reconnected to power and water.'

'You really didn't need to, I only want somewhere to write during the day. Please don't go to any trouble. I have no intention of sleeping here, I thought I'd keep my room at the motel.'

He seemed a little bit disappointed at my lack of enthusiasm and so I quickly retracted my statement.

'I suppose it would be good to have somewhere to escape to, and after all the writing doesn't always fit daylight hours. Suppose some nights I'll be too tired to drive back into town.'

'And you probably won't always want the mayor breathing down your back.'

He was right, being tracked by the town's elders could become quite stifling.

I grabbed my cleaning supplies and went to where I wouldn't get in the way. The bedrooms needed no repairs, just a good scrub. I tackled them first, washing down the walls, cleaning the windows and mopping the floors. The rooms were stark, white walls, dark floorboards, and quite frankly a pleasant change from the claustrophobic, overly decorated motel room, the antithesis of the cool minimalist chic that I had come to take for granted. If I was to use this as a retreat, I would need some furniture, at least a mattress, a desk and a chair. I didn't want to get too attached to the old place but I knew it still had to be practical.

We worked hard all day and by five all the necessary repairs had been done and the cleaning was complete. Such a tiny little house didn't take much time. The young station hands left and I found myself sitting on the steps again with Andrew, beer in hand.

'Thanks Andrew, you've been really great, you'll have to let me know if I can return the favour.'

'Can you cook?'

'Actually I can.'

'Well, maybe you could come over to my place and cook me dinner one night?'

'Easy,' I said clinking bottles to seal the deal.

'What are you doing tonight?'

'What do you mean?'

'For dinner, where were you planning on eating?'

'I hadn't thought that far ahead.'

'The pub in town does a decent steak on a Friday night, want to eat there?'

'What about your kids?'

'They're at their mum's, she's got them for the next week. We share custody.'

'God, I'm pretty knackered. I thought I might curl up in bed with a packet of Tim Tams.'

'That's not dinner, come on, come to the pub. It's a bit of a Friday night tradition, decent feed, a few beers, chat with the locals, you'd love it.'

'Well, I guess I could be tempted. What time?'

'Six? They eat early here, the kitchen often runs short, best to get in first if you want the steak.'

'Alright, you win, we'd better get moving. See you there.' I said, looking at my watch, finishing my beer.

He followed me out the drive and I looked in the rear vision mirror to see him stop and close the gate, he must have repaired that as well. Then, instead of turning left, he followed me into town, and to my surprise pulled into the carapace next to mine at the motel.

'What are you doing here?'

'Usually book a room if I come in on a Friday night. The local cop always sits at the turnoff, booking me for drink driving would give him something to do. And look at me, I'm covered in twenty years worth of dust, couldn't be taking a lady out to dinner looking like this?' he said, the lines on his weather beaten face pleasantly wrinkling as he smiled.

'This is not 'dinner', it's just the pub, Mr Andrew Cameron.'

'Still need a shower, Miss Maxwell,' and with that he took out a key and opened the door.

'See you at six.'

Cheeky bastard, I thought, smiling at his flirtatiousness.

I showered and put on one of my simple linen shifts, a bit Jackie O, not too dressy. It felt good to be out of the jeans and sweats that had been my uniform over the last few reclusive weeks. I dried my hair, leaving it down skimming my shoulders. Some mascara and lip gloss would be enough, I didn't want to give the wrong impression. Andrew was very charming, his attention was flattering, but I wasn't ready for any type of relationship.

At six a firm knock on the door told me he was ready. He whistled and stood back to take in the view.

'You polish up alright Maxwell, shall we go?'

Looks like an impression had already been made. I would have to be very careful.

He was right, it was some kind of Friday night ritual, the pub was surprisingly full. Andrew walked next to me, his hand against the small of my back, guiding me through the crowd to the bar. People were looking, I was the new face. I wondered what they were thinking. A table of elderly women huddled together, hands to mouth whispering amongst themselves. 'Who was this out of towner walking in with the district's most eligible bachelor?' I could almost hear them say and instantly I was transported back to a time when I was that insecure teenager who didn't fit in. I reached behind, grabbing Andrew's hand, pulling him towards me stretching on tip toes to reach his ear.

'We've got to go, this place it's freaking me out,' I pleaded.

'You'll be ok, I won't let them get to you, they're harmless,' he said, squeezing my hand reassuringly and directing me to a stool at the bar.

I felt only slightly reassured, having my back to the crowd was a small consolation. And in truth, these were all old people. No mobile phones taking pictures, no hurried texts spreading the word that the pariah from the big city was in town.

'Now, if you let my hand go, I'll sit next to you and order us a drink.'

I quickly released him, embarrassed by my panicked response. We were served quickly and I nearly downed the entire glass, the cold liquid giving me a slight brain freeze, the alcohol calming my anxiety.

'Sorry, I guess I wasn't expecting so many people, must be the heat.'

We ordered our food. People came up to chat, Andrew was well known. He politely introduced me as Edward Maxwell's daughter. Many of the older men knew my father and told tales of their youth. I no longer felt threatened, I felt I belonged. When the food arrived, Malcolm called out over the din of the crowd, inviting us to sit with him and his wife Shirley Goodchild. We were welcomed like old friends. It wasn't so bad after all.

I knew why Andrew had booked into the motel. The beer had flowed, many locals bought jugs for us to share, and we were both quite drunk as we walked out the door and headed home.

'Where you goin'?' he yelled, as I crossed the road.

'Back to school.'

The old play equipment sat begging, I jumped on the swings, the screeching sound of the rusted hinges echoing up the street. He ran across the road, following me, and jumped on the other swing.

'Race, see who can go highest.'

Like a big kid he held onto the chains pulling himself higher. I followed and giggled as the butterflies in my belly took flight. I loved this, swinging higher, feeling a childlike sense of daring and freedom.

'Jump!' he yelled, as he flew into the night, and I did.

We fell in a heap on the soft red sand, laughing out loud at the sheer idiocy of our behavior. He got up first, dusting himself off, reaching for my hand, pulling me to my feet. He didn't let go and we walked, playfully knocking into one another as we stumbled home. It occurred to me briefly that I could let my guard down, not worry about what people would think, and invite him inside, but common sense stepped in and saved me from myself. I knew he wanted more, but I presented my cheek as he attempted to kiss me goodnight and retreated, quickly into my room. I heard him drunkenly wishing me good night on the other side of the closed door and smiled. What a lovely night.

It was 10am when I woke, my head pounding, mouth parched, desperately trying to find some paracetamol and water. A coke from the mini bar and a packet of salty chips helped slightly. I had slept in my dress and smiled at the red dirt stains on the white linen. Last night had gone so well and I loved that I woke without regret, glad that I hadn't slept with Andrew or compromised this pleasant friendship. The shower helped clear my head. I walked over to the window, pulled the curtains, surprised not only by the grey overcast sky, but also by the absence of Andrew's truck. I noticed a piece of paper on the floor near the door. A note from Andrew, thanking me for a great night and inviting me to his place today, suggesting I might want to borrow some furniture. A map showed me how to get there.

He must have left early.

I would head out after lunch.

He was right, the turnoff was almost halfway between the two towns, ten minutes past my farm house. A few kilometres up the dirt road I saw the giant cypress hedges, sentinel like, guarding the big old property, blocking the view. The sign welded on to the massive steel gates told me that I was indeed at Cameron Pastoral Holdings. I got out, released the catch, pushed the heavy gates open and drove through, remembering to shut the gates behind me. I didn't want to look like the complete idiot from the city who let his prized livestock out.

Tall lemon scented gums lined the driveway and as I got closer to the homestead, grassy paddocks were replaced with lush green lawns and manicured gardens. Sitting in the midst of this botanical splendour was a very stately old two storey bluestone mansion. Ornate cast iron lace, wide verandas, purple wisteria climbing up the posts and walls. Big bay windows overlooking the grounds. This was not your average farm house.

I knocked on the heavily panelled front door and wondered, after trying for quite some time, if anybody was even at home. I should've called first. I dialled his number and just as the call connected, he opened the door.

'Come in,' he said smiling, still cheekily holding the phone to his ear. I walked into a dark hall, walls lined with the portraits of the Cameron ancestors. I had lived in a mansion like this once and resisted the urge to turn around and walk straight back out.

'Don't let the relics get to you, they're all dead,' he said, irreverently, sensing my unsettled demeanor.

'I was married once and lived in a place like this, it always unnerved me.'

We walked down the long corridor and I caught glimpses of the grand rooms. Like mine, it was big and rambling, but unlike mine it felt like a real home. The furniture was worn, there were kids' toys strewn around, the dog was stretched out on a rug. Country radio was playing, windows were open, curtains billowing, birdsong bringing the sounds of the garden inside. The house seemed to sing with life. It was obvious a family lived here. I remember how sterile my own place had been, each room kept immaculately clean, the priceless antiques in pristine condition, more like a museum than a home.

'How long have you lived here?'

'Camerons have been here since the district was first settled. My great great grandfather built this. He made a fortune selling wool, the English couldn't get enough of it.'

'But I thought you said you grew up on your grandparent's farm in Horsham?'

'Yeah, we did, it was a much bigger property than this and my mother's father needed help. Dad wanted me to take over this place and I moved back when I finished university. He was starting to buy up a lot of the smaller farms, the land was cheap. He could see the unrealised potential of the area. The climate is perfect for canola, grapes. He was an innovator and trusted me to follow his vision. He never moved back, pretty much left me up to my own devices. He stayed on the Horsham farm until he died.'

'So did this place stay empty while you were away, it looks to be in really good condition?'

'George, my Dad's farm manager, stayed on. Kept it running and helped me out when I returned. He's still alive, lives somewhere in north Queensland.'

I followed Andrew into his office. Spreadsheets flickered on the computer. Aerial photos and a map showing all the properties, vast tracts of land almost interlinked between Horsham and Ballarat. Shelves stacked high with folders and files. This was not the kind of farming I'd grown up with. This was a very big business.

'Sorry, I won't be long, just getting the sugar reports for the grape harvest, vintage is about to start. Need to know which properties need the machinery first.'

After a few minutes he was done and we went to the kitchen. It was massive and I imagined the large number of servants it was designed to employ.

'Drink?' he asked.

'Depends what you're offering. Felt a little bit shabby this morning, one too many welcome home beers. How about you?'

'Fine, you've gotten soft city girl. I was back here working at six this morning. Miss me?'

'Didn't even hear you leave.'

He filled our glasses with iced water and we sat down at the work table.

'I thought about your offer and realised some furniture would be good. I probably only need a table, something to work on, a couple of chairs and maybe a bed?'

'I've got sheds full of stuff. Finish your drink and we'll have a look.

The back of the property was more like a small village, bluestone buildings dotted about the place.

'What are all these?' I said, surprised at the vastness of the estate.

'Stables, dairy, shearing sheds, workers quarters, foundry, a glasshouse, even a chapel. Farming used to employ a lot of people, most of the staff and workers lived on site. We were too far away from town to make the trip on horseback every day. At one stage there were enough children living here that my great grandfather employed a teacher and a governess.'

We walked into a small two storey cottage filled with furniture.

'This used to be the manager's cottage, George was the last person to live here. Now all my managers and workers live in Smithfield.'

The interior appeared to have been modernised in the thirties, the furniture looked to be from that era.

'There's a nice old table here, it would fit your kitchen well.'

It would, big enough to write and eat on. There was enough furniture for the entire farm house, and although I had been briefly redecorating in my head, I had to remind myself this would only be a temporary tenancy. There was no point in filling the house, as it would all be coming down when the canola crop was planted at the end of autumn. Two slatted wooden chairs, a miners couch and a single bed would do. Andrew said he would load them into the truck and deliver the furniture tomorrow morning.

I sensed his spreadsheets and computer were calling him back. The grape harvest was only days away, he was preoccupied. I knew it was time to leave.

Rather than spend the remainder of the day stuck in my motel room, I decided to go into Smithfield and do a bit of shopping. I couldn't live entirely like a monk and would have to pick up a few essentials if I was going to make my retreat liveable.

It was a Saturday and the tourists were wandering around in their droves. The cafes buzzed, the farmers' market filled the town square. I enjoyed shopping this afternoon, my mission now had purpose and by the end of the day I had purchased enough to see the back seat crammed full.

A pretty little bench under a tree opposite the square was a good place to sit on this beautiful balmy afternoon, have a coffee and think about the last few days, and in particular, Andrew Cameron. There was no question I had enjoyed his company, was even attracted to him, but I couldn't quite pinpoint how he felt about me. On one hand I was pretty sure he would have jumped into bed with me without any hesitation last night, if I had let him in. On the other hand, he seemed to be offering a genuine friendship. My problem was that I didn't know how to have men as friends. In the last two years since Paul's death any man, apart from Sam, that I had become friends with, had very quickly become my lover. I loved sex, the power it gave me had been thrilling, but I now had very mixed feelings about having sex without love. Sex with Adam had been deeply satisfying, loving him made it so much more intense. The brutal ending of our relationship a few weeks ago had left gaping emotional wounds that had only just begun to heal. Being away from Melbourne protected me from the unwanted intrusion of the press. Being in Greenhope, finding the farmhouse, connecting with my past was a good way to distract myself from the intense emotions that simmered just below the surface. Keeping busy, thinking about new things, helped to lessen the sting. Making choices, rather than being a victim of fate, rebooted my natural pragmatism and gave me the resilience I now drew so heavily upon. And being here also removed me from the possibility of any chance meetings with Adam. After what had happened, and what I'd done, there could never be even a friendship between us.

I vowed to take things slowly. Andrew would become a friend first, I would not let him become a lover just yet.

Writing Again

I woke with a new enthusiasm and raced over to the farm, keen to set up and keen to see Andrew.

When I pulled up I was expecting to see his truck. Inside I saw he'd already been and gone. The lovely old table and chairs were set up in the kitchen, the couch in the lounge and the single bed, squeezed into my old bedroom. To my amusement, the decorating had not stopped there. Andrew had placed a big double bed in my parent's bedroom. My belly fluttered at what this might mean, my sex warmed at the thoughts it provoked. Perhaps Andrew Cameron was making his intentions clear?

A wine bottle on the table sat next to a note, 'Happy writing, Andrew. PS, hope you like Shiraz, it's one of mine.'

It was amazing what a difference the furniture made. Bringing things back into the house, to give it warmth and humanity. A whistling kettle for the stove, a real teapot and a caddy of Earl Grey on the mantle above the oven. Cups hanging on hooks, two plates in the rack above the sink. A cashmere throw rug and a couple of cushions on the couch, an indulgent spend at one of those naff stores in Smithfield. My one and only attempt at 'country chic', a secret vice that would never rear its head in my Fitzroy home. And my little bedroom, with the bed now invitingly made, a safe place to snuggle into after a long day of writing. Next time I was in town I would buy linen for the double bed. I wondered when or if it would ever be used.

Outside I wandered around, looking for traces of my family's history. Nothing but a 'Fowlers Vacola' preserving jar that I filled with green fronds and pink berries, bringing indoors the pleasantly evocative spicy smell of the ancient peppercorn tree.

Satisfied after my morning's procrastination, I was finally ready to write. It did occur to me not to write at all, but I knew the story would never go away unless I told the world what really happened. Moses had been brutally honest, but his diary had only been his story. I needed to tell mine. To explain why it had been so tempting to give everything up for a simpler life. So I started at the very beginning, right here in this house. A story without context meant nothing.

The time flew past, the story of growing up here, of always feeling like an outsider, of not fitting in. Being in this house brought back all the memories. Of dancing to Mum and Dad's old records, dressing up, pretending I was someone else. Being stuck here in this strange place waiting for that indefinable 'something' I so intuitively craved. My parents craved it too. My father didn't want to be a farmer, he left for the city in pursuit of his dreams, but returned, with my mother, naively thinking that finding each other would be the answer.

By late that night I had written thousands of words, the story was pouring out and my life was beginning to make some sense.

Day after day I wrote, talking about what it felt like to leave home, discover a world that other's took for granted, a wide eyed innocent, hungry for what the city would reveal.

Leaving the motel early and coming back late at night, I barely saw a soul. I was driven. Malcolm knocked on my door Friday morning, just to check I was ok and I told him I'd fixed up the old place and was spending all my days writing there.

'Will you be coming to the pub tonight?' he asked.

Of course, it was the thing to do around here. I lost track of the days and had become so absorbed in my writing that I'd completely forgotten about this Friday night ritual. It felt like I'd been here forever, yet it had only been just over a week.

'Not sure, it completely slipped my mind, depends on how much writing I get done. Will you and Shirley be there?'

'Never miss it. You've gotta eat girl, you're as skinny as a rake. When was the last time you had a decent meal?'

He was right, I'd been living off the few bits and pieces I'd picked up at the farmers' market. The house had no refrigerator, so lunch was often chocolate or cheese and crackers. I had become too involved in the story to think about food.

'Perhaps you're right, I'll see how I go.'

The car almost drove itself, the route to the house hard wired into my brain. Two beautiful old wicker arm chairs were sitting on the back verandah when I arrived. I read the note.

Thought these might be a bit more comfortable than the step. Sorry I haven't been around, the harvest is in full swing, no time to think. See you soon, Andrew.

I had seen the trucks laden with grapes, travelling along the bypass, the smell of sticky fermenting juice in the air.

It had only been last Saturday that I'd gone out to his place, almost a week since I'd seen him, I really had lost track of time. It would be good to catch up, he would probably be at the pub tonight.

185

I finished a little earlier, showered and headed off to the pub. It was as full as last week, the terror of walking through the front doors, into a room full of strangers, not quite as daunting. The place was beginning to feel a bit more familiar, a bit more like home.

'Over here Tina.'

It was Malcolm, waving from across from the room. Before sitting down I grabbed a tray full of drinks, remembering what they'd had last week.

'Shirley, here, a Chardonnay I think?' I said, handing her a glass.

'Thanks love, you remembered.'

'Malcolm, Coopers light I believe, cheers!'

'Cheers Tina, thanks.'

We spent the next hour chatting. Shirley filled me in on the local gossip and the men talked about some town regeneration project they were sure would be the next big thing. I tried to concentrate, but was keeping my eye on the door, hoping Andrew would walk through. Sensing my distraction, Shirley took my hand and whispered in my ear.

'He's not coming tonight, he's got the kids.'

I was embarrassed at her almost sixth sense intuition, she had read my mind and I blushed.

'And it's vintage, grape harvest is in full swing. Took over a week's worth of food, put it in his freezer, poor man, barely has time to sleep. You'd think that wife of his would at least take the kids during harvest!'

Shirley most definitely disapproved of this woman. I wonder what the story was. Maybe I could ask Andrew one day.

The next week was more of the same, the writing flowed. Cindy called to say the press had bought the story of my disappearance to Adelaide. Jane, my editor, was also deeply ensconced in writing her half of the story.

'Have you been able to get anyone to talk?' I asked

'Yeah, most people have been pretty good. I've let them read the transcripts, so there are no nasty surprises when we publish. The only person I haven't been able to contact is Adam. Seems he's dropped off the radar, nobody can find him anywhere. Sam said he was in Cambodia and didn't want to be contacted.'

'Sorry Jane, I'd be the last person he wants to talk about right now. I guess you'll just have to wait, he can't stay away forever. Is this holding you up?'

'No, not really, there are enough newspaper stories to fill in the gaps. We are refocusing on what it was like here in the office. It's better to write about what we know.'

She was right, and that is exactly what I had been doing. Cindy and Jane knew only that Adam and I had split, his response to the Diary scandal was to be expected. I didn't tell them about the abortion. When I took back control, I completely compartmentalised this part of my life, locking it up in an impenetrable steel vault, sealing it off never to be thought of again. It was the only way I could cope. I'd had years of practice, it was frighteningly easy to do.

187

The week ended with me trying to write about my marriage, a much more difficult task than I expected. I had to be aware that Kate would read about it and needed to remember that she had loved her father. I didn't want to go into every graphic detail, just the bits that were relevant to the story. I tried to paint a picture of a shaky start, but a partnership that grew over time, a bit like an arranged marriage. She didn't need to know I had never loved her father.

Friday came around quickly, but this time I did not expect to see Andrew, the number of grape trucks had increased substantially over the last week.

As usual I sat with Malcolm and Shirley and this time even the barman welcomed me with a 'G'day Tina'.

'Mind if I join you?' said the familiar voice.

I had my back to the door, I hadn't even seen him come in, my heart skipped a beat. Shirley moved up one seat. I felt like a schoolgirl when he sat down, close, next to me.

'Hey, thanks for those chairs. It's been ages, how are you?'

'Absolutely fucked, but I think we've turned a corner. Should have most of the crop off in the next week, need to get it in before it rains. What are you drinking?'

'No, let me, sit down. I'll get us a jug, you look thirsty,' I said with the confidence of a seasoned local.

We ate and talked and Andrew held court. Malcolm may be the unofficial Mayor, but Andrew was most certainly king.

'You staying at the pub tonight?'

'No, gotta be in Smithfield early tomorrow, have to watch what I drink. How's the book going?'

'Good, the house is working like a treat, the ghosts are doing all the talking.'

He seemed to be less flirtatious than usual, I was getting mixed messages. Maybe the double bed thing had been my over-active imagination. By eight he said his farewells, apologised for not staying longer, and left. Malcolm walked me home. It was like he was my father escorting me from a failed date. I felt like a teenager, a little forlorn and ever so slightly heartbroken.

The writing became more intense and the nights got even later. On Thursday at 2am, too tired to drive back to Greenhope, I crawled into the double bed. I was being kept awake by the rumble of trucks, a sound I had failed to notice whilst so absorbed writing in the kitchen at the back of the house. I was instantly reminded of how this had been when we lived here. Dad had put shutters on the front rooms to block out the noise. I dragged myself into the back bedroom, the smaller one that was once mine, where the noise was less invasive. Eventually I went to sleep.

Bang bang bang. What was that? My fuzzy brain took awhile to register that someone was knocking on the back door. I grabbed a sheet to cover up my nakedness and went to see who had disrupted me.

It was Andrew.

'Didn't expect to see you here,' he said, way too cheery for six am.

'What the hell? The sun is barely up. Come in, sit down.'

189

I put on the kettle, the coals in the stove were still glowing from the fire I'd lit the night before. I'd almost forgotten how cold it could get at night once summer had ended. A few more bits of wood would get that kettle boiling in no time.

'So what brings you over here so early in the morning?'

'Checking the soil, thought I'd bring you over a little gift.'

I heard the tailgate of his truck open and went out to see.

'Found this at my office in town, didn't need it anymore, thought you could use it?'

It was a small fridge, hardly romantic, but something for the half finished wine, the milk.

'Grab the end.'

I did as he said and awkwardly tried to shuffle in my sheet gown.

'How ya doing? Not too heavy?'

'Fine.'

No sooner had I tried to step up onto the veranda when my foot caught the edge of the cloth and the rather precariously draped sheet slipped to the ground. He smiled and laughed heartily, at no point did he think to look away. I was not ashamed of my body and didn't want to let him think that I was fazed by my predicament, so I put the fridge down stepped over the sheet and walked, completely naked, back into the house to retrieve my clothes. He wolf whistled as I went past.

'Jesus, you've got a great ass!'

He couldn't see my grin.

By the time I'd returned, fully clothed, he'd made tea. I sat down, he handed me a cup.

'Thanks,' I replied with a wry smirk.

Again I could easily have let this be an invitation to my bed, but I showed restraint. I would not instigate anything, he would have to woo me.

'So why the urgency?'

'Can't sleep in, getting the kids back tonight, wanted to get a few things done before they come home.'

'You coming to the pub tonight?'

'No, might grab something from town when I pick up the kids, I'm sure they can put up with another night of Maccas.'

'Hey listen why don't I cook for you? You've done so much for me. I do a pretty mean lamb roast.'

He sat scratching his chin, thinking about what I had just said.

'What time?'

'Well, it would take a couple of hours to cook, how about five?'

'How about four and I can take you on a tour of the farm while the sun's still out?'

'What about the kids, don't you have to pick them up and bring them back?'

'They finish at three, we'll come straight home.'

His phone started ringing, some problem with a delivery at the winery.

'Gotta go, see you at four. Oh, and bring your pyjamas, you can have a sleepover. I've got a few bottles of last year's vintage that are just starting to come good...and don't buy the lamb, I've got a freezer full.'

'Great, can you take out a leg?' I yelled, as he went out the door.

'No worries, see ya tonight,' and with that he drove off.

Roast Lamb and a Sleepover

I could no longer concentrate on writing and drove back to the motel for a shower and change of clothes, my mind buzzing with the prospect of seeing Andrew tonight. He had suggested a sleepover and I was most definitely ready to explore the possibility of what this might mean.

My personal grooming had been quite neglected, some pampering in town was much overdue. The stylish and smart looking salon in Smithfield offered all the treatments I desired, waxing, massage, hair, facial, nails. It was strange to think just two years ago I had spent the day, at Raphael's insistence, being given these wonderfully indulgent treatments for the very first time. It was transformative and after my day of pampering, I had been seduced by Raphael, confident to show my body, confident enough to be gloriously fucked by my charming Italian friend. And for the first time experiencing orgasm, satiating a desire to have fulfilling sex. It had given me a hunger that had definitely been suppressed for long enough.

What was I preparing myself for, what would happen tonight?

The various treatments were given by a small team of young women, overseen by the owner, a tall, beautiful, almost androgynous woman, Ava. When my body had been overhauled, she moved me to a private room at the back of the salon, dismissing the other girls, and sat me in front of a mirror. She would cut my hair.

'I much prefer to work in here, the light's better and it's more private. Champagne?'

I looked at my watch, it was well after midday.

'Why not,' and pushed the glass towards the opened bottle.

I warmed to her immediately.

'A special occasion?' she quizzed.

'No, not really, just needed a bit of attention, as you have seen I've been a bit neglectful of the basics,' I joked, not ready to make a full confession just yet.

'Do you live here?'

'No, I'm staying in Greenhope, doing a bit of writing, needed to get away from Melbourne,' and with that she magically began to extricate the first details of my story.

What strange powers do these women possess? In the hands of a hairdresser I was talking as if on a psychologist's couch.

'Greenhope, why there? You do know we have some very good places to stay, eat and get away from it all in Smithfield. Where on earth are you living? Greenhope's virtually a ghost town.'

'I was born there, moved out when I was seventeen. Hadn't been back for over twenty years. I'm renting my family's old farm house, you may have seen it, it's on the bypass just before the turnoff.'

'That old place, it's been empty for years. I know the owner.'

'Andrew Cameron, yeah, nice guy,' I said almost territorially, wondering if they perhaps had more than a friendship, after all she was beautiful, wore no ring and Andrew was single and the hottest catch around.

She laughed.

'What's so funny?'

'He was my husband,' she replied.

My God, how would she feel if she knew of my true intentions? I didn't know how to proceed and felt an unnerving claustrophobia.

'And you're right, he's a really great guy, we share custody of the kids. I'm surprised you haven't met them yet.'

'I keep to myself pretty much and he seems like a very busy person,' I commented, hoping she would buy my indifference.

For the next hour or so we chatted about things to do in Smithfield. She filled me in on a bit of the gossip, the best places to eat, the good wineries... food and wine a shared passion. Time passed, and after more champagne, I decided I liked her.

'Can I ask you something?' she said, stepping back slightly from the mirror and looking directly at my me.

'Like what?'

'Your face is really familiar? Are you Chris Brown or should I say Christina Maxwell?' she said hesitatingly

I hadn't given my name, just walked in off the street and cringed at the thought of the loss of anonymity. I had also dressed to blend in and thought that Smithfield, being a much bigger place, would be easier to disappear into.

'Well, yeah, but I had hoped to keep my presence here quiet. Please don't say anything.'

'Absolutely not, your secret's safe with me. I can understand why you would want to get out of Melbourne, the press has given you a bit of a hammering.'

'You bet. I've been intentionally keeping a low profile, didn't think anyone in Smithfield would know who I was.'

'People know who you are, the local paper has done many a story on you over the last couple of years.'

'Really? When I lived here all those years ago I didn't think anyone in Smithfield thought much of Greenhope. We always felt looked down upon.'

'We're a parochial bunch, love to bathe in the glory of a 'local girl done good', and you've done very good, which makes you most definitely one of ours,' she said smilingly.

It was a curious thing to be claimed by a town full of people who I had very little connection with.

'And please don't worry, no one knows you're here. Believe you me, we hairdressers would be the first to know, it would be the hottest gossip in town.'

It was nice to know that the few people in Greenhope who knew of my recent return had kept their word. I felt very protected by the town folk.

'And as long as you don't ruffle any feathers, keep on everyone's good side, you should be ok. Small towns can get a bit ugly if you don't play by the rules!' she said with the faintest hint of sarcasm in her voice.

'Sounds like you're speaking from experience?'

'Well, you don't divorce the town's 'golden boy' without copping some flack!'

'So what happened?' I asked emboldened by our new found intimacy and the second glass of champagne.

'I'm surprised you haven't heard some of the rumours. He has a lot of fans in Greenhope. The woman who runs the general store cleans his house and is fiercely protective of him, absolutely hates my guts.'

'Shirley, yes I've met her. She did mention your shared custody arrangement, couldn't understand why the two of you couldn't work it out. Seemed to put it down to you not being one of them, the city person who didn't fit in. But what business is it of hers anyway?'

'You really have been away for a long time, don't you remember how gossipy these small places can be?'

I chuckled.

'And so Ava, what happened between you and Andrew? Why would you ditch the town's favourite son if he was such a nice guy?'

The roles were now reversed.

'To put it simply, I met someone else and that someone else was not a man!'

'Ava! You wicked woman, that's absolutely scandalous. I'm surprised you weren't marched out of town. How did Andrew take it?'

'He already knew before we were married. I guess for a short while he felt he'd conquered some kind of final frontier. Don't most men harbour some fantasy about lesbian threesomes?' she said, grinning cheekily.

'So why did you marry him, how come you switched sides?'

'He was very charming, I was new to the town and enjoyed his company. My sexuality had always been somewhat ambiguous and I was upfront with him right from the start. The more I got to know him, the more I thought about the possibility of spending my life with him. I wasn't getting any younger, I wanted children and eventually I convinced myself it would work.'

'What changed?'

'I couldn't be the type of wife he needed. We gave it a good go, ten years, but in the end I needed more, we both knew.'

'Do you have a partner?'

'I do, she lives in Melbourne. We get together when I don't have the kids. I keep it quite discreet, Smithfield hasn't come that far yet. The kids go to a small Catholic school, it's bad enough that we are divorced, I don't need them to be teased even more. Small towns can be a brutal place if you don't fit the social norm.'

'Don't you think you should be a bit more honest with them?'

'I guess the longer I've put it off, the harder it's become.'

'What did you tell them when you split up?'

'Just the usual bullshit about mummy and daddy not getting on, that we still loved them very much. Luckily Andrew and I have stayed good friends. He agreed not to go into details with the kids or anyone else, and quite frankly, the separation was really amicable. We try to go to most of the big things together, birthdays, school plays. I'm sure the townspeople still don't understand what went on, and for now I'd like to keep it that way.'

'Your secret's safe with me.'

Ava and I chatted as if we were old friends. I understood her need to talk about the secret life she lead and knew she could be trusted, because we both had something to hide.

Before I left, I felt the need to confess.

'Hey Ava, I haven't been completely honest with you.'

She looked taken aback.

'What do you mean?'

'It's about Andrew, he's invited me over to his place. I'm going over tonight to cook dinner,' I said sheepishly.

'Is that all! I'm surprised he hasn't invited you sooner. It's cool, Christina. Give the kids a hug from me,' she said, finishing up, removing the cape and brushing off a few stray hairs.

'Have you got a hat I could borrow?' I said, confident that we had formed a bond.

'Yeah, take this.'

She grabbed a baseball cap bearing the insignia of a local winery, pulled my hair into a loose ponytail and threaded it through the gap in the back. I looked in the mirror, putting on sunglasses to complete the disguise.

'You'd better get going, you've got a big night ahead... now what was your name again?' she said grinning as I paid my bill.

Just before the door closed, she called out.

'Oh, and beware of the Andrew Cameron charm, it's quite intoxicating!' she said, winking, as I left the salon.

My watch said two, just enough time to pick up the groceries, get back to the motel and change.

Dinner with Andrew

He greeted me like we were old friends, taking the bags from my hands and leading me into the kitchen.

'Here's the lamb, I picked some rosemary from the garden. Love to eat, but don't cook, not really interested. Shirley always stocks up the freezer, but her casserole repertoire leaves a lot to be desired. Got a bit of stuff you might like to use in the pantry, come and have a look.'

At first I could only see packets of cereal and two minute noodles, but as my eyes adjusted to the dimly lit room, I was surprised to find a veritable cornucopia of supplies. Bottles of olive oil, jars of olives and pickled condiments, organic flour, pasta, pink salt, lentils. Many of the labels were familiar, brands that I'd seen in gourmet food shops in Melbourne. He opened the fridge. There were cheeses, smoked meats, hams, salamis and bacon and the freezer was jam packed with cuts of meat, poultry and game.

'I don't get it? You implied you needed a home cooked meal, yet you've got an overstuffed pantry looking more like a gourmet deli than your average farm kitchen. I pay a fortune for these things back in Melbourne.'

'Like I said, I don't cook and these thing are completely beyond Shirley's understanding of food. Her idea of a good meal is any old stewed meat, flavoured with a packet of soup powder. It all gets to taste the same after awhile. Thought maybe a city woman like you would know what to do with it all.'

'My God, it's brilliant. I love to cook and your kitchen and pantry are heaven to me. But I still don't understand why you've stocked your shelves with things you don't know how to use?'

'Because most of it is my stuff, and I thought you might be impressed,' he said, smiling proudly.

'What do you mean, your stuff?'

'Well, when Dad and I started to buy up a lot of the smaller farms, we realised we were putting people out of jobs. Our big machinery did the work of many men. Smithfield could easily have gone the way of Greenhope, and we didn't want that to happen. We liked living in the country and didn't want to see our town die. We started small at first, sinking money into different crops, olives, lentils, canola, grapes. Looking at ways of utilising the land that was no longer suitable for wheat, sheep or cattle. Then we started to see how we could value add to the things we were growing. At about the same time the politicians in Melbourne were threatening to close the railway line and I knew that this would cut off a vital link to the city. I got together with a group of like minded townspeople and put up a plan to develop tourism in the region, food tourism in particular.'

'How on earth did you do that, a place doesn't develop overnight?'

'I spent a shit load of money paying Melbourne's top chefs to come to Smithfield for a long weekend. We hired all the catering equipment and set up temporary restaurants in the empty shops in the main street. The papers loved the feel good story and after a feature in the food section, the tourists flooded into the town. It was a raging success, we were completely overwhelmed.'

'So what happened next?'

'Firstly, it gave the town hope, silenced the naysayers. We realised there were many possible businesses that could grow from this small event, accommodation, retail, cellar doors, restaurants, things that would bring life back to the town. Dad and I worked out a way of providing seed capital to fund people who could put together a viable business plan.'

'Ah, the White Knights of Smithfield ride in and save the day!' I teased.

'We gave money to the projects the banks weren't adventurous enough to take a risk on. Don't think we were giving away our hard earned dollars, all the loans were secured. The other thing we had going was ridiculously cheap property. We talked to some of the chefs who wanted out of city life, wanted to bring their kids up in a place a little kinder to families. A place where they could afford to buy a house and a shop. Our dying town was abundantly oversupplied with this kind of real estate. Much of it owned by Cameron Holdings. And the more these people came, the more the value of the real estate went up. It was a win for everyone.'

'When the railway was still under threat of closure, we backed an independent candidate at the following state election. She convinced the locals to vote for her with her 'save the Smithfield line' campaign. It was a close call, but in the end, not only did she win, but she held the balance of power in state government. The party that guaranteed to keep the line open got her deciding vote.'

'White Night, Kingmaker and Powerbroker. Andrew Cameron you sly devil, you hide it well under that affable country boy exterior!'

'Don't give me that bullshit Maxwell. I know for a fact that you're no business slouch yourself. I was reading an online business site that claims your property holdings in Fitzroy alone are worth millions, that your blog generates 'rivers of gold' in advertising revenue and your fashion business has been touted as a leader in clothing retail.'

'Well, I guess then we are not so very different Mr. Cameron, except that I can cook and you can't.'

Our little chat was suddenly interrupted by the sound of children giggling on the second floor landing. I'd completely forgotten about the kids.

'Come downstairs kids, come and meet Christina,' called Andrew.

The dull sound of feet bounding down the carpeted stairs came to an abrupt halt as the two children stopped, a little wary, before entering the kitchen.

'Don't be shy you two, Christina won't bite, get in here.'

Slowly they walked up to their father.

'Christina, this is Sophie.'

The fair haired girl quietly said 'hello'.

'And this is Tom.'

The boy reached out to politely shake my hand, 'hi'.

'Pleased to meet you both, do you like roast lamb?'

'Yes, thanks,' they replied in unison.

'Now, if you're good, Christina has brought a treat for dessert.'

And instantly the true boisterousness of the kids surfaced, both noisily demanding to know what it was, and I lifted the lid to show them the decadent chocolate cake I had bought in town.

'If you're good, you can have some after tea.'

'Aw dad, we're starving, can't we have some now?'

'Have an apple, there's plenty in the bowl.'

The children's faces dropped with disappointment.

'Andrew, if you don't mind, I've got some treats. Dinner will be at least two hours away?' I said tipping a bag of chocolates, sweets and chips onto the table.

'Please, please, Dad!' they begged, looking at the bounty spread before them.

'Alright, but just this once, and if you don't eat your vegies at dinner, you'll have to clean out the chook shed tomorrow.'

They were ripping off wrappers almost before he had finished the sentence. I saw Andrew looking lovingly at his kids, and thought he secretly liked being the soft touch, the fun parent. The divorce must have been hard for his children to comprehend. After they had taken their fill, they chatted to me. Asking where I came from, how come I was living in the house, did I have kids, talking as if we had known each other for ages.

I had won over Tom and Sophie. Would I win over Andrew, too?

'Hey Dad, are you going to take Christina on the 'special tour' of the farm?' asked Tom in a conspiratorial fashion.

'What do you reckon Soph? Do you think she's up to it?'

Sophie giggled her assent and I wondered what kind of tricks they were up to.

'Wanna have a look round the place?'

'I thought that was part of the deal, I'd love to. Just give me a few minutes to put the lamb on. It can cook while we're out.'

'Sure, I'll get the machine warmed up. Kids, will you bring Christina out when she's done?'

I easily navigated my way around the kitchen, found a roasting dish, rubbed the lamb with pink salt, stuffed the cavity with garlic and rosemary and drizzled over the olive oil.

Still giggling, the kids dragged me out the back door and as we were passing one of the massive sheds, my ears were assaulted by a deafening loud noise. It was a helicopter, and it was to be the farm touring vehicle. The kids were bent over laughing at their well planned joke. Andrew signalled from the cockpit for me to get in. I crouched down and tentatively approached. He belted me in and placed earphones and a mike over my head. The screeching sound abated and I felt less afraid when I heard his voice, as he grinned at me.

'Welcome aboard. You ready for the tour?'

Wide eyed and a little bit nervous I gave him the thumbs up and braced myself for takeoff. We flew low over my old farm, a mere patch on the vast territory that was owned by Cameron Pastoral Holdings. It seemed so insignificant, I asked why he was even bothering to plant it up. He said that he was trialling a new strain of drought resistant canola and didn't want to commit to more land until he was sure it would be suitable. Our old farm had been reduced to a test patch, barely worth bothering about, no wonder my father could never make it pay. There were no small farm blocks left, he owned everything, mile after mile of land, coloured according to the crop. Bare red earth waiting to be planted, grey green orchards of olive groves, latticed grape vines, bright with autumnal colour. Green pasture dotted with the black specks, that were prime, grass fed cattle waiting to be snapped up for the lucrative export market. For an hour we flew over the land that was his, covering a huge part of the state. No wonder he could fund the smaller businesses that were helping to keep Smithfield booming.

'Mmm... something smells good,' said Andrew, as we walked back into the kitchen.

I opened the oven and tossed in some root vegetables. The roast looked good, the old wood stove had worked its magic while we'd been flying over the countryside.

'Thirsty?'

'You bet.'

'What would you like?'

'First, I could do with an icy cold beer and then, didn't you mention something about a prized Shiraz?'

'You remembered, here, follow me,' he said, as he handed me a beer and pointed to the back door.

Under the wide veranda and down an external stairway we entered his cellar. A familiar damp musty odour briefly made my heart race. I quickly shut out the memories it evoked, putting them to the furthest reaches of my mind. A more pleasant smell soon overtook, the spicy mustiness of wine. Thousands of bottles filled row after row of wine racks. The dustiest specimens were extremely old. It appears the Cameron family had been collecting wine long before the vines were planted in Smithfield, that is what rich people did. Andrew took out a bottle.

'Twelve years old, one of our best years for Shiraz, great with lamb.'

'I trust you, but what are these?' I said, walking past a section labelled with familiar Italian names.

'New stuff we're trying, Italian or more specifically Sicilian, Nero D'avola.'

'Yeah, I know it well, it's a favorite, I love Italian wines.'

'Really, most people have never heard of these old world varieties, I'm surprised you have.'

'It's a thing of mine, some very dear friends introduced me to them when I was in my early twenties. I always keep my eye out for them, they are sometimes really hard to find. Have you got much planted?'

'A little bit, we're trying out a stack of Spanish, Italian and French grapes more suited to the dry climate to the north and some cool climate stuff further south. If we get it right, we can be first on the market, sell it before over production lowers the price. Grab anything you like the look of. You are staying the night, we can drink till we fall over.'

That was not a question, but a statement and I wondered where I would actually end up sleeping.

The kids came in, puffed out, smelling of horses and covered in dust.

'Jesus, where've you been? You smell like rotten hay and horse shit. Get in the shower before I hose you off,' said Andrew, playfully whacking each of them on the bum as they skipped past.

'Dinner will be ready in twenty minutes.'

As I finished preparing the meal, Andrew set the table.

'Hope you don't mind, but I much prefer sitting around the kitchen table to eat, the main dining room is far too formal. I usually only use it at Christmas, special occasions. The table seats twenty, you need a microphone to talk to each other.'

'No problems, it's your place, I'm just the cook.'

The kids wolfed down the food, the ride had made them hungry. The chocolate cake I'd bought from the bakery was devoured with equal gusto. After the plates had been cleared and the dishes done, the kids begged to be allowed to stay up late and play on their computers. Andrew acquiesced and said they could have an hour.

We retreated to the den, a room with a club like atmosphere. A hint of cigar smoke, overstuffed leather couches and high backed armchairs, worn through years of use. Old books on the towering library shelves and hunting memorabilia from a time when killing tigers was perfectly acceptable. Andrew carried a few of the bottles I had chosen from the cellar and before long we were settled in, debating the merits of each wine.

We talked about the week, about the book, what I had done today.

I told him I'd met Ava. I knew the story and that his secret was safe with me. He seemed to relax just that little bit more, knowing no explanations were needed. I felt a little bit closer to him.

The mood shifted as we were interrupted by the yelps and screams of Sophie and Tom fighting over something. They were great kids, had been really friendly towards me and were comfortable enough to let their guard down and have a full blown argument in front of their father's house guest.

'Alright you two, I'm coming up and you'd better get yourselves sorted before I make both of you sleep in the chook shed,' he yelled in mock chastisement.

'Where's your bag? I'll show you your room.'

I followed him up the grand staircase to the landing and down a long corridor to a large bedroom on the right.

'This is yours. Ava renovated it before she left, there's an en suite. I hope you'll be comfortable. I'd better attend to the kids.'

The room had whitewashed floor boards, Persian rugs and antique Chinese furniture, subtle and understated, paying homage to the age of the home, but not sticking to the usual heavy, dour style of mid nineteenth century rural architecture. The bathroom was lavishly stocked with expensive toiletries. Ava had done a brilliant job. As I unpacked, Andrew tapped lightly on my door.

'Sorry to bother you, but Sophie was wondering if you would read her a story. Sometimes I have to remind myself she's only seven, they've had to grow up a lot in the last two years.'

Keen to have me read 'just one more page' I spent longer than expected upstairs with the children. I glanced in the mirror as I anxiously returned downstairs, not quite knowing what would happen next. The house was quiet. Stretched out on the couch was Andrew, fast asleep. I had my answer and retreated back to my bedroom. It had been a really lovely day. Perhaps this would take a little longer than I expected. Things went much more slowly in the country.

Planting Time

Autumn was rushing past, the days grew shorter, the nights much colder, the book was nearly finished.

I'd seen a lot more of Andrew and the children. During his weeks with the kids, they visited often and I went to their place to cook. The kids dominated his life. When they were with him they were his sole focus. When the kids were with Ava, Andrew spent much of his time away. I could understand why, I'd seen the vastness of his domain. When we were together I felt accepted, almost part of the family, but I sensed a real reluctance by Andrew to make the next move. Perhaps it was just too soon.

What was looming, however, was canola planting time. I couldn't bear the thought of losing the house and wondered if it could be saved. I rang Holmes House Removals. Terry Holmes scratched his head as he walked around the house, inspecting the exterior, crawling between the stumps, tapping the timber as he went.

'No white ants, seems to be solid enough. Reckon if we cut off the verandas we could move it in one piece, she's only a little place.'

He gave me a quote and said he'd need at least a week's notice. I told him not to say anything just yet, as I hadn't discussed it with the owner, but if it went ahead I was happy to pay the price.

I'd grown so fond of the old house, it made me feel safe and let me write freely about the many things I'd kept bottled up for so long. I'd gone online to see what land was available and had found a beautiful block, closer to Greenhope, on the banks of the Little Thames River in an ancient Red Gum forest. A joke really, as the river was barely a trickle. At least it wouldn't flood. It would be perfect, a peaceful retreat, away from that hellish road, a place my parents would have loved, a place to call home.

I called Andrew and he came over to discuss my plan. He didn't think there would be a problem, in fact he was quite happy I would handle the removal of the house, wanted no money for it and was pleased I was investing in the area.

'I like the idea of you finding something more permanent. The kids were getting quite worried about you leaving, they've grown very fond of you and so have I,' he said, as he put his arm around me and gave me a bear hug squeeze.

'Me too,' I responded and snuggled in a little closer.

And just when I thought the mood had shifted, his phone rang. Another bloody drama over at the winery that only he could fix.

Finally I'd finished the book. Jane was done too and the publishers were eager to get it ready for a Mother's Day release. Cindy was keen for us to catch up face to face and I sensed a slight disappointment in her voice when I told her of my plans to buy the land and save the farm house.

'Jesus boss, I thought you hated living there when you were a kid?'

'I did, but things have changed, I've met some really nice people.'

'Yeah right, who is he?' she said sarcastically.

'Bloody hell Cindy. You jump to conclusions too easily, it's just a really nice place that I could call home.'

'I can see it now, you knitting tea cosies in your shabby chic cottage, caring for litters of kittens.'

'Shut up, it's not like that.'

'You've got a life here, a beautiful home. You seem to have forgotten I grew up in a small country town, too. You can't fool me with your misty eyed delusions. We'll see what it's like when you crave a walk down Gertrude street, are sick of being the centre of gossip or wish to have a conversation about more than how successful the local footy team is this season.'

'Ouch! You've really got your bitch on today!'

'Ok, ok, I'm sorry. Not all places are like that, but I do know that this place is not for you. I've seen you come alive in Melbourne and as much as you're in denial, for whatever fucking reason, you are a fully fledged city woman and we miss you!'

Talking to Cindy had thrown me. I felt confused. She'd tried to spark my enthusiasm, reminding me of the life I'd left behind. But what was that life? A life of no privacy, under the spotlight? A life without Adam, without love? I seemed to have been beaten, I'd lost my drive. The business was being managed magnificently by Cindy and didn't really need my input. It no longer interested me and slowly I was coming to the conclusion that I wanted out. Was Andrew and his family filling some kind of gaping emotional void? I had loved the way in which he and the kids had so warmly welcomed me into their lives and the way that Malcolm and Shirley had become almost like surrogate parents. It felt good to belong.

Andrew had rung, inviting me over to dinner. He wanted to talk to me about something important. No need to cook, dinner would be organised. I was curious. What was on his mind? He sounded excited. The kids were at Ava's, we would have the house to ourselves. I wondered if he was finally about to make a move.

'Jesus, you look hot Maxwell!' said Andrew, with a broad grin, as he opened the door. I had decided to wear a little black dress and killer heels.

'You said dinner had been arranged, so I decided to dress appropriately.'

'Come in. I thought we'd eat in the dining room, it's a pretty special occasion. I've got a bottle of champagne on ice.'

He took my hand and walked me down the long corridor. His enthusiasm was palpable. I loved seeing him this relaxed and happy, away from the kids, not being a father, but a charming flirtatious man.

He pushed open the heavy door to the magnificent room.

'Christina Maxwell, there's someone special I want you to meet.'

Standing next to the bay window, illuminated by the setting sun was a very beautiful tall, blonde woman. She was dressed in jeans, cowboy boots and a cream turtle-neck sweater, a single long strand of pearls completing the picture of casual country elegance.

'Sarah Shawcroft, this is Christina, the woman I've been telling you so much about.'

I reached out my hand and she shook it firmly, confidently.

'Pleased to meet you. Andrew can't stop talking about you, and now I can see why I should feel quite jealous.'

What the hell was going on here, who was this woman and what did she mean by 'jealous'?

'Christina, you've been such a great mate over the last few months, cooking, helping with the kids. We wanted you to be the first to know. Sarah and I are getting engaged.'

Engaged! What a fuckwit I'd been. I'd completely misread the situation. I wanted to crawl out the door and run. Trying to compose myself I took a big sip of champagne while my heartbeat settled from the shock of what I'd just been told. Instantly I felt like the young student in the uni bar all those years ago, overhearing a conversation that put me back in my place. I was the once again the intruder who'd foolishly thought she fitted in. I was a good friend, but not good enough to be one of them.

'Congratulations,' I spluttered.

'Andrew, you really are a sly dog, where have you been keeping her?' I continued, directing my conversation at him, attempting to regain my composure.

'Sarah's my chief winemaker. She's based in Dunkeld and has been overseeing the production of our cold climate whites. This sparkling is hers, it's the one that's been giving us so much grief in the past few weeks.'

I sipped again, the bubbly liquid left a bitter taste.

'Excellent drop,' I lied. I was good at that.

I remained composed throughout the night. Andrew had gone out of his way to impress, he'd hired a chef from town to put together a sumptuous feast to mark the occasion. There was even a waitress to do the menial work, at least I wouldn't be doing the dishes.

Andrew spoke of how he'd rekindled their friendship when he'd put word out amongst his old uni friends about the problems he was having with that year's vintage. Sarah had been at Roseworthy University with him and agreed to act as a consultant. They held hands and spoke romantically of it being love at first sight. Their courtship had been remarkably brief. I now understood why Andrew had been away so much when he didn't have the kids. They both mentioned they would love it if I could be around when they broke it to the children. I had now become the spinster aunt!

Thankfully I was able to make my excuses for an early exit, tomorrow morning the Holmes brothers were moving the house. I would leave her in the big old house, to spend time in the bed, with the man I'd thought so naively, would be mine.

The empty motel room was a fittingly ugly retreat for me to return to and wallow in my own self pity.

Moving Day

We were all up bright and early. Sarah and Andrew greeted me warmly. They both had that 'just fucked' glow.

The verandas had already been cut off. The poor old house looked forlorn, like a face with an overly short, home haircut fringe. The Holmes brothers assured me they could take the house in one piece. It was only a short distance to the new block and the local cop had given his tacit approval by volunteering to escort us through town.

Slowly the house began to move off its stumps as the jacks did their job. Creaking and groaning, the old place seeming to be complaining at the indignity of it all. Eventually it was high enough off the ground for the truck driver to attempt to back under the structure, to get it onto the flatbed and take it on its final journey, saved from destruction.

But something wasn't quite right. The driver missed the mark and accidentally backed into one the props. A thunderous crack signalled the disaster about to come and, as if in slow motion, we watched as the poor little house break in two and crash heavily to the ground. We were all horrified by what we'd just witnessed. I burst into tears and found myself sobbing against Andrew's broad chest.

'I'm so sorry, Christina,' he said soothingly as he gently stroked my back, calming me like he would a distressed animal.

Once the dust had settled, we walked over to the mess of shattered glass, splintered timber and twisted corrugated iron, and to my surprise, at the point where the house had split, a flurry of pages drifted to the ground. I recognised my mother's neat handwriting instantly. These were her diaries, she must have secreted them somewhere between the walls. Sarah helped me gather them up, Andrew chased a few errant pages blowing towards the road.

The house had given me a gift.

This is Who I am

Back in the motel room, journals of different shapes and sizes were laid on the bed, loose pages stacked on top, sorting through the mess until finally all was in order. I started reading from the earliest date, neatly written in the top right hand corner of each page and this is what I learnt.

My mother Mary was a war orphan, shipped to Australia from London in 1946 at the age of ten. Her single mother, missing, her father unknown. She wrote of the brutality of the wardens during her years spent in a home for displaced girls. Then of the abuse at the hands of her employers when she was sent out to work as a domestic help at the age of fourteen. Saved by her good looks at sixteen, she got a job as a shop assistant at the prestigious department store, Georges. Perhaps helped with a reference from a jealous wife? She mentioned a friendship forming with another new employee working in the menswear department, a man called Edward, my father. She talked of him frequently, they became 'dear' friends, he took her out dancing. I remember Mum and Dad telling me about this. In 1954 she became a house model and told of dates with dashing young men, sons of the wealthy families who shopped at this exclusive emporium. I wondered how my dad fitted into this, obviously he was still just a friend? In 1956, at the age of twenty she was photographed by the famous fashion photographer, Helmut Newton. Newspaper and magazine clippings folded out to reveal her beauty in black and white.

An engagement to a man called Charles, who she wrote about gushingly at first. Gradually she began to describe an insanely jealous man who beat her, blackening an eye before a photo shoot for Vogue.

217

She talked of finding shelter with Edward, who allowed her to share his small room above a shop in Flinders Street. Charles discovers them and bashed Edward to teach him a lesson. They planned their escape and secretly took the train back to Greenhope. Edward introduced her to his mother and father as his fiancé. They married in 1958, photos showing the old Presbyterian church. She wore a stunning full skirted white gown, a small pearl tiara in her hair. Two anonymous bridesmaids accompanied her, my dad beamed with pride, she was smiling back. What a hero, my dad saved her, won her heart and took her home. They were both twenty two.

Not many photos. A clipping from the local newspaper showed them attending the Greenhope debutante ball, her brunette hair swept up in a stylish French twist. She wore a long figure hugging sheath gown. I remembered it's navy satin elegance, it had been one of my most favorite dress ups. Other women in the shot looked dowdy by comparison. What did the townspeople make of this glamorous woman, my mother?

She wrote of moving into the farmhouse upon the eventual death of Edward's father, of the endless backbreaking work, of the longing for a child and of the understanding that it would never be so.

Never be so, I didn't understand?

She talked of an insatiable desire and unfulfilled need. I read on, sensing a weariness in her tone, still not understanding what she was inferring.

And then the bombshell hit. She described her undying love for my father, but at the frustration she felt at being with a man who had no desire to touch her. She wrote that she knew what she was getting into when they married. She always understood that Edward was not interested in women, that they truly were 'just good friends'. But she thought it would alright, because he could provide her with the sanctuary and safety she had craved all her life. Was she saying that my father was gay? Did she even have a word to describe it?

I stopped to take stock of what I'd just read, pouring a glass of Andrew's red to help calm me. It seems so obvious now, my father's brief fling with city life, his loathing of the farm and unsuitability to country life. I was reminded of the performances in the lounge room where he taught me to dance, his sing-along to those old musicals, his slender piano playing hands.

The writing continued, little changed during the sixties, just more of the same unrelenting cycle of drought and poverty and longing, barely enough to fill more than ten pages.

In 1971 things have become so grim financially that she took a job as a housekeeper. The advertisement is clipped and glued on the page.

Live in housekeeper wanted for three months, must be able to care for infant. Applications in writing to Mrs James Cameron.

Fuck! Andrew's mother. She got the job and moved into the Cameron household.

The diary writing becomes more animated. She describes the house and I immediately see what she sees. She marvels at the small luxuries, an automatic washing machine, central heating and instant hot water. Unlimited credit at the store in Smithfield where she shops for the weekly groceries. An account with Georges where she orders some of James Cameron's more expensive food requests, tinned pâtés from France, jams from England and single malt whiskies and shortbread from Scotland.

She wonders about the life she could have lived if she'd made different choices. Perhaps stayed in the city?

She can't understand how Mrs Cameron can bear to leave her baby son, Andrew, choosing instead to tour Europe with her aging parents.

She looks forward to telephoning my father with tales of how the other half live. He seems to be ashamed that she needs to go out to work and reassures him it's only for a short time.

Slowly she starts to describe James Cameron, and the tone shifts from one of employer to that of friend. She writes of drinking wine, dancing in the drawing room, picnics with James and Andrew on the lawns of the beautiful front garden. How a gardener is employed full time to keep the grounds looking magnificent all year round, an ornamental lake supplying as much water as the thirsty and exotic plants need.

She no longer refers to him as Mr. Cameron but as James, and the words of endearment, then passion, start to flow. She has fallen in love with him. I am shocked. I hate her and her betrayal of my kind, gentle father and can barely read the flowery prose which takes up many more pages.

After three months she knows Mrs Cameron will be returning and hopes to be able to stay on. She writes lovingly of the little boy in her care and her heart aches at their inevitable separation.

She is informed that the Camerons will be moving to Mrs Cameron's parent's station in Horsham, where James will take over the running of the family property. George will be managing the Smithfield property and her services will no longer be required. Her employment is terminated abruptly.

She returns to my father and is grateful for his love. He tells her he has missed his closest friend. She writes of loss, of missing both Andrew and James.

The diary entries resume with a depressing familiarity, same old struggles, same old life.

And then, about two months later, things change dramatically.

I can't believe it, she writes. *Today I have discovered I am pregnant, I am finally going to be a mother. Edward is a little shocked at first, he knows he is not the father, but understands my longing for a child. His mood shifts and he tells me that he will love this baby as if it were his own and that we will never discuss this with anyone else. He pats my belly lovingly and tells me he is very happy. He too had carried the sadness of thinking he would never be a parent.*

James Cameron is my real father, Andrew Cameron is my brother.

My head was reeling. I could barely comprehend the enormity of what I'd just read. My world shattered around me, so much of what I knew had been a lie. I was nearly sick at the thought of what almost eventuated with Andrew.

I drank the last of the bottle and took a sleeping pill. It was only early evening, but I had read enough, I hated my mother and I needed to sleep.

The pill only lasted for four hours and I woke at nine that night with a shitty headache and aching heart. A hot shower and a cold lemonade restored me somewhat, but the diaries called and before long I continued reading.

I had completely underestimated both my father's and my mother's need for a child. She spoke of the joy of my birth, of the times she would catch my father, completely transfixed, staring at his sleeping baby girl. He would tell her that their lives were now complete.

My anger was slowly abating, remembering how much I too, loved my own baby daughter and what that kind of unconditional love felt like. My feelings toward the affair changed. James Cameron had given them both a most treasured gift.

My birth kept them sane, brought them closer together. Every small step of my life was recorded, and as the pages filled, I slowly began reading of things that were part of my own memories, birthdays, Christmases and the occasional holiday.

The last entries were the most poignant, my mother writing of how proud they were of their daughter, of her moving to the city, of having opportunities never open to them. She knew I never really fitted in to small town life. She knew, because neither had she. Dad and Mum lived in their own private fantasy world, two misfits who had found each other.

The last entry was the saddest. She wrote that she was looking forward to seeing me the following night at the graduation ceremony. She told of the late nights she had spent putting together an album of photos and clips of when she worked in the fashion industry, so long ago, from a time that seemed like another world. She almost didn't recognise the woman in the photos, but hoped I would appreciate the little archive of her more glamorous past life and that maybe the signed original Helmut Newton photos might be of some value to me. I never saw these albums and guessed they must have been destroyed in the crash.

I weep at what was lost, but am overwhelmed by the quirk of fate that gave me the chance to reconnect with this women I barely knew. The house, although gone, had given me an amazing gift.

I loved her and forgave her.

Who was I to judge?

Farewell

Andrew came into the small motel room, unsure about why he'd been summoned.

I gave him the diaries. He was shocked by what they revealed. He had absolutely no memory of that time of his life, although he did say that his mother never returned to the Smithfield property. Not even to visit when he and Ava had lived there. Andrew never knew why she had such a deep loathing of the place, now he understood. His mother must have hated what had happened to her family while she travelled the world. That this woman, my mother, the outsider, had loved her husband and her only child. That the only way to keep them, was to take them away.

Andrew and I drank wine, it eased the discomfort of the truth.

'I hated my mother when I first read this, but then thought about some of the decisions I've made and realised we're all just human, we're all fallible,' I said.

I'd had a bit longer to process the information and was much more resolute about what I'd learned. Andrew was still coming to terms with it.

'Me too, but I read these diaries and I feel I hate my father even more for letting your mother go.'

'I don't understand?'

'Your mother talks about looking after me when I was a baby. I could almost feel the love in her words. A love I never felt with my own mother. She left me with a complete stranger when I was an infant, then sent me to boarding school when I was six. She was more like a distant aunt. When I had my own kids, the pain deepened. How could my mother so easily abandon me?' his eyes searched mine for answers.

'I envy you, you always knew you were loved. I was just an inconvenience,' he added.

'But your father, he loved you, trusted your decisions when you were a young student. Perhaps it was his way of showing love?'

'I think you're right. We had a great relationship when I was older. I miss him a great deal, wish he could've lived to see my kids.'

As the wine flowed, the conversation became more depressing, we were both mourning the loss of things we'd never had. I was heading back to Melbourne Sunday and realised it was stupid to be spending these last few days like this.

'You bloody dickhead, you've completely forgotten the best thing about all this,' I said, looking him directly in the eye.

He began to smile intuitively, second guessing what I was about to say.

'That I've got a little sister and you have a big brother!'

'And nieces and nephews and a brilliant fucking family! I came expecting ghosts and found you! Very much alive.'

We drank into the night, talked about things we could do in the future and collapsed, fully dressed in a drunken stupor on top of the bed. And again I woke up expecting him to be there, only to find a note.

'See you on Sunday little Sis. PS you snore!'

What a great day, my new family were all there to say farewell. Sophie and Tom were thrilled to discover they had an aunt and a cousin. Kate, although still a little shell shocked, flew into Melbourne and caught the train up. The kids insisting Kate not leave their side, their little hands always close by. Ava thought this was also a good time to introduce her special friend Deb, as did Andrew who presented Sarah to his extended family. The kids thought all these new friends were just great. Even Malcolm and Shirley were invited, the new surrogate grandparents to their adopted family. Shirley had softened and seemed to be quite pleased with the way things had turned out.

Everyone brought food to share. Andrew toasted the day's events with a bottle of Sarah's new Prosecco and this time it tasted like nectar.

And just before the dreaded farewells, Andrew presented me with a beautifully wrapped gift.

'There's just one more thing. Deb is a curator at the National Gallery and she found a few things you might like.'

I ripped open the package. It was a large album of the most exquisite Helmut Newton photos, showing his beautiful, elegant model, my mother.

I was speechless and burst into tears.

We hugged and kissed with promises of more family dinners, vowing to return soon, not waiting twenty more years to make it back home.

Part 4

Back to Reality

It should've felt better returning to my Fitzroy house, with its elegant minimalism and uncluttered spaces. But I had changed, nothing felt right, not even my home. I felt a restlessness, didn't want to be tied down or accountable.

The business had run smoothly without me and I was no longer necessary in its day to day operations. Cindy was pleased that I'd come back to Melbourne. However, she was completely unprepared for the proposition I presented to her.

I wanted to give her a half share in the blog. A gift to a very capable woman who had been my right hand and voice of reason over the last two years. I had my lawyers draw up the agreement and after some hesitation she signed. Her reluctance was short lived when she began to tell of the ways in which she would like to grow the company. She had been thinking about starting a new blog for a younger audience, employing younger writers and, cheekily, capturing the huge advertising revenue that this market had the potential to attract. I instantly agreed and knew she would be brilliant.

The task ahead of her was not so onerous as I had employed a team of managers to run all the different divisions of my business. This would remain unchanged and all of these senior staff would be answerable to Cindy.

The UDressU business would be overseen by a board of directors, chosen from business and community leaders who would maintain its integrity. A twenty percent share was given to the workers in Cambodia, enabling them to vote on key changes within the company. Chenda would still be in charge and, along with a substantial pay rise, I too gifted her a ten percent share in the company. I would attend board meetings and sign off on all the designs. Cindy would lead the team that looked after the everyday running of that business, the IT guys, the designers, the logistics people.

I would be available to help with all major decisions within the various businesses, but I no longer wanted a hands on role. My books and my property portfolio earned me money in excess of what I needed, in fact I was wealthy way beyond my wildest dreams. If I chose, I would never have to work another day in my life.

The book hit the shelves for Mother's Day and was a runaway best seller. Thankfully, after a few key interviews, the press left me alone. I had told them everything, the book had been my confessional, there was nothing to uncover, nothing new to find, I was of no interest to them anymore. I wanted out of this very public life.

Not long after the autobiography came out, a letter arrived.

Dear Christina,

My older sister, Jessica was married to Moses. I was moved by your account of the kidnapping. Moses diaries were the one sided ravings of a delusional mad man and failed to show the abusive, evil, manipulating bastard I knew. You were lucky to escape. My sister was not so fortunate.

We came from a very poor family. My father was violent. Moses was Jessica's first boyfriend. I think she married him because he offered her a life away from the poverty and abuse in her own family. Moses seemed ok at first. Jessica talked fondly of him and of the house they were building. What he offered her must have been so attractive. For the first time she had hope of a better life.

As time passed things changed. I would see her when she came into town. She looked broken, I saw the bruises. She told me that her quiet husband would sometimes erupt into violent fits of rage. Once she tried to get out and came back to our house, but my parents were furious, told her she was not their responsibility and that she had no place here in Lands End away from her husband. Anyway it didn't matter what they thought, Moses tracked her down and forced her to return.

They hardly ever came into town after that and I was getting increasingly worried about my sister and so decided to pay her a surprise visit. I was shocked by what I saw. The shack was barely habitable and, after so much time, the new house was no more than a slab of concrete and a few mud bricks. She was thin and almost feeble. Moses was obviously not happy about me being there. A bruise on Jessica's face the next day was dismissed as being the result of her clumsiness when she walked into a door. I didn't believe it for a minute, I had heard them arguing in the shed.

I asked whether she wanted to come back home with me, but she said no. I imagined her punishment last time was enough to deter her, and anyway I knew he'd track her down if she tried to leave. She claimed that Moses needed her and everything she wanted was here. But the so called 'everything' was not very much. She had barely enough food and struggled to live on the meagre crops the garden produced. She had no money and he wouldn't let her drive. He'd isolated her and had total control. She had no means to escape and by the end of my visit I knew she no longer had the will. Their marriage was almost no different from the one she had observed between my mother and father. It was what she knew and she seemed to have no expectations of anything else.

When she got sick the second time, I asked why she didn't want any treatment. She said she was tired and didn't want to go through the chemo. again. I didn't believe her and sensed she wanted out and this was the only way she knew. She must have died a lonely, fear filled death.

The way the press has treated you has been disgusting. They didn't know the Moses Smith I knew. I'm glad you got out and was able to tell your side of the story. My sister never had that chance.

Yours sincerely,

Beth.

It seemed that Beth could see right through Moses' one sided account that his diaries and the journalists' stories had portrayed.

Although the most poignant, this was not the only letter I'd received from abused women. Many talked about men who start by offering so much, but ultimately take everything away. Some described being lured in by the concept of finding a soul mate, of someone who truly understood them. But then wrote of the gradual loss of liberty and the slow descent into violent, controlling relationships. Many wrote of not feeling good enough, of feeling worthless and not deserving of anything more. All of them wrote of ultimately being trapped.

When I thought about it, I realised some of what they said reminded me of my own experience with Moses. He did everything at first, fed me and even cleaned me. I was completely dependent and when I understood what the boundaries were, I seemed to thrive on pleasing him. I had been so seduced by living up to his ideal of the perfect woman that I was able to ignore the reality and brutality of how I'd arrived there in the first place. Conveniently forgetting the verbal abuse, the shackling and isolation he'd used to keep me under control. It wasn't till the end of my incarceration, after the savage beating, that I got a taste of the monster he really was. Thank God I'd been rescued. Some of the women who had written painted a very grim picture of what my life would have been like, if I'd stayed.

It still troubled me that I had been so easily seduced by Moses Smith. What on earth would a therapist make of me? Had I been looking for a father, a husband, a place to call home? Is that what Moses had offered me? Had I never really believed that I deserved happiness and love? Was that pathetic woman of my past still only a wrong decision away?

Perhaps I would never truly know why I had almost chosen Moses, but at least it made me aware that I was not the only woman who blindly went looking for sanctuary in the wrong place, with the wrong man. Perhaps I also needed to understand that there is no such thing as closure, just a lessening of the sting as time goes by.

Unfinished Business

Andrew, Sarah and the kids had made a few trips to Melbourne. I loved having the house full, having them close, getting to know them just that little bit more. We went to my favorite places, ate great food, tried different wine. The kids regularly Skyped and told me they'd repainted one of the old bedrooms, so that I would have my own room when I came to stay. It was so nice to have found these people, my new family.

Andrew called, wanted us to meet at a restaurant in Flinders Lane. I was hesitant at first, the restaurant's proximity to The Imperial, Adam's hotel, made me reluctant to attend. Andrew said he was meeting with a few restaurateurs in that street and didn't have much time between appointments, but it was important he see me. Curiosity got the better of me and we agreed on a place.

Andrew stood to greet me. I smiled and felt a growing sense of love for this man, who was my darling big brother. We sat down at a table in the window, Andrew poured me a glass of his new Aglianico.

'So what's this important thing you spoke about?' I asked, before taking a sip.

He handed me a piece of paper.

'What's this?'

'I found where George, my old farm manager, was living. This is his address, maybe one day you can look him up. Perhaps he can remember what is was like when your mum was at my farm.'

'Do you think he'd talk to me?

'I'm not sure. He's a pretty quiet individual. We'd lost contact over the years. It took quite a bit of detective work to track him down.

'I could ring him if you like. See if he wants to talk.'

I was barely able to concentrate during lunch, my mind was totally distracted by the thought that there was someone out there who could perhaps fill me in on my mother's secret life and her time spent with James Cameron, my real father.

Although the meal was rather rushed, Andrew was able to keep me up to date on the kids, the farm and the people of Greenhope. He looked at his watch and I knew he was keen to get to his next meeting. We kissed goodbye and he gave me a playful slap on the bum.

'Still think you've got a great ass!'

'Cheeky bastard!'

'Hey, I'll phone you, let you know how things go with George,' he called back, before walking away.

I headed up the street, completely distracted by the lovely lunch, the wine and the note. I unfolded it and saw an address in Queensland.

'Oh God, I'm so sorry,' I spluttered as I tried to extricate myself from the person I'd just run into.

To my horror it was Sam.

'Tina,' he responded, just as shocked as me.

'Sam, ah... how've you been?'

'Good, and you?

'Not bad.'

I was embarrassingly aware of how awkward this was. I hadn't seen Sam since Adam and I split. Sam had been so much a part of my life once. I missed his cheeriness and enthusiasm. I could only imagine what it had been like since the stuff about the mining deal had appeared. The papers said Adam had left the country, no one had been able to pinpoint his whereabouts. I'm sure Sam missed his boss dreadfully. But there was a look in his eye that signalled all was not lost.

'Hey you, why don't you come back to the hotel? I think we could both do with a drink,' he said, smiling sympathetically.

Sam had not completely closed ranks and slowly, after a glass of wine, started to open up. Eventually I was able to establish that, like me, Adam had withdrawn from the day to day running of his empire and had appointed senior people within his company to take on managing roles. He too, wanted to be out of the public eye. I learned that Adam was most definitely not in Tasmania. The land he bought had been gifted back to the people of Tasmania and the money from the China deal provided all the funds required to turn it into a national park. Joe was overseeing the building of a visitors' centre and restaurant.

A second wine had now considerably loosened Sam's tongue and he was very pleased to tell me that Justin and his bitch of a wife Fiona were no longer in the country. They had fled to Ecuador, to escape the tax office, and the police, over one of their very dodgy business deals. I hoped there would never be an extradition agreement between Australia and Ecuador.

'Even Adams mother has gone over there. Seems she went to keep an eye on her errant son and has apparently hooked up with some kind of plantation owner. For the first time in his life Adam's free of them all.'

It was hard to believe that the man who had been such a problem between Adam and me was no longer around. Momentarily I was saddened that Adam and I would never know what a relationship without his interfering brother would be like. Sam's and my mutual loathing of Justin built a bridge and with another glass of wine, the Sam I'd remembered, opened up a little more.

'He's not in Cambodia. He's been travelling around somewhere in Australia. He rings every so often to let me know he's still alive.'

Sam was being distracted by the demands of his staff and I sensed he really had to get back to work.

'Thanks Sam, and sorry, I know you must miss him.'

Sam looked at me sadly and paused before he spoke.

'Hey Tina, I wish things were back to normal. I liked it when you two were together, when things were good. I'd never seen him happier. Keep in touch?'

I nodded and waved goodbye.

North

I was free.

The business was running smoothly, thriving in fact, and for the first time in ages, I had time on my hands. No books to write, no appointments to keep, no press on my tail. The trouble with my early retirement was that all my friends and acquaintances were at work, busy. The house had been cleaned from top to toe. I had tried every new restaurant in need of discovery and had walked my way around just about every laneway, street and park of inner city Melbourne. By mid June, the winter cold and boredom set in. Maybe I'd been just a bit too hasty in withdrawing from the world.

Why stay?

Like a moth to the flame, I was being drawn to warmth. I set off and after a two week drive found myself, thousands of kilometres away, on the outskirts of Tully, in hot tropical north Queensland, knocking on the door of George MacDonald's house. The piece of paper in my bag had been eating at me. I needed to talk to the man who knew both my mother and my biological father. Andrew had called and arranged the meeting, George was expecting me.

'Hi, my name's Christina Maxwell, I'm looking for George.'

'Speaking, you must be Andrew's friend. He told me you wanted to have a chat.'

'Ah, yes, if you wouldn't mind?'

'Long drive, come in.'

George looked weather beaten, his face heavily lined, his skin crusty and damaged by years spent outside, under an unforgiving sun. He looked ancient, his back bent, his gnarled arthritic hands those of a man who had worked physically hard all his life. He lived in a small transportable home in a caravan park. His cabin was in a row of semi permanent houses, all with the neat and lovingly tended gardens that told me the occupants had much time on their hands. Probably elderly people like George.

He gestured for me to sit down on a faded cane sofa in a small, sparsely decorated lounge room. The place looked like the kind of cabin occupied by someone who was unfamiliar with home ownership. No clutter, no family photos and apart from a television, almost no other furniture. He offered me a drink and opened a packet of biscuits, pulled out a chair from the kitchen table and sat down.

'Andrew tells me you wanna have a chat about James Cameron and your mum, Mary. Tells me you found some diaries?'

'Yes, and I suppose he told you I discovered he was my brother.'

'He did.'

I told him I needed to know what happened, what did he see, what did he know of that time?

'Poor little bugger, couldn't believe that his mother was going away for such a long time. Was pretty pleased when Mary, your mum, got the job. She took to him like he was her own, never seen the little fella so happy.'

'Mary brought a warmth to the house we never felt with the boss's wife. It didn't take me long to realise there'd be trouble.'

'What do you mean?'

'My boss, James, I could see he was fallin' for her, told me so himself after a few weeks. He'd often talk to me about things that were troublin' him, bit like a big brother. We were pretty close. I was a few years older, eighty six next birthday, he'd be seventy nine if he were alive today. Died just eight years ago, never got to see his grand kids. Too young to die, if you ask me.'

Andrew had told me his father had died of a heart attack just before Tom was born, his mother two years earlier of breast cancer.

'Can you remember much about my mum?' I asked trying to get him back on track.

'Yeah, beautiful lookin' woman, fancied her myself. You look just like her. Could never understand how she ended up in Greenhope.'

I told him what I knew of her life in Melbourne, of why she'd married my father and her longing for a child.

'I think my father was gay, not interested in women. Although he and my mother loved each other deeply.'

'I'd heard the odd rumour, we were all a bit surprised when he brought her home. It was something you just didn't talk about in those days. Anyway, back to your mum. Happiest time we'd ever had at the old property. She brought life to the place. We were all sad to see her go. Sad for the boss and sad for the little fella. The missus had returned home from her trip oversees, knew something wasn't right and gave James an ultimatum. Her parents had loaned him a ton of money. If James made the wrong choice he'd lose everything, his wife, his son and the farm that had been in the family since the area was first settled. The missus couldn't stand the place, they moved back in with her parents, to get him away from your mum. Left me in charge.'

'So do you think he, James, loved my mother?'

'No doubt whatsoever. Would've taken up with her in a flash, if there wasn't so much at stake. But he wasn't the problem, it was your mum. She couldn't leave your dad, loved him too much. If it wasn't for that, I'm sure James would have fought for her to stay, tried to work something out. But your mum was adamant, she was not deserting her husband.'

'Do you think James ever knew about me, knew I even existed?'

'After your mum left, James didn't come back much, trusted me with the property, didn't want to be reminded of what he'd left behind. The missus never came back at all. I remember seeing your mum in town, could tell she was pregnant, often wondered about the father, but didn't want to cause any more trouble. Best to let sleeping dogs lie.'

We talked for another hour or so, George rambling on about the past, pining for the good old days. He seemed world weary, not afraid of death. Happy to live out his last days in this austere little cabin, keeping to himself, a loner uncomfortable in the company of others, a bit uncomfortable with me. We said our farewells and I sat for a while in my car thinking about what I'd just learned, pleased to discover that my conception had been the result of love, not just some rich bastard screwing with the domestic help. I wondered what my life would have been like if my mother had chosen a different path? And then I stopped this game of 'what if' and, with a new found resolution, accepted what had been. The past would no longer rule my life. What I'd learnt was enough and now I was ready to let go and see what the world had in store for me next.

It was getting late and Cairns, my destination, was still more than a two hour drive away. The landscape was a lush green with banana plantations, sugar cane and intermittent tropical rainforests. Dark mountains loomed inland on my left, the sky above heavy with brooding storm clouds. The road was busy with trucks carrying cane and bananas, unfriendly drivers, keen to reach their destinations, intolerant of annoying tourists like me taking up space, flashing their lights, beeping me as they overtook. The aggressiveness was freaking me out and I was doubting whether I could keep going. It had been a big day, I was tired and finding it difficult to concentrate.

The sign said *SANCTUARY BEACH, next turn right*. I turned off and drove toward the coast, following the sign, not knowing what I would find at the end of the road. Glad to be off the busy highway.

It was dark when I pulled into the resort. The most expensive suite was available. A two roomed apartment, bedroom upstairs, very stylish, brand new, built after the cyclone according to the brochure. I was very happy to take it. I ordered room service and contemplated the events of the last few hours.

What a day, talking to a man who knew my mother, who could shed light on the discovery I'd made not that long ago. I felt calm in the knowledge that the choices she had made were her own, thankful she'd chosen my dad, the only man I thought of as father. They were both misfits who'd found each other and after years wondering where I fitted, I finally had a sense of closure, journey's end. The bed was comfortable, the quiet swishing sound of the ceiling fan lulling me into a relaxed and, for the first time in a long while, undisturbed sleep.

I woke to the sound of waves not far away and got up, drew open the curtains and pushed back the bi-fold door to the balcony. It was paradise, a long white beach, palms dotting the shore, where the rainforest met the sea. Sun rising over the water into a warm pink sky. Coffee in hand, I wandered the short distance across the manicured lawn of my private garden and straight onto the beach. Not a soul in sight, no one to see me in my pyjamas as I sat on the soft white sand, contented and utterly at peace. The voices in my head silent at long last. This would be a good place to stay for the next few days.

The woman at the desk was happy to take my booking, business was slow, she said.

The town was nothing more than a single road following the three mile beach. Houses, small hotels and boutique accommodation nestled either side, almost hidden in the rainforest. A scattering of buildings, a general store, small restaurants, hairdresser, beachwear and post office, signalled the centre of town. All rebuilt tastefully in old Queenslander style after a devastating cyclone almost wiped out the town two years ago. Picture perfect white weatherboard shops with long verandas, wooden benches encouraging you to linger. Glorious purple and pink bougainvillea climbing the posts, weaving through decorative wooden lattice, ridiculously pretty. Smiling owners welcoming you inside. Across the road ancient dark mango trees canopied the park in the town square, beckoning me to sit under their shady branches, away from the heat of the midday sun. On the foreshore, a gorgeous old church, overlooking the sea, like something straight off the set of 'South Pacific'. I hummed the tune 'Bali High', from my father's record collection, smiling at the thought of how easily the words came back to me, remembering our impromptu performances in the lounge room of that tiny family home. My meditative reminiscences were interrupted by the sound of a school bell ringing, a real bell, and the voices of excited children spilling out into the playground. What a joyous sound of life.

I spent the day reading books on the beach, swimming in the afternoon, luxuriating in the steamy tropical heat. I strolled the street at sunset, deciding where to eat, my cool linen dress perfect for the evening passeggiata. The eager owner of the seafood cafe suggested the coral trout and a glass of sauvignon blanc. Delicious.

It had been a perfect few days, but I was beginning to think I really should be heading back to Melbourne, finishing my road trip, getting on with life.

Friday morning and I was driving, unwillingly, away from Sanctuary Bay. I'd decided to put my car on a truck, and catch a flight back to Melbourne.

Cairns was a large city, a hub servicing the vast area that was far north Queensland. With sprawling suburbs, busy shopping malls and high rise hotels it was much like any big tourist town. I found a restaurant at the regional art gallery in the heart of town, always a safe choice in a strange new place. The food and the art were good, but I was just killing time and felt that nervous anxiety which would be eased if I just stopped fucking around and went straight to the airport.

The polite young secretary at the transport depot, where I dropped my car, volunteered to take me to the airport. As we drove, she said the vehicle wouldn't leave till late that night and would take about a week to get to Melbourne.

'Which terminal, domestic or international?'

'Domestic,' I replied, surprised that there was an international facility here.

In the entrance hall I looked up to see the electronic board flickering through its list of exotic destinations. I could easily jump on board a flight to Cambodia and wondered how Chenda was doing with the new business arrangement.

Suddenly I felt reluctant to leave. Why the rush, what was I actually going home to? Cindy didn't need me hovering. I had no book to write, no business to conduct, no one to go home to. I had never been freer.

That little town, Sanctuary Beach, was beckoning, its siren song calling me back. I was under its spell and felt a sudden, desperate need to return. A quick phone call to the resort, yes, Ms Maxwell your room is still available. I ran outside hailed a cab and raced back to stop my car from being loaded onto the truck.

Little Shack to Call Home

I had been back for a few days and couldn't help but notice how undervalued property was in the area. Perhaps this could be a new hotspot for investment? Saturday morning saw the town buzzing with life, a few more tourists, locals catching up, doing their shopping and me looking through the window of the real estate agent's office. Photos of many cheap houses and units, the boom had ended, no one wanted to invest in a town where cyclones threatened. One house stood out, an ugly little blockwork shack. The agent, Pam, overenthusiastic in this dead market, offered to drive me. Full of beans and ever so charming, she filled me in on the local real estate.

'Shouldn't be saying this, but we're all just barely hanging on. The cyclone was in February 2011, totally wrecked the place, killed the tourist industry, flattened all the crops. Took ages for the insurance companies to come good on their promises, was well over a year before we rebuilt. People have been reluctant to return, can't seem to make the tourists understand that we're open for business. All the money is being spent in Cairns, we don't see any marketing dollars down here. We feel forgotten about. Sanctuary Beach is just a little town, made up of small businesses and young families. We don't have the same clout or dollars to run a glitzy campaign to bring the tourists back.'

'It's a gorgeous little place, I can't understand why people aren't coming?'

'Most tourists fly into Cairns, then head further north to Port Douglas or the Daintree, places the whole world knows about. We're over two hours south on a road to nowhere and it seems nobody knows we even exist. They rarely choose us.'

'But the town looks amazing now. I was meant to go home to Melbourne but couldn't bear to leave. Cancelled my flight and came straight back. It seems to have gotten under my skin.'

'I understand, happened to me a few years back. Was working in Sydney, came here for a holiday, never left. Lots of people like me, refugees from city life, looking for something simpler. We've all invested heavily, but unless something changes soon, it won't need another cyclone to turn it back into a place of ruin.'

Ironically its remoteness and lack of tourists made it even more attractive to me but I understood that Sanctuary Bay would become a ghost town if the tourists didn't come. Perhaps I could do my bit to help.

At the far end of town, we pulled up in front of a letter box marked number 7, my lucky number. Bigger blocks, houses hidden in the jungle, fewer neighbours, more privacy. No fences, just a path through the undergrowth. And no surprises. The house was as ugly as the photos, a seventies cement block rectangle, painted asylum green. We entered through the back door, laundry to the left, bathroom to the right and walked into a dark kitchen/lounge. She flicked on the fluorescent lights and, although fully furnished, it felt like I'd landed in a waterless backyard swimming pool, a hideous aqua blue room, decorated by someone who had absolutely no idea.

'I know what you're thinking. It's horrible, but just wait.'

Pam had seen the look on my face, as my eyes squirmed to adjust to the colour and the harsh lighting. She walked to the windows and pulled back the garish 'Finding Nemo' curtains, and suddenly my perception changed. Along the entire front of the house were sliding glass doors, light streamed in and beyond the modest garden, a palm fringed glorious white beach and blue ocean. This was the real beauty of the house. She saw my jaw drop and smiled, no words needed. Either side of this main room were two identical bedrooms, with the same floor to ceiling glass doors, front and back, ocean on one side, forest on the other.

I walked around the lush garden. A filthy swimming pool on the north side, protected from the winds, would bring welcome relief in summer, when the poisonous jellyfish kept everyone out of the sea.

'What do you think?'

'How much?' I asked, trying to hide my enthusiasm.

I was very rich, I would never have to work again and by five o'clock that night, I had willingly paid far too much for my own little piece of paradise. It was rather a rash decision, but somehow felt right. The previous owners were cane farmers from Tully. It had been their beach shack for years, the cyclone was the last straw. Too old to start from scratch they sold their farm and 'did up' the shack to maximise its value. They had retired south to Surfers Paradise, to a more friendlier climate. It was vacant and the owners had said I could move in straight away.

Sunday morning saw me rise early, keen to get back to the shack. It wasn't as bad as I remembered. The furniture was awful, I would donate it all to the local church charity and, once freed of its ugly accoutrements, the house only needed a coat of paint.

Back in town I noticed a market had sprung up under the mango trees in the village square. The local people were out selling their wares. Home baked goods, pickled, dried and fresh produce. Potted plants, herbs and bright tropical flowers. Sugar cane and pineapple juice. Yummy smelling food, ready to feed the breakfast crowd. Pearl and silver jewellery, handmade clothing, wooden toys and brightly coloured kites.

'Nice kites.'

'Thanks.'

'My niece and nephew would love them.'

He was friendly, a bit hippyish and very relaxed.

'Where you from?' he chatted amicably, as he packed the two kites into cardboard cylinders.

'Melbourne.'

'How long you up here for?'

'Don't know, just bought the shack, at the end of the road, number 7. Might be here for quite some time.'

'You're bullshitting me, you've really bought something, you're staying?' he said, smiling in disbelief.

'Yep, absolutely love the place, couldn't leave.'

He called out to the stall holder next to him, a gorgeous brunette, dressed in fifties looking retro gear, sexy siren, neat little apron.

'Annie, Annie, come and meet..., sorry what was your name?'

'Christina.'

'This is my wife Annie. Christina's just bought the place at number 7, and sorry, I'm Jake, welcome to Sanctuary Beach,' he said enthusiastically.

'Hi Christina, pleased to meet you. Love to chat, but I'm flat out. Great news about the house, let's catch up for a drink some time,' she replied.

Annie had a stall selling rice paper rolls. The sign described the delectable fillings. BBQ duck, wood ear fungus and water chestnut, blue swimmer crab, coral trout, were just some of the delicious offerings that saw a queue of people waiting to attract her attention. I left her to her customers, Jake handed me the kites.

'Nice to meet you, see you around,' he said, as he finished the transaction.

The entire market was full of great things, people with an enthusiasm for what they made, their town and the people in it. I could see this becoming a Sunday morning ritual.

The last stall, near the church, was the St. Bertulph's Ladies Guild. Second hand books, trinkets and yummy homemade cakes and biscuits, with furniture and clothes in the church hall next door.

We will happily collect all your old furniture and goods, said the sign. They were raising money for the ongoing restoration of the church. A rather formidable woman, Norma, gave me the phone number of the man who would clear my house of the unwanted furniture. She too welcomed me to their town, I told her how pleased I was to be staying.

'By the way Norma, who was St Bertulph? It's a really unusual name, I've never heard it before.'

'He was the patron saint of protection from storms, guess he was on holiday when the cyclone called!'

It was a busy week. I looked at the furniture again. Some things were worth keeping, the fridge, washing machine, dryer, dishwasher, the bed bases, but not much more. Norma came with the driver, she wanted a bit of a nosey around and couldn't believe I was giving all this brand new stuff away. The wide screen TV took up most of the lounge room wall, the clam shaped bed heads still had the protective plastic wrap on them and the occasional tables with the shells and bright coloured seaweed set into their resin tops would find a more suitable home than mine.

I followed in the car with the boxes of trinkets I had packed and was delighted to find our destination was a huge old shed crammed full of mid century modern pieces. They were still considered 'old fashioned' by the ladies, who were young wives when the furniture was first produced. Norma couldn't understand why I was swapping perfectly good new stuff for all this 'old junk', but happily took my money, shaking her head in disbelief. Both of us quietly thinking we'd won.

It took a whole day to soak and scrape off the photographic wallpaper mural in the lounge room depicting a scene of the Waikiki beach front, and three more days and three coats of paint before the aqua blue walls were finally white. The floors were covered in large white tiles and would be ok. Some rugs would soften the harshness and remove the sand from feet before climbing into bed, a problem of beach side living. By Saturday, the interior was looking ok and I was ready to take delivery of the furniture items Norma was holding for me.

My market visit was much more fun this time as I looked for things for my little house, linens, soaps, lotions, mosquito nets. Jake greeted me like an old friend. I noticed his stall was covered with an elegant white sail. He told me he made them. I knew a white sail would make a perfect replacement for the ugly aluminium veranda clumsily stuck onto the front of my home. He was also happy to earn a few extra dollars painting the exterior of the shack, a job I had been dreading.

During the week, I went to Cairns to look at second hand catering equipment. I fancied I might like to cook a little more now that I had so much time on my hands. I struck gold with a free standing stainless steel kitchen bench and small commercial oven. A warehouse full of used equipment spoke volumes about the fickle nature of tourism and the restaurant market.

Jake, with the help of a couple of backpackers, got the exterior painted quickly, leaving him free to make and fit the sail. The whole job took three weeks. Cool white interiors, simply furnished, outdoors white as well. Under the new sail, I placed a teak refectory table and eight chairs, a splash of colour with two huge bright orange glazed tubs planted with dark green, primitive palm like cycads.

The house was now a home and tonight would be my first night sleeping there. Jake, Annie and their two boys came over with a bottle of champagne to celebrate. I'd felt the same sense of pride many years ago, after fixing up the old flat in Brunswick. Perhaps I loved this little old shack in the just the same way.

Welcome Party

Things went at a much quieter pace in Sanctuary Beach. I needed something to do and wondered if I could be of any help to the ladies of St. Bertulphs?

'Can you bake?' was Norma's blunt reply.

I had an idea.

Annie rented the kitchen of a vacant restaurant, the owner had grand plans, but the cyclone took away his customers. She said she would love to share the kitchen and the money for rent would help take some of the financial pressure off.

Bread, I would bake bread to help the ladies. It was something I had once done a lot of. And so began the 3am Sunday mornings with Annie in her kitchen. I mixed the dough, watching it prove at astonishing speed in the warm moist tropical heat, almost overwhelmed by the growing monster threatening to take over.

She preparing her rice paper rolls, while I baked hundreds of baguettes. We chatted like peasant women around the well, stopping occasionally for a blast of espresso then, as the sun was rising, contentedly looking at the bounty of our labours as we exhaustedly loaded up her van.

The ladies were pleased to accept my offerings, sceptical that anyone would pay $4 for a baguette, but utterly surprised and delighted when the bread sold out long before the markets had finished.

This is how I spent the next few Sundays, getting to know this small community, earning their respect.

'It's about time you got to know a few more people,' proclaimed Annie, as we sat around the kitchen bench one Friday afternoon.

I had spent the day with her, helping her cook for a wedding, she was being paid handsomely to cater for. The food had been delivered to the venue and we were just cleaning up.

'Where do you get your energy from? I'm so knackered after today I can't believe you're even thinking about another party!'

'Christina, I used to be a chef in Sydney, had my own restaurant, this is a walk in the park compared to that! And we only have a short season to make enough money to live on for the next six months.'

I understood, in November the poisonous jellyfish would start to populate the warm sea water, the heavy summer rains would fall and the tourists would stay away until the more hospitable weather returned in April. She would have plenty of time to kick back and relax. We hadn't talked much about our pasts, every one around here seemed to have run away from something, though questions were rarely asked. I told her I owned a bit of real estate, lived off the rents, she pried no further. We had become firm friends and she wanted me to get to know some of the locals. Annie checked her calendar and we agreed next Wednesday night would be good. The school holidays were over, the southern tourists had departed, now only the weekends were busy. We would have a BBQ at her place. I would bring wine and bread, nothing too fussy. I looked forward to meeting her friends.

I wore the white linen dress from Kep, but left my shoes at the bottom of the cupboard. I'd learned to go barefoot like the locals. The mirror showed my lean tanned body, the tropics suited me. A longing surfaced, I had not had sex in six months, not since Adam. My body was hungry to be fucked. I wondered if there would be any available men at the party?

No need to drive, Annie's place was a ten minute walk along the beach, Sanctuary's other highway and tonight would be a full moon to light my path home.

Annie had dressed the trees with Chinese lanterns in her beautiful tropical garden and one long table had been set up on the lawn, facing the beach. We would all have a view of the moon when it rose. People, couples, families gathered and talked. I felt like the only single woman there and was uncomfortably aware of the stares of men, looking up from the BBQ, as I walked towards Annie.

'Hi gorgeous, you look amazing, come and meet some of the locals,' she said, taking my hand, giving it a reassuring pat, sensing my awkwardness.

She introduced me to her friends and sat next to me when the food was ready. The table looked stunning, linen tablecloth and embroidered fifties napkins, dusky mauve lotus flowers strewn down the middle, junk shop silverware and an eclectic mix of floral china plates. Tarnished candelabra held breeze flickering candles, very Annie. I complimented her on her great style. Jake poured the wine and there was the low hum of contented eaters. I was relaxed, the guests included me in their conversations, welcoming me into their fold.

We were interrupted by a woman emerging from the jungle driveway, commanding the space as she made her entrance. They all looked up.

'Annie darling, sorry I'm late, problem at work, bit far away to get to paradise on time!'

She was tall, earthy, a wild beauty with untamed red hair, tight curls escaping the twisted raggy turquoise silk tied around her head.

'Indy, wondered when we'd get to see you.'

They kissed affectionately.

'You must meet my friend Christina.'

'Hi Christina, Indigo Bell, Annie's notoriously late friend!'

Indigo leaned forward, taking my hand pulling me towards her, giving me the same effusive welcome. She smelt of musk. We all wriggled along the bench, letting her in.

'It's been ages, what have you been up to?' asked Annie.

She lowered her voice and we drew close to hear what she had to say.

'I've brought someone with me, a man, met him through work. He's still in his truck, on the phone. I came to warn you, don't eat him alive. I'll see if he's finished.'

Indy got up and disappeared into the trees.

'Indy works as our youth officer, government appointed her after the cyclone. She travels to all these far reaching towns, keeps her eye on the kids, not much for adolescents to do around here. Everyone loves her.'

She was one of those people whose presence filled a room. The dinner guests waited for the life of the party to come back and a crunching of leaves and a sultry laugh heralded her return. He emerged from the shadows, tall, bearded, dark skin, unruly hair. Black tight fitting tee shirt, low slung jeans, boots, the look of a tortured poet. Indy held his hand, dragging the reluctant man into this bright happy crowd.

'Annie, this is Adam,'

'Pleased to meet you,' he responded, his deep husky voice resonating through my head.

'And this is Christina.'

I reluctantly looked up, straight into those cold hard eyes.

'What is it?' said Annie, seeing the shocked expression on my face.

'Actually, we've already met. We know each other from Melbourne.'

I took his hand and shook it firmly, hoping to hide my spreading anxiety, trying to keep calm as my heart raced a million miles an hour.

'What are you doing here?' he said quietly, menacingly.

'I live here.'

'Hey you, come over here,' yelled Jake from the far end of the table, and instantly Indy broke the uncomfortable nexus, dragging Adam away.

I gulped my champagne, it ran down my chin. I grabbed the napkin and coughed as the liquid went down the wrong way. Annie gave me a firm thump on my back as I gained my composure.

'You alright? You look like you've just seen a ghost.'

If only she knew!

The night continued. I tried not to look his way, tried to remain cool, collected, but my eyes were drawn to him, nervously blinking every time he caught me out.

By 8pm a faint glow began to appear on the dark horizon.

'Come on everybody, moon's rising, let's hit the beach.'

We followed Jake to a giant pile of leaves, sticks and logs set down on the cool white sand. We sat and waited silently as the first bright arc of light sprang from the inky water. Almost imperceptibly a great golden orb rose up from the sea and slowly lit the beach. We clapped and cheered at nature's magnificent performance and when it was high in the sky Jake lit the bonfire. We scuttled back as the fire and heat roared at us and when it had calmed, we continued to drink and talk. The glare of the fire meant I could not see across it, see many of the guests, see Adam. It was difficult knowing he was so near. Annie handed round a joint and I breathed in hard, almost enjoying the burning in my lungs, craving the mellowness that would soon be upon me. The weed did its job and I started to chill, felt like a naughty teenager. We gorged on Annie's lemon tartlets, raved about the homemade ice cream cones and declared that the nougat was the best ever eaten.

By ten pm the day was starting to catch up, I was tired. I got up, said my farewells and started off down the beach.

'I'll walk you home,' said the deep, quiet voice of the man striding beside me.

Anna Buckley

I was too stoned to reply. My house seemed so far away, neither of us spoke, the longest kilometre of my life. The distant light on my veranda signalled our arrival. We stopped, an uncomfortable silence. Having walked up the cobbled path to my house I looked back and saw he had not moved, his dark profile silhouetted against the moonlight. I sat on the fallen log that marked the boundary between the grass and the sand. Eventually he sat next to me and we stared out to the infinite night sky. I broke the silence, the weed giving me the confidence, and spoke with surprising clarity of things that had been gnawing at my heart. The words came tumbling out.

'I never knew where I belonged, where I fitted, not in Greenhope, not at university, not with Paul, his friends or with you. When I got married I locked up my emotions, my body and lived behind a facade. I operated at this emotionally starved level for so long, that I didn't know what was real. I even wondered whether all that I had created would be exposed as some kind of fraud. I didn't feel worthy of my success.'

He put his head in his hands.

I breathed deeply then continued.

'Moses played on those insecurities. He lead me to believe that only he truly understood who I really was. He reinforced that I was a loner who didn't fit in. Didn't fit in with my husband, his family, my daughter, you. That where I fitted was with him. We were alike, spoke the same language, had similar pasts. He was driven by his visceral hatred of you and all that you stood for. He showed me press clippings of you, my family, friends, getting on with their lives without me, reinforcing the idea that I wasn't really one of them and that nobody really cared. Being with him, hidden away, I would be protected from this vulnerability, be with someone who cared and understood.'

256

I paused.

'It was very seductive.'

His chest rose as he breathed deeply.

'And even with you, before and after the kidnapping, I didn't understand what you were offering, didn't know how to be loved. My only understanding of love was that given unconditionally by my parents, something I had taken for granted until they died. Nothing could ever fill that loss of innocence, of that most purest form of love, that void when a child becomes an orphan.'

'I didn't understand your relationship with your father, brother, mother? How it could be so destructive. The anger it made you feel. I had no reference point to understand it or you.'

Now I took the deep breath.

'I'm sorry for the pain and hurt all this has caused you'.

We sat there staring out to sea, silent. Eventually he got up and walked away. I returned to my empty house, to my empty bed. Finally I'd had the chance to speak to him. I drifted into a drug hazed sleep.

I woke with a fright, someone was inside. Footsteps padding on the tiled floor of my bedroom, my sheet violently yanked away, my naked body exposed. I heard clothes being torn off, the clanging of a belt to the floor, then a pair of strong arms, his heat, his body, his desperate mouth on mine. Adam had come to my bed and I responded with an animal longing, my tongue forcing its way into his mouth, reciprocating his aggressive assault. His rough beard coarsely rubbing my cheeks, my jaw, hungry for more. I opened my legs, wrapping them around him, gripping firmly, feeling his hard cock pushing against my wet swollen cunt. He rammed into me and I bucked at the intensity of his force, pulling him harder against me, demanding he go deeper, desperate to be filled and fucked. His hands held my ass, his fingers slicked and lubricated by my wetness, brutally entered my anus. He pumped me, sweat pouring from him as he fucked me harder than I thought my body could ever endure. It was animal and he grunted as he thrust. I groaned at the sheer abandonment of self. My orgasm came in wave after wave of explosive energy. I felt the force of his cock pulsing as he reached his own aching climax, spilling his hot angry seed deep inside me. Panting he collapsed onto me, and before I could fully comprehend what this all meant, he got off the bed and walked away.

I heard the door slam.

Four am, no sleep. At dawn I got up and went for a walk along the beach. The bonfire was still smouldering, coals glowing. A chill rush of cool morning air, tumbling down the mountains made me shiver. I squatted near the fire, blowing it, poking it with a stick till it reignited, small flames flickering around the unburnt timber. I watched mesmerised and warmed.

'Penny for your thoughts?'

It was Annie.

'Hi,' I responded, happy to see my friend.

'Saw you from the kitchen window, thought you might need this,' she said, handing me a mug of coffee.

'Up early?'

'Couldn't sleep.'

'Hangover?'

'Yeah.'

That was all she needed to know. I would have to tread very carefully. Indy seemed like a close friend and I had just been fucked by her new boyfriend. Jealousy, guilt and longing haunted me.

We both watched the fiery orange sunrise.

'I never tire of this. Sometimes when things get tough I come to the beach in the early morning to centre myself, remind me of why we're here,' said Annie.

'This morning, is that why you're here?' I asked, concerned that something was wrong.

She grinned at me,

'Nothing so profound, hangover, just like you.'

We looked at each other with furrowed brows, shaking our sore heads.

'But great party.'

'Yeah, I swear I'll never get that drunk, but each time the full moon beckons, I do it all over again.'

Contemplatively she poked the fire, although the warm tropical sun was rising higher, heating the air, lessening the need for the flames.

'So how did you know that guy Indy turned up with last night?'

'Adam?'

'Yeah.'

'He was the brother of my husband's business partner. After my husband died, we had a bit of a thing. Didn't work out.'

'You're a widow? I'm really sorry, I had no idea. You look too young.'

Although we were friends, I had given little away, no one in my new home knew very much about me at all. I liked my privacy, but on this quiet morning I was happy to reveal something of myself.

'Don't be sorry it was more than two years ago.'

'What happened?'

'Heart attack, he was only forty. The marriage wasn't very good. We stayed together because we didn't care enough to leave. We led separate lives under the same roof.'

'Kids?'

'One, she's in her final year at uni in Canberra.'

'That's a long way away, you must get lonely?'

'She very independent, we catch up during holidays. And honestly nothing is more lonely than a loveless marriage.'

She took my hand a gave it a squeeze and asked no more questions.

Annie was a bit of a hippy at heart, said they didn't have TV or internet. She really had no idea of who I was or all the shit that had gone down. They had chosen their isolation. Different to some of the older locals who thought this was the centre of the world, only read the local paper, watched the local news. To them Melbourne barely existed and if it wasn't for the tourist dollars, most of them wouldn't care if the southerners disappeared off the face of the earth.

The remoteness suited me just fine.

Before long the kids and the dog came scampering down to the beach.

'There goes our peaceful morning! Better get these guys ready for school. See ya later.'

Farewell Drinks

Another early Sunday morning, dough up to my elbows, usual girlie banter.

Annie filled me in on the Indy gossip. Apparently she met Adam in Tully, he'd been teaching some of the kids a few building skills.

'Indy doesn't really know where the relationship's going, but she did mention it was worth staying for the mind blowing sex.'

I felt a surge of jealousy and pretended to laugh at the bawdiness of the statement. I was still pretty shaken by my own encounter just a few nights ago.

'Oh, by the way, a few of us are having drinks at the Boathouse tonight. Wanna come?'

'Jesus girl, you and your never ending supply of energy! I'll see how I feel.'

As it turned out all the baguettes had sold by mid morning. So I left early and spent the day enjoying the beach that was my back yard, swimming, reading and warming my bones under a tropical sun.

Anna Buckley

The Boathouse was an institution. No designer chic interiors, just a corrugated iron shed sitting on top of the disused wharf. The bar was filled with locals, drinking cold beer and debriefing after another weekend accommodating demanding tourists. A place far too scruffy and intimidating for southerners. Annie and Jake were at the bar, the place was unusually packed, lots of familiar faces, people from the party.

'Hi, guys, what's the occasion?'

'Not really sure. Indy rang to say she wanted to catch up, everybody around here knows her.'

My heart sank. Would Adam come as well? What would I say? What was last Wednesday night about? He'd come to me intensely, aggressively aroused. I'd reciprocated lustily. Had he left Indy's bed for mine? I'd smelt her musk perfume on his body. How did he explain his disappearance to her or the smell of sex when he returned?

And just like her arrival a few nights ago the room quieted and people smiled when she walked through the door, holding Adam's hand. She worked the room like a true professional, introducing Adam to all her friends. He was so painfully shy, this must have been torturous. Before she reached us, she pulled out a chair, stood on it and whistled us to attention.

'Thanks for coming guys.'

Jesus I didn't know this was her party!

'Yesterday I got some news and thought it would be good to share it with you. As you know, Australia has been having some 'boat people' issues and our esteemed prime minister has decided that Australia would be a much safer place if we shipped them off to Manus Island. And in his wisdom, Mr Kevin Bloody Rudd needs people to be there to help

262

the poor bastards when they arrive. So it looks like they've picked me to run their adolescent mental health unit, and I said yes.'

There was silence. This wasn't what her friends had expected to hear. What would they do now that the life of the party was leaving? At least I might get another chance to get dirty with Adam without feeling like a home wrecker. He had reignited something inside me I thought had died.

'Unfortunately, they need me up there tomorrow to help set up.'

The crowd booed loudly.

'Ok, ok, that's enough,' she said, gesturing with her hands, calming the crowd.

'So I don't know when I'm going to get to see you guys again, and I'd hate to leave without a party, so help yourselves to drinks. Bar's on me, or should I say, this lovely man, Adam. Cheers!' she declared and they all cheered back.

She kissed him and he kissed her.

'And just in case you're wondering, he's not available ladies, he's coming with me.'

I felt sick, she'd claimed him, Annie had got it wrong. I wanted him back, needed his body, his mind, him. This was a farewell party I didn't need to attend. Adam was getting his revenge.

Anna Buckley

Just Another Sunday

As usual grumpy old Norma was already waiting at the stall when I arrived. She helped me unload the baskets brimming with freshly baked bread.

'How about I get you a coffee?'

'No thanks, got my own thermos out the back. Can't see why you southerners spend all that money on that fancy stuff, tastes the same to me.'

Norma was a hard nut to crack. Even though I had been in the town for many weeks and never once failed to deliver the loaves, she still saw me as an interloper. Assuming I would return to Melbourne when the season was over.

I came back to find her looking very smug.

'Guess what?'

'What?'

'Just sold a heap of your bread sticks to a bloke. Left us a $500 donation, said he liked the old church. Reckon we could just about shut up shop.'

Did I detect a smile?

The market was exceptionally busy that morning, the town had been crowded all week, unusual for this time of year, no school holidays, few tourists. I'd been sending Cindy weekly posts about Sanctuary Beach, gave myself a pseudonym, and spruiked the joys of this idyllic place. Perhaps it had sparked some interest? Annie had doubled her profits and, after some photos posted of Jakes colourful kites, he'd taken on a young kid to help him keep up with demand. Both of them agreed that the coming low season would not be such a worry this year, although neither of them could understand why things had picked up so much.

Annie was being swamped with customers, so I helped her until the market closed.

By 2pm I was stretched out on the beach, reading all the weekend papers, soaking up the sun. A balmy 27 degrees, luxuriating in the thought that in Melbourne, thousands of kilometres south, in late August, it was only eight degrees, coldest maximum in ten years.

I was aware of a warmth, fingers on my sex, circling my clitoris, heating me up, waking me from sleep. Was I dreaming?

'Keep your eyes closed, don't look up,' whispered the deep familiar voice.

I'd heard no footsteps, was a little frightened, but very aroused. I parted my legs, inviting him in, sensing his body next to mine, recognising the feel of his erection against my leg. What was happening? What was my mystery lover doing here? The sound of a zip. His hand in mine guiding me to his cock, holding my fingers firmly around his swollen shaft, moving them up and down, his breathing heavier. The familiar smell of him, earthy, masculine. I needed more and edged closer, my back against his chest, still unseeing, but filled with hot, wet desire. My hand bringing his cock between my butt, sliding it toward my needy cunt. He thrust hard, I cried out at the unexpected pain of his attack at the wall of my womb. His hand moving up my torso, searching for my breast, tugging roughly at my nipple, more exquisite pain, electricity to my brain.

Thud! A coconut landing dangerously close woke me, from my erotic dream, my sex wet with arousal, hungry with desire, desperate to be loved. Had I spent too much time in the sun? Perhaps I should head inside, get a drink, something to eat? What I did know was that Adam was the man I'd dreamed about. He'd been on my mind and I'd wondered whether distance had truly made the heart grow fonder. I contemplated that in a place like this, away from Melbourne and all the things that had derailed our relationship, we could possibly have found happiness. But it was too late. He'd really found someone this time, was committed to her and they'd started a new life together.

A bottle of wine at my door. I'd lent Annie my car, it was back in the yard. She mustn't have seen me hidden away. I'd moved further up the beach to a more secluded spot under the shady palms.

'Hey, thanks for the wine. How did you know?'

We were at the boathouse for the usual Sunday night catch up.

'What wine, I don't know what you're talking about? Think you're going troppo, Christina,' said Annie looking at me quizzically.

'The bottle of Nero D'avola, I thought you left it at my back door when you dropped off the car.'

'Wasn't me. Kids were going nuts, went straight back home.'

Only one person knew about my love of this wine. But he was in New Guinea, with his girlfriend.

'A drink for my two favorite ladies?'

Lovely Jake brought back beers for us both. I missed the companionship, was sick of being the single woman and longed for what this couple had, what they would go home to tonight.

Perhaps I could find out more?

'Do you ever hear from Indy. The refugee situation is hotting up, she must be flat out?'

'Indy is the world's most hopeless communicator, she rang me once. Said the situation on the island was hopeless. Absolutely nothing there, lived in a tent for the first few weeks, overwhelmed by the amount of work to do. Barely had time to breathe.'

'Adam, that guy she's with, he's a builder. Surely they could have put him to good use?'

'Didn't last, they fought all the time. She said he left after a couple of weeks.'

Where was he, had he come back? My head spinning, my heart happy with the thought that they were no longer together. Did he leave that bottle? Was he looking for me? Would he walk through the door? I missed him, longed for his body, still loved him, needed him to make my life complete.

I stayed until the very last of the stragglers left the bar, desperately hoping he would arrive, but knowing in my heart this would not be.

Looking

Who would know if he was still here? Indy had said they'd met through the work he was doing with kids. I drove to Tully first thing Monday morning. The woman at the community services office said I might like to try the industrial estate. Apparently there was a construction guy there who'd built the temporary dwellings after the cyclone, he might be able to help.

It was easy to find, a big corrugated iron warehouse, the only place that seemed to be operating. FOR SALE signs on most of the empty sites. I knocked, no answer, so I walked in. Inside there was a buzz of activity, sounds of power tools and bad country radio, young men and women working on shipping containers. They seemed to be in the process of converting them, some into sheds, some into dwellings. This had to be something Adam would do, he had to be here.

'Need some help?' said the gruff voice.

I jumped slightly, surprised by the man behind me. Tall skinny guy, dark blue work gear, steel capped boots, bright green hi-vis vest, face giving nothing away. I felt intimidated as he looked me up and down. The pretty little dress I'd worn for Adam was not appropriate in this place. I sensed he disapproved of me already.

'Sorry, there was no one at the front office. I don't know if you can help me, I'm looking for someone, Adam Darcy. Does he work here?'

'Who wants to know?' said the man, eyeing me suspiciously.

'I'm a friend of his from Melbourne, thought he might be here.'

'Leave me your number, I'll ask around. Now you'd better get outta here, you're not dressed for a place like this.'

I'd met my first hostile local and was slightly shaken by the experience, upset that my search appeared fruitless, certain that the piece of paper I'd scratched my number on would be tossed aside.

I called in to see how George was going, but he too was not that keen on a surprise visit and stood awkwardly tripping over words, the screen door separating us, I wasn't invited in.

The phone didn't ring, sitting around home waiting didn't help. I'd hardly seen anything of the countryside and decided on a trip further north, past Cairns, to the resort town of Port Douglas.

Lunch for one, it was becoming so tedious. The food was good, the view from the restaurant on the wharf spectacular, sparkling clear water, blue skies, a fecund humidity. I sat there watching couples, sharing food, knowing looks, relaxed, just fucked languor. Not me.

A table across the room was beginning to fill, men in suits reminding me this was a town where deals were still done and millions of dollars traded for the outrageously priced real estate. He walked in with an immaculately dressed blonde woman on his arm. He wore a dark fitted suit, showing off his perfectly lean muscular body. He had shaved, looked powerful and arrogant. She exuded a quiet confidence, assured, they looked like sex. They sat with their backs to me and I was glad they couldn't see the sad lone diner. I wanted to crawl under the table. Champagne was poured, obviously a successful deal had been struck, they were all completely engaged by the event. The table became noisy, the men all playing games of one upmanship, vying for the attention of the one beautiful woman. Adam, superior to them all, confidently touching her arm. The others weren't even in the race. I quickly made my exit before having to face another humiliating introduction.

The suite had a private pool, a penthouse cantilevered amongst the palms. Sleek interior, no gaudy tropical carnival interiorscape. I was learning to spend the money I'd worked so hard to earn, enjoying it even. I liked the look of Port Douglas, a small town that hadn't succumbed to over development. Low rise architecture, lush rainforest plantings, a vibrant main street, beach at one end, marina at the other. No theme parks or fast food joints. Restaurants where Melbourne's chefs had been seduced by the prospect of warm weather and feeding the rich. A town where millionaires and celebrities could enjoy a casual blending in, shorts were the great leveller. A stay for a few days felt right, I had nothing much to go back to.

My phone buzzed, a text, unfamiliar number.

'How was your meal?'

'Who is this?' I replied to the nameless text, wondering if the restaurant was following up with a courtesy call, I'd given my number when I'd booked.

'The restaurant, don't you remember?' I did, the gorgeous young waiter had flirted mercilessly, and like some desperate spinster, I had given him way too much information, stupidly thinking the teasing was real.

'Are you the waiter?'

A brief pause and not the answer I'd expected.

'Meet me at Havana for drinks at ten.'

Ten at night, that was the clue, he would finish work by then.

'Maybe?' I cheekily replied.

If nothing else, I could do with some uncomplicated casual sex. In all my adventures I'd never been with a young man before. My body was hungry for attention, I could easily match his stamina, it had been a very long time. I wanted to be fucked with abandon, until I couldn't walk. If Adam could be with a beautiful young woman, I could most certainly take this waiter to my bed.

Luckily I had packed a few nice things and it felt good to get out of the casual beach wear that had become my uniform. An afternoon of pampering, prepared my body, readied my mind. A short black elfin haircut, thanks Audrey, took years off. A little more makeup, bedroom eyes, built the mood. A strappy short black dress would do, something to show off my tanned legs and a pair of elegant black low rise Chanel slip-ons completed the picture.

The review site said Havana was a favorite haunt of both locals and tourists and buzzed with a late night after work crowd, once the kitchens around town had closed. I was late, ten thirty, no need to seem too eager, too desperate. The music was pumping, the lights low, a party crowd had taken over. I walked in, heads turned, giving me a boost of confidence. I scanned the room, hoping to remember the face of the boy I would seduce. Who was he? The room was filled with potential 'waiters', he could be any of the men partying before me, I had absolutely no idea. Who cared, I might just try them all.

The drinks flowed, I danced with a number of willing young men, whispering sweet nothings, tempting me with their outrageous propositions, and I flirted back, grinning at their playfulness. I had not felt this carefree for a long time. Had I ever?

By two a.m. the party was still raging, but I was ready to depart. I didn't want to bed any of the men I'd danced with, and although I'd enjoyed the cheeky seductions, I didn't fancy having to make excuses as to who would be chosen. They were fun, but they were really not my type. I slipped out quietly.

Once away from the hypnotic beat, the heat and the noise of the crowd, I realised I was very drunk. Slipping off my heels helped a little, one foot in front of the other, that's all I had to remember to walk home. By the time I reached my apartment my head was spinning, the corridor was moving and the key wouldn't fit the lock. I sat against the door, hoping this would all stop... and then went blank.

My head hurt, my mouth was dry, the bright morning sun seared my brain. Where was I? I looked around and slowly my eyes focused. Thank God, I was in my room. How did I get in? I got up, needing to pee and saw the sad reflection of my makeup smeared face and my wrinkled, crushed dress. I felt like shit, swallowed some painkillers, guzzled the tap water, stripped off and went back to bed. I was not ready for morning just yet.

By mid morning my head was still bad, a cooling swim might help and I wandered out across the deck to the pool.

'She emerges,' a voice from behind, quiet applause.

Who was that? I thought I was alone. Had I let one of them, drunkenly, into my room at night? With nothing to cover my nakedness, I dived quickly into the pool. The coolness was soothing as I swam under water to the end, wondering who was there. I emerged and turned around. He was standing there, dark suit pants, bare chested, no shoes.

Adam.

'At least I dressed before I came out,' he said, grinning with wry amusement, walking towards the pool.

He looking amazing, his hard body leaner than I remembered, barely clothed, certainly not undressed enough.

'What the hell are you doing here? How did you get in?'

He sat on the edge, dangling his feet in the water, not caring that his trousers were getting wet.

'You had trouble getting your key in the lock, it was in your hand when I found you.'

'What do you mean, 'you found me'? How did you know I was here?'

'I followed you home, saw you had a bit of trouble walking straight.'

'Were you at Havana as well?'

'Yeah, for a little while, was supposed to meet someone there, but she didn't show. Too many people, not my kind of place, so I went to a quieter bar around the corner. I walked past Havana on my way home, you looked to be having a great time. I was surprised to see you leave.'

I wondered if the blonde woman had stood him up?

'I found you in the corridor, outside your room, picked you up and carried you to bed.'

'God, I can't remember that at all. Where did you sleep?'

'On the couch.'

'You idiot. Why didn't you sleep with me? The bed is huge.'

'Didn't know if that would be a wise thing?'

A knock at the door, Adam answered and was followed by a waiter pushing a food trolley.

'I took the liberty of ordering breakfast, thought you might need a bit of a fry up and a pot of coffee.'

'Thanks, I think you're right, I'm starving.'

'Wait there.'

I watched curiously as he went into my bedroom, only to come out, moments later, carrying a robe. He held it out for me and smiled playfully as I stepped into it, not looking away, eyeing the full length of my body.

'Thanks, you cheeky bastard!'

The waiter had set up the table under the shade of the giant umbrella on the terrace. It was comfortingly familiar.

'This reminds me of that first morning back in Melbourne, during the lock down, when we had breakfast together outside, by the pool,' he said smiling, gesturing for me to sit.

My thoughts wandered to the beautiful day when we had first made love, back to a more innocent time, before all the shit occurred. Tears sprang to my eyes, the raw emotion still there. I wiped my face with the sleeve of my robe.

'You ok?'

'Yeah, bit of mascara in my eye, didn't get around to removing it last night. I might just wash my face before we eat.'

The splash of cool water helped. I looked much better, skin glowing, surprised at my reflection. I'd completely forgotten about my new hair cut. My phone beeped, I grabbed it on the way out, that same number, a text from my mystery date.

'Did you have fun last night?' it read.

I returned to the table.

'Excuse me, I should reply to this.'

Adam poured a coffee as my fingers tapped the screen.

'Yeah, how about you?'

An innocuous enough comment to someone I didn't know. Had I even danced with him last night? I pressed send.

Adams phone beeped.

I looked at Adam, he smiled.

'It was you, where were you, I didn't see you. You stood me up!'

'I think we said ten? I was there, I waited, and as I said, it really wasn't my scene. It was just by chance that I saw you leave and you know the rest of the story.'

'So I still don't understand?'

'I saw you at lunch, by the time I could get away, you'd left.'

'But you were there with someone, that gorgeous woman. You looked to be very friendly.'

275

'We were, we had just secured a deal with those guys at the table, we were both very happy.'

'I still don't understand?'

'Those people were investors who had just agreed to buy one hundred containers for an eco lodge in the Daintree. Heidi was the real estate agent who brokered the deal. She was very pleased and I think she thought there might be a little bit extra afterwards.'

'And it looked like you were happy to lead her along?'

'I wanted to show the other men at the table how it was done!'

'You evil bastard, always the alpha male.'

We sat and ate, the food was good, the conversation so familiar, so easy.

'So tell me about the containers, do they have anything to do with the factory in Tully?'

'The one you visited?'

'How did you know?'

'Pete rang me, sorry if he wasn't too forthcoming, but he knows I like my privacy. He's pretty protective of me and the project.'

'The project?' I asked.

'Yeah, the stuff going on in Tully. We convert shipping containers into temporary accommodation, my company got the contract after the cyclone. The towns around here were a mess, we were the only ones big enough to handle the massive scale of the job. We do this sort of thing all over the world. Pete ran the job right from the beginning and he stayed on long after it was finished.'

'We identified that once all the permanent housing was constructed, we'd have to do something with the redundant containers.'

'So you thought of converting them to luxury pods like the one at Lands End Lagoon,' I said, second guessing him.

'Correct, but more than that. Normally I send a team of guys to fit out the containers, it's quicker and more efficient than training locals. They move on once the job is done. After the cyclone there was a lot of unemployment, especially for the unskilled labourers and kids. It was Pete's idea to run the training program. I came up here to see if I could help.'

'It was a bit hit and miss at first. The kids had no idea, couldn't see who would want to live like this, after all most of the poor bastards had been living in the containers while they waited for their houses to be rebuilt.'

'So how did you get them to change their attitude?'

'I set them a project, to design their own pod, to use in whatever way they saw fit. Some were just basic, but others were quite over the top. It showed me what different skills, ideas, they could bring to the project. I put them into teams and set them a real task, to convert a container into a dream home. Each team got to build one. We got a bit of publicity up here and the orders started to trickle in. A design blog did a story, took lots of pictures and now they've become the hottest thing. We're being swamped with orders. We're not just training welders and tradesmen, but designers, I.T. teams, managers. The level of sophistication is extraordinary, some of the kids are really gifted. Nothing leaves the factory without my approval. I've set really high standards. It's reignited my passion for architecture. I've never been more excited about what I'm doing. I feel like it's the first time I've been truly happy.'

I smiled, I knew that feeling.

His phone rang.

'Gotta go, photo shoot in the Daintree. Why don't we finish this conversation tonight? Want to have dinner?'

'I would really love that, what time?'

'How about eight? I'll come past and pick you up. Don't want you standing me up again!'

He got dressed and left.

I couldn't wait.

There was so much I wanted to talk to him about, it was like we were meeting for the very first time, nervous first date. I wanted him to be in my bed tonight, I needed him so badly. Did he feel the same? What if he only wanted us to be friends, how could I live up here so close to him if he wanted nothing more?

I spent a few hours shopping. New dress, heels and outrageously sexy underwear. I booked myself into the hotel spa and indulged in a ridiculous number of treatments. It helped kill time.

I got the text at five.

'Ferry broken down, stuck here overnight, don't know when we can make it back. Sorry about dinner. Will catch up soon, Adam.'

My disappointment ran deep, it wasn't just the cancelled dinner, but the tone of the text. It seemed so casual, hardly the words of a lovesick suitor. My quiet little 'happily ever after fantasy' was just that.

What a fool I'd been, indulging myself all day with thoughts of a perfect seduction. The new dress, shoes, the almost ritualistic preparation of my body, just for him. I even booked Oceania, the beautiful and very romantic restaurant where president Clinton dines when he secretly flies in. On reflection the entire scenario had been a fiction thought up in my stupidly needy head. I put on my pyjamas, ordered room service and had an early night.

Alone again.

Island

A knock at the door woke me. I was disappointed to see the hotel manager standing there.

'Sorry to interrupt Ms Maxwell, but we have a maintenance problem. The apartment below has flooded, seems your pool has a leak.'

'Could I at least have a shower first?'

'Sorry, but the problem is quite urgent, all the electrical systems have been compromised. The apartment is very unsafe. You'll need to pack an overnight bag, we don't know how long it will take to fix.'

I threw some things together and got dressed. I felt disgusting, no shower, the dense humidity made me grumpy.

'Well, where am I meant to go? I had planned on staying in today?' I whinged, pissed off at not being able to sit and sulk all day, wallowing in my own self pity.

Anna Buckley

'We have arranged to take you to one of our other properties. A driver is waiting for you in the foyer.'

'Why can't you just transfer me to another room? This is really inconvenient!'

'I'm terribly sorry, but we are completely booked out, there is no other alternative.'

'Well, maybe I should just check out now and find a more acceptable place to stay!'

'Ms Maxwell, we are sending you to one of our most exclusive properties. I'm sure you will be pleasantly surprised.'

'And if I don't like it, what then!'

'I will personally look harder until we find something that meets your high standards.'

Jesus Christ, why me, why today? I liked this hotel, it was conveniently located in the centre of town. I didn't have to drive, the beach, the main street and the restaurants just a short stroll away. This new place better be bloody good.

The black limo was heading along the main road. I wasn't happy and had no desire to spend my time stuck in some out of town resort, confined to a generic hotel chain's idea of a good time. We passed all those resorts. He pulled up to the small local aerodrome, a helicopter was waiting. The driver took my daypack and escorted me to the noisy whirring bird, buckled me in and signalled to the pilot, thumbs up, that we were ready for takeoff.

The view of the Great Barrier Reef was spectacular, bright turquoise water, small white sand islets and further out the occasional, bigger, green island. After about twenty minutes he flew low over one and I could see just how beautiful it really was, dense jungle, blue lagoon on the sheltered side and ocean rolling onto a broad beach. Picture postcard perfect. He landed.

'This is your stop, you will need to walk a little way around the island to the lagoon. There you should find everything you need.'

I got out and walked clear of the blades, expecting him to turn off the engine and escort me to my destination, instead he took off. What the fuck! He'd left me here stranded on a bloody desert island. Was I being punked? This couldn't be happening. No buildings, no sign of life, I didn't know if I was even heading in the right direction. Who would send a lone female to a place like this?

'Everything I need', he'd said. Is that what I was seeing? A pebble path guided me off the beach, into the jungle and there before me were steps. I climbed into a tree house, a big white canvas canopy sitting on top of a huge wooden platform, shrouded under luxuriant leafy boughs. The bed surrounded by billowing white curtains, mosquito nets. An outdoor shower with expensive toiletries. A fully stocked kitchen, fridge filled with food, wine, champagne, bowls of tropical fruit, flowers everywhere. They had delivered me to paradise... alone. I threw myself on the bed and wept. Would I share my life with anyone ever again?

The outdoor shower refreshed and revived me, the uninterrupted views to the sea cleared my head. I felt remorseful at my petulance. Looking around me I was surrounded by breathtaking scenery, wasted if I chose to continue this indulgent melancholia. It was only one night and honestly it was magnificent.

I breathed in the sweet smell of frangipani flowers blooming in the ancient gnarled tree growing within reach and plucked a flower for my hair. A sarong tied loosely around my hips felt decadent, no need for more clothes, I would go native. My nipples became hard as I rubbed sun block onto the delicate pink skin, my sex tingled with faint arousal.

There had been a lagoon, I'd seen it from the air, its blue waters had looked inviting, a swim would be good. Glimpses of water spied along the path through the jungle told me I was near. It was magical, a natural secluded pool, ultra white quartz sand made the water a surreal turquoise, hypnotically drawing me in. A distant splash broke the trance. Someone was swimming towards me. As they got closer they dived below the surface, the ripples obscuring the view.

And just like that time almost two years ago, he emerged, naked, from the water. My Mr Darcy. Adam strode silently towards me, water beading off his body, pubic hair in tight black wet curls, soft velvet penis hanging, tantalisingly, between his strong muscular legs. He swept me up in his arms and kissed me deeply. I was breathless with desire, utterly transfixed by this erotic spell. He nuzzled my neck and groaned, his chest rose as he took in the scent of me, and pulled the knotted fabric away from my hips.

'Mine,' he whispered and gently placed me on the silk that floated to the ground.

I lay back and parted my legs, he knelt before me, eyes heavy with desire, tracing his tongue along the soft skin of my inner thigh, coming to rest at my swollen wet sex. His tongue searching, prying, teasing, tasting me, my back arching as he found my clitoris, sucking, nibbling till it sat proud, hungry. I pull him towards me, his mouth tasted salty, musky, of me. And as our tongues explored, I felt his penis, now thick and hard, easily glide inside. I moaned at the pleasure, the completeness of the sensation of being filled, of the gentle rhythm that we both danced, as if our bodies were made for each other, a perfect fit. Slowly we connected, the tenderness of our recoupling almost too profound for me to comprehend and a long rapturous orgasm washed over every nerve, every cell of my body and soul. I was complete.

He held me close, kissing my closed eyes, my forehead, my lips and we stayed together, basking in the warm glow of this most perfect love making.

I woke to find his deep brown eyes looking into mine, I reached out and touched his mouth, tracing the line along the edge of his lips, parted sensuously, he playfully bit, then sucked. I smiled.

'You hot?' he whispered, I nodded.

He got up, taking my hand, inviting me into the water, we walked together. The water temperature was perfect and I dived under, surprised that it was not salty but fresh, I drank thirstily and wondered how long we had been lying in the sun. I swam further, each stroke invigorating, replenishing, giving me life, I felt reborn.

He sat back outstretched along the water's edge, the faint rippling of water causing his penis to sway. I swam up and kissed him, he gathered me close, I straddled his lap, he licked my nipple, then bit, pulling gingerly with his teeth till it hardened. I sensed his cock awakening and lifted my hips to accommodate him, engulfing it, taking him into me, relishing the feel as he stiffened inside. We had all the time in the world, no frantic scrabbling, happy to let the gentle waves rock us. I leant back, stretched my torso, aware of how extraordinarily deep this allowed him to enter me, he moaned as his cock swelled. The sun was warm, he held me tight and slid us both into the water, till it was deep enough for him to stand. I held him tighter, mounted firmly astride him, my legs clinging around his waist. We kissed, he dribbled the cool water into my mouth, I drank willingly from him, he did it again, then smiled. His strong arms gathered me into him and he held me under my ass as he walked out of the water and took us back to the tree house, the same intense sensation against my womb as I held him tight, deliciously impaled. I felt like Jane as my Tarzan stealthily mounted the stairs, back to the treehouse and delicately placed me on the bed, careful to not break the connection. And there we remained, all day, all night, never letting go of each other. I woke only to arouse him again, to feel him swell, then pump his seed into me. Waking and fucking till we surrendered to exhaustion.

'Morning beautiful,' he whispered, awakening me with a kiss.

'Morning,' I whisper back.

We lay there in the magical pre dawn light and watch in awe as the sky turns hot pink, heralding the rising sun.

He kisses the top of my head, and I nestle into him. He wraps his arms protectively around me and we stay like this for what seems like ages, listening to the birdsong, the waves, the faint sea breeze rustling the leaves. He has delivered me to nirvana and I could explode with happiness.

He is the first to rise, his early morning erection almost tempting, my cunt stings as it involuntarily responds... not just now. I watch as he puts together some breakfast, I realise we haven't eaten for over a day. He brings a bowl of fruit to the bed and feeds me, licking the drops of succulent sweet juice dripping onto my chest. I feed him with my mouth and I kiss when our lips touch. Sticky, sore and sweaty I take his hand and lead him to the shower. I get in first and he watches as I uninhibitedly pee standing up, right in front of him, the water washing everything away. He copies me and also pisses into the water, I love the sheer abandonment of the act. We wash each other clean, he dries me, neither of us feel the need for clothes.

He spends the morning sketching ideas for this new project, I read, we catch each other looking up, smiling. We do very little and eat when the fancy takes us. We have no idea of time.

I go for a swim in the lagoon and return wearing the sarong.

He looks up in displeasure.

'What?'

'I want you naked the whole time we're here.'

'Why?'

'Because I want to be able to fuck you whenever I feel like it,' he answered mischievously

'But I'm really sore. I think you've mortally wounded me. It's been such a long time, I feel like the virgin bride.'

'My poor baby, lie on the bed, let me see.'

I am suddenly embarrassed and hold the sarong firmly against my body.

'The bed,' he commands and I reluctantly obey.

He yanks off the offending sarong and eases my legs apart.

'No, we can't, you're making me aroused, it hurts just thinking about it,' I plead.

'Shh, shh, relax.

Anna Buckley

He gets up and goes to the bathroom. I close my eyes, my nostrils flare at the familiar smell, coconut oil. I feel the oil dribble onto the chafed skin and am immediately aware of how soothing this is and ever so gently he begins to massage, stretching my legs further apart as he rubs deeper into the sensitive folds.

'You are a very bad man Mr Darcy. Do you have any idea of what you are doing to me?'

'I do, I can see your cunt blossoming and I know what I would love to do to it, but understand that I really could cause you serious harm and that would make for a very boring holiday.'

'But it's not fair, I want you to fuck me, your fingers are driving me wild. You have to stop!'

'Who said there was only one way to fuck you, Ms Maxwell?' he replied with a roguish smile, spilling more soothing oil onto me, letting it run between my cheeks, the burn abating.

'What do you have in mind?'

'Something that needs a bit of practice, but first some preparation.'

He stopped what he was doing and poured oil into his hands and rubbed meticulously between his fingers and palms.

'Watch, Ms Maxwell.'

And with that he poured oil over his flaccid cock then began to rub.

'This is what I would do when I thought about you, when you weren't there.'

I watched lustily as he brought his cock to life, stroking it's length slowly.

'Adam,' I breathed, 'would you like me do that?'

'No, no, don't touch, I'll come too quickly,' he hissed.

He continued until it was rigid and proud.

'Roll over, let's play ass fucking, I think this is what I have in mind?' he proclaimed.

We had been in Cambodia when I had tried this for the very first time, I had been a little bit drunk, my senses dulled by the alcohol, not really cognisant of the experience. What would it feel like with my senses fully awakened?

Adam stacked some pillows on the bed and draped my body over the mound, lifting my ass high, open and exposed. I loved the thought of what he was about to do and shuddered with excitement as I felt the oil dribble between my cheeks. He teased the tight muscle and I remembered the secret was to relax. Slowly a finger circled, then pushed, easing me open. Two fingers, stretching, until I felt ready. I reached behind taking his fingers, withdrawing them. Adam looked uncertain. I wanted more control. Assertively I rolled over, dashing the pillows to the floor and forcefully pushing him onto his back, this time I poured the oil over him and stroked his cock till it was impossibly hard. Then I kneeled, straddling him and began to slowly rub the glistening tip between my ass, stopping at my anus, teasing the muscle open, slowly, allowing my body to accommodate this willing invasion. I had forgotten about the sweet sensation the pain caused and arched my back in pleasurable response. Adam groaned, I knew he would not last long. I let gravity work and slowly eased myself down on him, pausing as the tight muscle adjusted till finally I reached the base of his shaft, resting against his hard pubic bone, feeling the stretching fullness of my complete submission to him. I could go no deeper. I began to rise and fall, Adam thrusting, anchoring me with his hands around my waist, looking for his own release. We rocked and moaned like wild animals, my clitoris grinding against his pubis, finding purchase, and blissfully exploding into a thousand shocks of pleasure and pain. I fell, exhausted, hot and sweating, against his chest, our hearts beating frantically, collapsing wearily, our bodies spent. He ran his hands up and down my spine, as if dispelling the charge that had taken over his body.

'God Christina, you possess me, I am nothing without you, don't ever leave me,' he whispered.

I looked into his eyes that seemed to reflect a desperate longing, almost fear.

'I am yours... forever.'

A gentle sea breeze blew across our bodies, cooling our heated skin and we lay together relishing the carnality of the act we had just shared and the contentment of the words spoken. Neither of us moved.

We both grimaced as he, finally, eased himself out of me, our bodies had both just taken a pleasurable beating.

'I think we've just fucked ourselves into some kind of nihilistic oblivion, my cock feels like your cunt looked. I understand now why your arousal almost brought tears to your eyes.'

'You mean it hurts when you think about sex, about fucking me, when I stroke your cock like this and it starts to throb?' I said, playfully running my thumb along the reddened shaft.

'Stop!' he hissed and grabbed my arm, holding it firmly against the mattress.

'How about a swim in the ocean, the salt water might help, perhaps that will ease the pain?'

The seawater did feel good. Sex, for now, was completely out of the question and we spent the day, snorkelling the reef, swimming, body surfing, like sea creatures, without a care in the world. Adam threw out a line, and to my surprise he caught a fish. It was attractive in a cave man kind of way, primitively sexy, his nakedness, very fuckable.

At the end of the day we retreated back to our tree house, showered and oiled our worn bodies. I cooked the coral trout, surprised at how delicious fish, caught that fresh, could actually be. We finished, took a bottle of vodka and a rug to the beach and Adam lit a small fire.

'When did you learn to fish like that?'

'Pete has been taking me out. I've learnt to do a lot of new things over the last six months.'

I had been curious about how he had occupied his time since our separation.

'Like what?'

'Like being less of a control freak, learning how to get a life.'

'What made you change?'

He paused before he replied and looked out to sea as he gathered his thoughts

My heart began to beat a little faster. What would be his reply? I didn't want to open old wounds. Why had I asked such a stupid provocative question? Was I prepared for his answer? I remembered the look on his face when he'd left, a broken man. Of the angry sex and door slamming of just a month ago. And now this. Would his reply ruin what we had just found?

His face looked blank, gave no clues. He took a long sip of vodka before he spoke.

'I contemplated killing myself after that night, I hated you, hated what had happened to what I thought were our perfect lives. I blamed you for all that had gone wrong, for what you had taken from me. I took no ownership of anything. Anger and contempt ruled all my thoughts. I behaved very badly, treated women appallingly, fucked senselessly, drank excessively and lived up to the reputation that had only ever been a fiction in the mind of the gossip columnists. It was pretty ugly.'

'For a while I submerged myself even deeper in work. It was Sam who called me out, saw what a mindless prick I was turning into and said I needed to get away, clear my head. When the press found out about the mining deal and my scheme was exposed, it brought home what a soulless asshole I'd become and what a waste of effort it had been.'

'I started to think about what you'd said on that bad night when we split. My drive for success, to beat my father, prove my worthiness, had made me oblivious to the affect my actions had on other people. And to make things worse my father finally did get in contact with me.'

'Your Father? I thought he lived in Greece, had nothing to do with you,' I questioned.

'It was about a week after the press broke the story of the fight with my father and the whole fucked up plan to mine Moon Bay. We hadn't spoken for years.'

'And so what did he say?'

'The bastard rang to congratulate me. Said he was impressed with my ability to outmanoeuvre him and was glad that at least one of his sons was like him.'

Adam took another slug from the bottle.

'And it hit me that finally we were equals. It felt hollow, empty. My father liked me for doing something that had turned me into a monster. Turned me into him. I didn't want to be that person anymore. '

'And then of course my brother had to add to the shit storm by fucking with the tax department. I paid for him to get out of the country and quite frankly it was the best thing that could've happened. I told him that this was the last cent he'd ever receive. I couldn't believe my mother ended up following him. I assumed she wanted to make up for all those years she'd been emotionally unavailable. And for the first time in my life I was finally free of them all. I felt completely changed and lost all my drive and ambition. I really wanted to leave my old life behind.'

'So what happened next?'

'I sold off any of the parts of my business that were underperforming, and put the ones that were working into the hands of my senior management team. When I was confident they wouldn't fall apart, I got in my truck and headed north. I didn't take the coast, but went straight through the centre. The dry barren landscape fitted my mood. I lived in a tent and spent days in isolation, thinking about those things you'd said and as the anger started to dissipate I began to wonder what my life would be like if I looked for something else.'

'Eventually I longed for a change of landscape, I had stopped beating myself up. I wanted green and something to do and found myself at the factory in Tully. I liked what I saw.'

He took another sip of his drink, he looked more relaxed.

'For the first time in many years I felt alive again, loved work, had a sense of purpose. And for a while I liked the single life. It was Indy who made me realise what was missing.'

My heart sank. Did I want to hear this?

'I turned forty two and needed something more. At first I thought it was Indy and could've quite happily contemplated a life with her,' he paused again.

'And then you turn up, at that party and I realised I hadn't gotten over you. I wanted to kill you for fucking with my mind. That night, when I followed you back to your place, I wanted to warn you off, tell you to get out and leave us alone.'

'Why didn't you?'

'Because the more I walked along that beach, the more I didn't know what to do, and then you talked to me about all that shit going on in your head and I realised you were still in mine. Anyway I walked back to the party, everyone was pretty wasted by then, so Indy and I went back to the hotel and I tried to fuck her brains out, but my head just wasn't in it. All I could think about was you. The drugs, the booze, perhaps that's what made me do it, but I found myself walking down the road till I got to your place. I sat outside, wondering what the fuck I was doing when I noticed the back door open and, well, you know what happened next. It was wrong of me, I should never have done that to you.'

'Stop, stop, don't beat yourself up about it. I wanted you in my bed, didn't you feel it too?'

'That was the problem, being inside you, feeling your body, touching your skin, breathing you in, just made it worse.'

I reached out and took his hand.

'The whole thing with Indy, going off to Manus Island, was all just a sham. I thought that if I could get away from you the problem would disappear. It didn't last, Indy and I didn't get along. She wasn't you. She saw I was unhappy and, to her credit, let me go. I also knew I'd let the guys at the factory down, what we had wasn't finished and I needed to get back.'

'So one day, I'm in Tully walking down the main street and I see this book in a shop window, your book, and the next thing I know I'm reading it, something I thought I'd never do. I'd thought I'd left all that bullshit behind me in Melbourne.'

He slugged from the bottle and continued.

'And it wasn't what I'd expected.'

'What do you mean?'

'First of all, it wasn't about me. I'd dreaded what you might have said, feared the truth. And then the more I read the more I realised how little I knew about the real you and the demons you lived with. I hardly knew you, we hardly knew each other. What you said to me was true, I had created this idealised version of you. It wasn't fair. But most of all the book helped me understand why you did the things you did and when I finished I wanted to talk to you, see if maybe there was a chance that we could be friends.'

'So why didn't you try to contact me?'

'After that bad night, the Indy thing, I didn't know how to go about it, or even if you would want to see me. So I bumped into Annie and, although we hardly know each other, she told me about what you'd been up to. That's how I knew you'd be at the market stall last Sunday and I thought it would be easier if it looked like I'd accidentally bumped into you.'

'But I didn't see you there?'

'Well, the old lady at the church stall said you'd gone, didn't give anything away, not even when I put $500 in the donation box, so I bought a few of those breadsticks and left.'

'The old cow, I was just up the street getting a coffee. She told me about the donation, but didn't say you'd been asking about me!' I exclaimed in exasperation.

'I had some business to do in town, had lunch at the resort and saw a bottle of Nero D'avola on the wine list. Couldn't believe it was there, had to buy it and bring it to you. It would be my excuse to visit you at your house.'

'So it was you! Why didn't you stay?'

'I knocked and no one answered, even went down to the beach. Your car wasn't there so I thought you weren't at home. I left the bottle and drove straight to Port Douglas.'

'And I went to Tully on that Monday to see if it was you who had left the bottle!'

'And I'm very fucking pleased I wasn't there or we might not have bumped into each other in Port Douglas. Come here!'

He took my hand, entwined his fingers with mine and squeezed.

'Very fucking pleased!' he re-emphasised.

Adam poked the fire and put his arm around me, I nuzzled into his chest.

'So what I don't understand is how you got here, on this island. Last time you contacted me you were stuck on the other side of the Daintree River?'

'Jesus, I couldn't believe my bad luck! Here I was stranded with a bunch of suits, when all I wanted, was to see you, take you out to dinner, seduce you and take you into my bed.'

I smiled at his words.

'We spent the night at one of the investor's resorts and even though we got to the ferry early, the queue stretched for miles. It would be hours before I got back and I worried that you might leave. Anyway one of the guys had to get back to town urgently, so he called up his mate who flies a helicopter and he offered me a lift. We got talking and he told me he had this island and wanted to sell. I was interested, but said I'd never buy anything sight unseen. So he told the pilot to make a slight detour and we flew over, and then I had this idea. I told him I was interested and he said it was mine for the week, see if I like the setup. And that's when I rang my resort,'

'Hang on, you own a resort up here?'

'Yeah, the one where you're staying,' he grinned sheepishly, 'And I told the manager to put together food and supplies and to spin you a bullshit story about a maintenance problem. I flew out early with all the stuff and the pilot flew back to collect you. I got the place set up just in time.'

I looked up at him and saw the pleased look on his face and tilted my head toward him, he kissed me.

'I can't believe you did this, all for me, that is just so ridiculously romantic. Adam Darcy who are you?'

'I'm someone who has found you again and will do anything to keep you with me.'

The sea air was cooling, he pulled the rug over my shoulders and I stared into the fire, caught in its spell and utterly captured by the man who had won me back.

'Are you cold?'

'A little.'

'Do you think I could take you to bed?' his voice husky.

'Mmm, I would like that.'

'Do you think I could make love to you?'

'I would like that, why don't we see?'

We stood, he wrapped me in the blanket and carried me up the stairs and across the threshold to our bed.

'Very gently,' I whispered, as he kissed me.

'Very gently, my beautiful woman,' he whispered back.

The next few days were spent blissfully naked, fucking, swimming, spending time together, getting reacquainted. He was relaxed, carefree and it wasn't just the island or our escape, it was him, he'd completely changed. The anger that always appeared to be simmering just below the surface, threatening to explode, was gone. I felt like he'd been liberated, the weight of the world no longer resting heavily on his shoulders. He was free for me to love.

I was stretched out in the double hammock, thinking about what would happen when we left the island. We couldn't stay here forever.

He climbed in next to me.

'What are you thinking about?'

'I'm thinking about us, what's next, what happens in two days time when the helicopter picks us up?'

'What would you like to happen?' he asked.

'I want to be with you. I don't want us to have separate lives. I like who we've become, it's as if the island has given us a brand new start.'

He smiled and kissed me.

'I'm scared of what will happen when we leave,' I whispered, tears welling up in my eyes.

He wiped them away and kissed me again.

'You and I have created new lives for ourselves, both of us have started afresh, shaken the shackles constraining us. Being here, finding you again, has been like getting a second chance. I always loved who you were, your feisty spirit, your dogged determination to succeed, your innate sexiness. Even when all that shit went down, I still felt empty without you. The stuff that happened blindsided me for a while.

297

Melbourne just wasn't the right place for us to thrive, to be together. Now we've found somewhere that's ours, a place where we can be ourselves, together. I want what you want. Don't be scared.'

The gentle swaying of the hammock, his strong arms holding me close, calmed the panic.

And my heart stopped racing, the fear subsided and at last I finally felt a sense of peace. He had found it, too.

'I want us to live together. Do you think we could try again?' he asked.

I looked up into his deep brown eyes. The pain and the torment had gone, I saw love.

'I would love that more than anything in the world.'

Monday morning arrived too soon, the sun was just rising above sea. I sat up, and to my horror there was blood everywhere. My period had arrived, the sheets were a mess.

'Hey, why so early?' he asked, as I left the bed.

'This!' I said pointing at the stained sheets, feeling the blood trickling down my leg.

'Don't worry about it, come back to bed, I have a present for you,' he said mischievously, uncovering his huge early morning erection.

'But the mess?'

'Let's just dirty it up a bit more, my cleaners have seen far worse. It's our last day.'

He won and we did dirty it up that little bit more...and then a little bit more again.

The cleaners who arrived when the chopper landed most certainly had a bit of work to do.

A Sanctuary at Last

We agreed that Adam should live at my place, he'd been sleeping in one of his shipping containers parked behind the factory. The twenty minute commute didn't bother him.

The house just barely fitted the two of us. We converted the spare room into a studio where we could both do our design work. It was good to have him arrive home at five, to have him really present, not on the phone to China, not fielding calls from his brother, not worrying.

Sometimes he didn't bother to go to work at all. Today was one of those days. We were walking along the beach.

'I've been thinking about the house, I want you to design something for us, the shack really is too small,' I said.

We had been living on top of one another which, while we were madly in love and could barely keep our hands off each other, was ok. But when the wet season arrived, confined indoors, the place would be just too small.

'What have you got in mind?'

'Nothing really, I want you to design us something special.'

'That's a big ask, you have to give me something?' he responded.

'Well, I would like some more space.'

'Sick of me already?' he said.

'No, no, it's just that I would like somewhere for our friends and family to stay. Somewhere that can hold a big dining table, a big kitchen, a place where we can entertain our friends.'

'That's better, and where would this place be?'

'On the beach of course! We could knock the shack down, rent something while it was being built,' I said.

'But I like your old place, it holds some good memories.'

'I can't believe you're so sentimental, what's happened to the ruthless property developer I once knew?'

'He fell in love with a good woman, left all that behind,' he said, smiling.

'No, Adam I'm serious, I really don't mind.'

'Why don't we fix this up and build something somewhere else, on a bigger block, something more private. I liked having you naked and fuckable on the island, I'd like more of that, away from the prying eyes of neighbors or tourists on the beach.'

'But the island is too remote!' I said in exasperation.

'No silly, I didn't mean that. I hear there's some land being opened up at the other end of the beach. Not sure when, probably in the next few months. Do you think you can wait that long? Could you put up with me in that confined space for a little bit longer?'

'Oh you bloody idiot, of course I can. Anyway I think it would be good to see what you come up with in the meantime. I'm curious to see what's inside that architect's brain.'

'It's been awhile, but I've actually been thinking about what I would do if I built from scratch, in this climate, living with you.'

I was touched that he had been thinking of our future together, that he hadn't pushed me out of the shack, respected the little place and waited till I was ready for change. We walked a little further, speculated about what this new house might look like, fantasied about the things we could do. Adam kept referring to the bedroom and what he might like to do to me in it. We walked some more, stopping occasionally to pick up a stone, inspect a shell, casually ambling along like two people who no longer rushed, who had plenty of time just to be.

'Feel like a swim?'

'No, not really, I think I'll just sit for awhile, why don't you go in, I'll watch.'

He stripped to his boxers and ran into the water, diving into the waves like a kid. My heart filled with love. My life was perfect.

Adam got out of the water, sat next to me, and covered my face in salty kisses. We sat silently, Adam poked around in the sand, his eyes ever inquisitive, taking in all around him, looking at the world through an architect's eye, marvelling at the shape of an eroded shell.

'Look at this,' and he showed me the bleached white circle of shell that was all that remained of what once would have been a small spiral.

He took my hand and delicately slid it along my finger, looking at the ring, looking into my eyes and then he spoke.

'It's you, it's always been you, I have found love and I want to be with you for the rest of my life. Tina please marry me?'

I was startled at this sudden gesture, it was completely unexpected, tears sprang to my eyes at the simple, raw innocence of the moment, the emotion in his voice. I knelt in front of him as he sat, took his face in my hands and left a trail of kisses, across his lips, along his jaw and to his ear.

'Yes,' I whispered, 'Yes'

Just Something Simple.

My initial excitement was fast waning. We had told our friends and family, they were quite shocked at first, considering what had occurred at the beginning of the year. It was to be expected, no one knew of the rekindling of our relationship. But it didn't take long for everyone to share our excitement after I'd told them the story of our reunion. We set a date for mid November, the only time the little white church was available. It was Kate who said it wasn't a great time, she had her final exams, Andrew and Sarah were launching their new Shiraz and Lola would still be in Italy. The people who I most wanted to share this day with couldn't attend. It was important that the ceremony happened here. Sanctuary Beach and the little church were so symbolic of the place where we had both found peace. Every other date I suggested didn't quite suit. People lead busy lives.

'Don't worry, we'll be seeing them all at your brother's place at Christmas time. We can have a second celebration then,' said Adam, trying to ease my obvious disappointment.

Before I left, I'd promised Andrew and the kids we would have a big traditional Christmas. I was looking forward to it and would now have to accept that this was the only time we would all get together.

'Annie and Jake can be our witnesses, we can keep it simple. It's not about them, it's about us.'

He was right and when the day arrived I was glad we had chosen something simple. Annie would host a small reception in her gorgeous garden and we would go back to the island for our honeymoon. I chose to spend the night before my wedding in an exclusive villa away from Adam. Annie joined me and we giggled late into the night, speculating what my honeymoon might be like.

The church was booked for eleven. We spent the morning being pampered and by 10.45 the limo arrived.

'You look gorgeous, Tina, that dress is truly stunning.'

I had made myself a simple cream satin gown, classic lines, no frills, something Greta Garbo might have worn.

We arrived at the church and I was touched by the small gathering of locals who had turned up a to see the bride, a country town tradition I remembered as a kid. The driver opened the door and for a brief moment my heart fluttered nervously. I calmed myself knowing my beautiful man was waiting inside. Annie lead the way and I followed her up the stairs, the ladies of the town greeted me warmly and wished me good luck. The first thing I noticed was the gorgeous big bowl filled with green goddess lilies, sitting on a pedestal in the small porch and then to my complete and utter surprise, Andrew stepped from behind the arrangement and took my arm.

'I am here to walk you down the aisle little sis'. Are you ready?' he said with a stupid great grin on his face.

I hugged him and couldn't get any words out. I was so choked with emotion. All I could do was nod. He took my arm, calming me with a gentle squeeze and lead me to the entrance of the church. It was full. All the people I had so wanted to be there were inside. I walked down the aisle, smiling as I recognised faces. Shirley and Malcolm from Greenhope. Ava and her girlfriend Deb, the Finestras, Margot, Cindy on the arm of that nice young detective Steve. Sarah with Andrew's kids, Tom and Sophie. Joe from Lands End Lagoon. Even Tim Nolan the painter. Chenda, Nary, Adam's little sister and her mum, Dara. And waiting ahead of me was Kate holding a bouquet of green lilies just like mine. She walked towards me and we hugged and cried. Sam, the best man, beamed. Adam stood proudly at the altar, smiling lovingly as my tears of joy flowed. I couldn't believe what I'd just witnessed and was overwhelmed by the love in the little white church.

'Yes!' I proclaimed to the world, as the celebrant asked if I took this man to be my lawfully wedded husband, and tenderly Adam placed the ring on my finger and passionately kissed his new bride.

'I love you so much,' he whispered, as the guests erupted into loud cheers and applause.

We left the church and were covered in clouds of confetti. Adam held my hand high punching the air, smiling, victorious, and again the townspeople cheered. No cars, we slipped off our shoes and walked barefoot along the beach for the short stroll to Annie and Jake's.

The garden looked beautiful, white tablecloths, crockery, silverware and more green lilies. The food, the friends, our families made this day the most perfect celebration I could wish for. We danced and talked and hugged and kissed, till finally our car arrived. Farewells were said, promises to meet tomorrow for breakfast before our honeymoon commenced. Tonight we would go back to the villa.

'I remembered your face, on that first wedding day. You had no one, you looked lost. I didn't want this day, our day, to be like that.'

'But all the excuses, the reasons why people couldn't make it? Kate's exams? Andrew's launch?'

'I flew Kate up in the jet. Andrew postponed, I convinced him that a launch at the Imperial next week would be much better than the event he'd planned at his cellar door. Sarah agreed and they joined in on the whole charade. Cindy made sure that everyone had an excuse and I think we quite convincingly pulled it off.'

'You are my love. This is the happiest day of my life.'

I kissed him and let him wrap his arms around me as we drove. I desperately needed to make love to my husband.

The car seemed to be taking a long time to get to the villa, we were miles out of town. What did he have planned? There were no hotels this far along the beach. We drove through dense tropical jungle and

305

suddenly Adam told the driver to stop. He got out, opened my door and the car disappeared. I could hear the ocean, but couldn't see why we had stopped. He took my hand and guided me along a candlelit pathway, through lush gardens, under the palms.

Before me stood a stark, but beautiful house. Two massive rectangular cubes, ribbons of white concrete with curved corners, encasing walls of glass. One mounted on top of the other at slightly obscure angles.

He picked me up.

'This is ours, welcome home,' he said as he kicked open the front door and carried me up a flight of stairs into an enormous room overlooking the sea. It was breathtaking.

'When, how...?' I was almost speechless.

'I've owned the land all along, started building when I first came up here, but my heart wasn't in it. Everything about the design was for you, I couldn't get you out of my head. Without you I couldn't see the point in finishing. After the island, I couldn't stop.'

It was perfect, a glorious cool white space. Doors pushed back, a deep balcony along the entire front, the smell of the ocean, a cooling breeze. Furniture we both loved, all the things we had talked about, the lists we'd made for our dream house, were here. He'd been turning them into reality all along. A beautiful testament to our love.

'Come with me, I have a wedding present for you.'

We went back downstairs and outside along a wooden bridge, connected to a separate building was a single cube, a slightly smaller version of the main house.

'What's this?'

'It's a studio, somewhere for you to work, look inside,'

I flicked on the lights and my jaw dropped, it was all there, my old cutting table, the crocodile skin cases, the bolts of fabric, the Clement Meadmore stools, the Harcourt chaise, the Contour chair, things I thought had been lost all those years ago.

'Paul asked me to help him clear out your flat. I saved it all, couldn't bear to see it tossed away, it reminded me of the girl you once were, it was my connection to you. I never got rid of it, had it in storage for years. Sometimes I would sit on this chair just thinking of you, wondering if you would ever be mine. These things, they were only objects, but they told me so much about you. I have loved you from the first day I saw you in that room, wearing that dress, being you.'

I wept as I walked around the room touching the pieces, thinking about the young girl with all those dreams, the life that had taken such a circuitous route, to get me straight back here, to be given the chance to begin again. I turned off the lights, the glow of the full moon gently illuminating the space, and slowly undressed him. I turned, he undid my satin gown, it fell, pooling on the floor. Taking his hand, I led him to the chaise. I touched his body, fingers running tentatively over every surface. We made love, deeply, passionately, he filled my body, my heart, my soul, as if for the very first time.

And when we lay quietly, holding each other, he still inside me, connected, I took his hand and placed it on my belly.

'My gift to you, our baby' I whispered. He lovingly stroked the soft skin, smiled adoringly, his eyes filled with tears.

Our lives were now complete.

Epilogue

It had been a long day, quarterly board meeting, signing off on the new range, generally catching up with the team in Melbourne. Just letting them know I hadn't completely abandoned them. We still used the house in Fitzroy as our Melbourne base which was now a lovely home that Sam would make ready before our arrival. Davina laughed that her prophecy of this becoming a family house had come true. She would often visit with her kids when we were in town. Couldn't believe that her former boss was now a besotted father. Nothing like the driven man she had once worked for.

Adam was more than contented to be the stay at home dad when I was called away. In fact I know Adam was almost reluctant to go to work at all and more often than not he was happy to leave the day to day running of the shipping container factory to his foreman Pete.

We always tried to travel as a family but sometimes this wasn't possible. Today I was returning after a week in Melbourne. I had travelled alone and was missing my beautiful boys dreadfully. As my driver finally pulled up to the magnificent house Adam had built for us, I felt that wonderful sensation of coming home, of sanctuary. I wandered upstairs to see who was there but was a little disappointed to find the rooms empty. I knew where they would be. I kicked off my shoes and headed to the beach. I could see them in the distance. A little boy being chased by his dad, giggling, running and falling in the water, playing happily without a care in the world. They stopped and looked up.

'Mummy, mummy,' I heard Jack squeal with delight. Adam picked up the little boy, lifted him up onto his shoulders and ran to greet me. We tumbled in the sand as they swamped me with hugs and kisses.

Adam whispered words of love, telling me he'd missed me, and made deliciously tempting suggestions as to what he might do to me when I was back in his bed.

It was good to be home, happy and very much in love.

Previous books in the trilogy.

Awakening the lost woman

(book one in the lost woman trilogy)

What if you woke up tomorrow unencumbered, free of all the constraints that have held you back?

Free to discover your body, your big ideas and maybe even free enough to let yourself be desired.

Christina Maxwell had put her life on hold for too long. This was not the plan of the ambitious and creative young woman who had dreamt of bigger things. Unexpectedly alone, she must begin life again, to discover what she has missed, and to find her true self.

Capturing the lost woman

(book two in the lost woman trilogy)

Christina visits America and sees her business expand beyond her wildest dreams. Amongst the success she receives some pertinent advice;

'Find someone to share the journey with.'
'Find a life away from work.'
'Find a place to escape to.'
'And lastly, have fun... '

Back in Melbourne things don't go to plan. Taking time out, she finds herself unexpectedly in the Tasmanian wilderness...

For information on Anna Buckley's books go to <u>annabuckley.com/books</u>

Available by order from most book shops, buy on-line at Amazon, or as an eBook from Amazon, Google Books, Kobo and iBooks.
For more information go to <u>annabuckley.com/buy</u>

www.ingramcontent.com/pod-product-compliance
Lightning Source LLC
Chambersburg PA
CBHW061515020726
47502CB00006B/2087